Dedication

To Michael, now at peace in the arms of the angels. I will love you forever.

Looking for Snowflakes

By Eden Monroe

Print ISBNs
BWL Print 9780228623991
LSI Print 9780228624004
Amazon Print 9780228624011

BWL Publishing Inc.

Books we love to write ...
Authors around the world.
http://bwlpublishing.ca

Chapter One

The young man set two bags of groceries in the backseat seat of his aging automobile, then slid behind the wheel and turned the key in the ignition. After three tries it finally caught and the engine roared to life, the muffler system also in need of repair.

It was two days before Christmas and traffic had certainly begun to pick up, shoppers shifting into high gear during the countdown for the holiday season. Christmas trees were everywhere. From last-minute tree lot finds tied to the tops of vehicles and those gaily decorated in front yards, to living room windows where bright lights twinkled. He remembered the great annual Christmas tree hunt when he'd worked at a nearby tree farm as a teenager. Sundays were usually hectic and filled with family fun. His home life had been nothing like what he saw there, the parking lot routinely jammed with happy parents and their children. They were there not only for a tree, but to enjoy hot apple cider, sugar cookies, hayrides and carol singing. That place had been one of the first to get into the Christmas spirit in a big way, he recalled fondly.

Those happy memories had no sooner gone through his mind when a shiny black pick-up pulled into the parking lot beside him. An honest-to-God cowboy got out wearing a Stetson, western boots, jeans, and a fleece jacket. He guessed the guy was maybe in his thirties.

What really caught his attention though was his passenger, a white toy poodle, riding shotgun. The top of her curly white head was barely visible above the window frame. The obvious joke was that he was married to a dog, but if she was this cute, he guessed it wouldn't matter.

The cowboy spoke to the dog as he was getting out. He called her Snowflakes and told her he'd be right back before making his way into the supermarket with loose-hipped confidence.

The dog, instantly bored, put her paws on the padded doorframe and stood surveying the parking lot around her, her mouth open, pink tongue lolling. Isn't that what they called a dog smile? It had to be a girl because no boy dog worth his salt would be caught looking that pretty. She looked super friendly. He found himself smiling too as he watched her, it actually put him in a better mood. If this was the Christmas spirit, he just got into it in a big way.

Then the dog noticed him watching and since the truck's window was down an inch or two to allow for fresh air, he lowered his too and talked to her.

"How ya doin', Pooch?" he asked, and was rewarded with a friendly little bark. Her expression clearly said she wanted to play.

And then an idea struck him. He could call it a Christmas idea because the holiday was only two days away. Since he was in the Christmas spirit now, or as close as he was going to get, maybe Pooch here would like to go for a little drive. He didn't have a present yet for his wife and he didn't exactly have the cash to buy one. Their credit cards had been maxed out a long time ago. How ideal could this be? It was as though the perfect gift had been dropped right in his lap and although it wasn't normally in his wheelhouse to take what didn't belong to him, maybe he'd make an exception this one time.

Lelia loved dogs, and he loved Lelia. He would score major points when he came home with Pooch there under his arm. He could see the dog had on a red collar with what was probably an ident tag hanging from it, but he could easily get rid of that. Throw it out the window on the way home. There, problem solved.

He continued to study the dog, the poodle never taking her eyes off him either. This was meant to be! He had a perfect view of the front doors of the supermarket, and there wasn't a cowboy in sight at the moment. It seemed that everyone was either shopping or standing in long line-ups, and that was definitely in his favour. He glanced around for security cameras, saw only one, and guessed he might be out of range. Did anyone ever look at those things anyway? The film image was usually so grainy it could be anybody. He'd seen that on television. So it was worth taking a chance because it was almost dark, and he would be hard to make out. Hmmm, if he was going to do it he couldn't sit here all night thinking about it. He had to act fast. To avoid leaving fingerprints he slipped on his gloves. Also, the little thing could also turn out to be a biter. You never knew. He'd heard that dogs in vehicles could get downright territorial and go after anyone who tried to get inside. And this was probably a silly idea anyway because what if the truck was locked? If it was, no harm no foul, he'd simply carry on his way, and no one would be any the wiser. But maybe the truck *wasn't* locked and the more he thought about it the more he believed it was meant to be that the poodle should come home with him. All that remained to be done was snatch the dog and be on his way.

Do it, Brett, the devil on his shoulder told him. Just think how happy Lelia will be when she sees her nice Christmas present. They were having major money problems lately with him unemployed, which meant lots of arguments. This could help ease some of that tension. The last thing he wanted was to lose Lelia, for any reason, so a cute little dog would obviously make things better in a hurry.

Before he could change his mind, he took a deep breath, pulled up his black cotton hood and quickly got out of his car. He cursed the squawky hinges that could draw attention to him. He couldn't believe his good fortune when he found the truck unlocked, and better yet, the dog didn't seem interested in biting him. In fact, she licked his face. Did he need any more encouragement from the gods? This little dog was going on an adventure, starting now.

He'd left his car door open for a speedy getaway although he tried to act nonchalant. Criminal activity was new to him, so he gave himself a mental pat on the back for getting it right the first time out. He set the dog on the passenger seat and made a quick exit from the parking lot, although not so quick as to attract attention. Thankfully, no cowboy materialized as he kept his eyes on the front doors, waiting for the traffic lights on the adjoining street to change before he could finally get out of here. Talk about a clean getaway! His Christmas just got a whole lot more interesting and now he didn't feel like quite so much of a bum for not having anything to give his wife. He had the best present of all, a cute little pedigree poodle puppy. Well maybe not still a puppy, but she was small.

He reached over and patted the dog who now seemed be getting agitated. She was jumping around on the front seat, whining, and in general making it clear she'd changed her mind about the trip and wanted to be back in the cowboy's shiny black truck. It could be that she was hungry, and he'd have to get something for her to eat. He couldn't very well turn up with a Christmas dog and no food. When he'd been shopping, he hadn't known he'd be snatching a dog so there was no kibble in either of the grocery bags. Besides, he'd barely had enough to get what they needed to eat *themselves*, let alone expensive dog food. Stealing the dog had been a spur of the moment thing. Where was he going to get the money to feed it and look after it? He'd heard vet bills could be very expensive if you didn't have pet insurance. It would probably need shots at some point too and regular maintenance. His Aunt Gina had a little dog and she was forever getting *something* clipped on it.

Now the dog was barking, sharp little barks that while not dangerous sounding, succeeded in getting his attention. But no matter, he was headed for home now and they lived far enough away that the cowboy would never find her. But what about the dog, his conscience asked him. Don't you think she'd like to be home for Christmas? Probably, he thought glumly. Funny how a person could be so decided that something was a good idea one minute, then just as quickly be buried in an avalanche of reasons why it was a terrible idea. He was now at the avalanche stage, but for sure he couldn't take it back. What would he say? The dog opened the door on its own? Nothing was that smart, or in this case, strong. He had to keep going or he'd be in deep trouble; in for a penny, in for a pound.

To make himself feel better he thought about how happy the dog would be once she met Lelia. She wouldn't even be thinking about home. And he could just imagine Lelia's reaction when she saw her. The thought of giving her such a great gift made him feel better about himself than he had in a long while. Maybe she'd be cool with him again, because he figured in her eyes, he hadn't been cool in quite a long time. Losing his job because of the fight he'd had with the owner of the company, a man who had been very good to him in the past hadn't been too smart. Once he'd cooled down enough to see things clearly, he knew his boss was right. He'd been on the other side of the gate by that time. His wife was right too, he needed to learn to control his temper. She wasn't the first one to tell him that.

He looked over at the dog, already completely smitten by the tiny poodle with the shiny button nose. "How ya doin', Pooch? You going to come home and live with your new Mummy and Daddy?"

Mummy and Daddy? Now where had that come from? If his friends ever heard him talking like that they'd have a good laugh. He wouldn't have to worry if *they* thought he was cool anymore, but deep down none of that really mattered when the dog cocked her head and studied him. She seemed to be pleading in the only way she could, sharp little barks as if to say: what you did back there wasn't right. You stole me right out of my truck and now I have no idea where you're taking me. Her eyes said: I want to go home. Now.

He thought of the cowboy, a pretty rugged looking lad if he did say so. He didn't have to wonder whether or not *he'd* think what he did was cool. He might not fare too well if he got his hands on him. These were serious second thoughts, but it was too late now to undo what he'd done. No, it was a fait accompli as they said and so he carried on home with his prize.

The dog, seemingly resigned to her fate lay down with a sigh on the seat, stretched her paws out in front of her and laid her little face down on them. It was clearly a sad gesture. If there was any mistaking how he read that, the eyes she turned on him again spoke volumes. Not cool, Brett! Not cool at all.

* * *

Lelia walked in the door after ten straight hours on her feet. She was exhausted. It was a busy day at the store with the countdown to Christmas in full swing. She liked working the checkout, a chance to put a smile on weary customers. Today, she was the one who needed a smile in the worst way because her life at the moment was not so great.

She kicked off her boots and plunked down on the sofa in her winter coat, slinging her purse onto the cushion beside her. She looked around at the small dreary apartment. They didn't have a tree yet, and she hadn't bothered to put up any decorations. She did not feel one iota of Christmas spirit, her mood not helped any by the fact that there was no sign of Brett. She'd hoped he would have supper ready when she got home, but no. She had a sudden urge to talk to her mother and was grateful when she answered.

"Hi, dear, are you just getting off work?" Beryl Thorne asked her daughter, as usual in a cheerful mood. "You didn't work a double shift, did you?"

"I just stayed four extra hours is all. I need all the hours I can get with Brett not working. We're barely making rent at the moment, never mind Christmas."

There was a momentary hesitation. "You could get help, Lelia. There's the foodbank…."

"Brett's too proud to go there and he doesn't want me to either."

"Where is Brett?"

Lelia sighed. "I thought he might be home when I got here, but he's not. He said he was going out to look for a job today. He thought they might be hiring over at the factory so maybe he's already working. Whatever way it went I hope he comes home in a better mood than he was when he left this morning. He's really down about this job thing, and I kind of got after him about it so that didn't help. It seems like all we ever do is fight lately."

"Things will get better, Lelia, dear. The first couple of years are always tough for newly weds."

Lelia forced a laugh she didn't feel. "You keep saying that, Mum, but I don't know. Brett is down on himself because he lost his job and he thinks he's letting me down. It seems to be like we're going from bad to worse financially. I don't know what else can happen to us. I heard today they could be closing the store in the new year and if that's the case, I might be out of a job. But I didn't call to be all gloomy and everything. I wanted to tell you I've got a gift for you and Dad, plus I wanted to know if you guys are coming over here for Christmas or do we go there? I think we went there last Christmas, so really, it's our turn."

"First of all, dear, you didn't have to spend money on your father and me. It's very thoughtful of you, but you need the money worse right now than we need a gift."

Lelia blinked away tears. "It isn't much, Mum. I got it on the deep discount counter, but I thought it was nice, so I picked it up. I know it's something you can use."

"That's sweet of you, and we certainly appreciate the gesture. How late do you have to work on Christmas Eve?"

"The store's staying open 'til ten o'clock but I'm getting off at six."

"Perfect! Why don't you come over for dinner on Christmas Eve? You could stay the night and then you can help me with Christmas dinner on Christmas Day. It will do you both good to get out of that basement apartment for a while."

"Mum, that sounds really good, but Brett doesn't want to be beholding to anyone. He keeps saying we're not a charity case, but actually at this point that's exactly what we are. We need all the charity we can get."

"There's no shame in taking help when you need it, Lelia. Besides, we'd love it if you could come. It would be fun. Your brother and his wife can't make it this year because he's stationed overseas of course. They'll be joining us by Skype on Christmas Day. It would be a chance to say hi to them too. Do talk to Brett and see if you can get him to change his mind about coming here. Your father thinks the world of him…."

"Mum, Dad does not think the world of Brett. You know as well as I do that he's never liked him. He says he's not good enough for me."

It was Beryl's turn to chuckle. "No one is good enough for his daughter, Lelia, or haven't you noticed?"

"I've noticed, but Brett really is a good guy. He just needs a little more time to get things straightened out in his life. Even though we argue, he's still very good to me, Mum."

"That to me is the most important thing because I know he has a temper. Are you sure…."

"He has never raised a hand to me. He does have a bit of an attitude, but you have to remember he had a hard time as a child. He didn't have a very happy home life. It's just going to take him a while to change how he thinks, to realize that everyone isn't against him."

"I know, dear."

"One thing he promised me when we got married was that he would make me happy, give me nice things like I had when I lived at home. He doesn't want anyone else to give me those things, he says it's his job as my husband to do that. I think a big part of our problems is that things aren't working out the way he wanted."

"Lelia, you and Brett are still very young. I would have liked it if you'd waited a couple of more years before you got married, but I believe you can make this marriage work. He has a whole lifetime to give you nice things. It doesn't have to happen all at once. He's putting too much pressure on himself."

"Brett is angry about a lot of things, and that worries me."

"Me too, sometimes," said Beryl seriously. "That's always on the back of my mind. Lelia, I'm going to ask you a straightforward question and I would like you to answer me in the same way."

There was no hesitation on the other end of the line. "I know what you're going to say, Mum, but go ahead and ask me anyway."

"All right then, here it is. Are you happy, dear?"

Happy. Lelia had been over-the-moon happy the day she'd met Brett Murdoch. She thought he was the cutest guy in the entire school, but he always kept to himself. He never seemed very friendly. One day while she was sitting alone at one of the tables in the library, she looked up to see him watching her. He'd quickly looked away, but their eyes met again and held and there was something there, an attraction. She'd smiled shyly at him, and he'd taken that as an invitation to join her at the table.

They'd talked well past the study hour. When the librarian approached them tapping on her watch to tell them the library was closing, he'd walked her home, carrying her books. And that was it. They'd instantly become a couple and were inseparable that summer. She knew he didn't have it easy at home although he rarely brought it up, only hinted at it a time or two. Other than that they told each other everything about themselves.

They were seventeen when he asked her to marry him. There was no ring, it was almost as if he didn't realize there was supposed to be. He'd told he wanted to be with her always, and she wanted the same thing. So they promised themselves to each other. They weren't out of school six months before they got married, but when fantasy met reality, there were understandable stumbling blocks. That's when they really got to know one another. They loved each other, that was a certainty for both of them, they just had to learn how to live together.

"I'm as happy as I can be, I suppose," she told her mother. "I don't run around laughing all day, but I am where I want to be. I can tell you that without a doubt. And I love him if that's your next question."

"It was, and can you guess what else I'd like to know?"

"Does he love me?"

"You're absolutely correct, that's what I was going to ask you."

"Sure, I guess."

"You guess! Lelia, you mean you're not sure?"

"It's just hard to tell sometimes, because he's so...."

"Angry...."

"Yes."

"Okay, honey, I don't want to overstep but you know if you're not happy you can come back home, even if it's just for a little while."

"I don't think Brett would care much for me running back home to Mummy and Daddy. I'm going to make this work. Besides, I have to now."

"What do you mean?"

"Because I'm pregnant."

"Lelia! That's wonderful, dear!"

That's when the tears came. "No, Mum, it's not wonderful. I cannot be pregnant," she sniffed. "I cannot afford to be pregnant. *We* cannot afford to be pregnant. It takes money to have a baby."

"Sweetheart, your father and I will help you any way we can. Are you absolutely sure? How late are you?"

"A month."

"Oh my goodness! And you're usually very regular?"

"As clockwork. Mum, this is the worst Christmas ever!"

"Money aside, are you happy that you might be pregnant? I know you always wanted children."

"I do. We both do, when the time is right. The problem is that now is definitely not a good time, and we were trying to be so careful."

"A lot of things in life happen when we're not ready, Lelia. We just *get* ready and get on with it. I'm sure everything will work out fine."

"Right."

"Have you told Brett about this yet?"

"Are you kidding me? He'd flip out. I can't tell him."

"Why would he flip out, dear? Didn't you just tell me you both want children?"

She could not forget the argument they'd had after Brett lost his job a few months ago. He'd been as down as she'd ever seen him, distraught over the loss of the job he loved and one that promised steady promotion. He thought the world of Wally, so it was also losing a valued friendship that bothered him. It was then that he'd said if he couldn't control his temper he shouldn't be around children. It was as though that was the straw that broke the camel's back because he'd obviously been having doubts that he'd not shared with her. That was the day that a lot of things changed for them.

"He's just not sure about it right now."

"Why ever not?"

"Because he's changed his mind. He doesn't think he'd make a very good father. He doesn't think he'd have the patience to deal with raising a child."

"Everyone has doubts. Everyone is nervous, that's not unusual. Bringing a child into the world can be a frightening thing, happy yes, but it's a very big deal and there will be challenges."

"He certainly has plenty of doubts. Honestly, I don't know what I'm going to do. I'm afraid he'd just walk out if I tell him I'm going to have a baby."

* * *

Brett glanced over at Snowflakes and knew he wasn't ready to take the dog home. Yet. He wasn't sure Lelia would be there anyway because she'd been working extra hours lately. All because he wasn't man enough to pull his share of the load. He'd lost another job because of his temper. He didn't have to get into an argument with Wally; he could learn to let a little more go. It was just that he felt frustrated because he'd imagined his life would be so much better at this point. He was too impatient. He'd had a five-year plan, and that included a nice house in the suburbs, him tinkering around the property; mowing the lawn, stuff like that. Instead they were living in a cramped basement apartment, and it wouldn't be long before they couldn't even afford that. They'd gotten a notice last month that the rent was going up in January. Thank heavens the big box store where his wife worked was only a couple of blocks away. That freed up their car so he could go look for work, but so far it had been a waste of time. He expected them to say no before he even asked. Factory work wasn't his thing anyway; that had been today's turndown. He liked construction but it seemed no one was hiring this time of year, not where he'd tried anyway. Maybe Wally had spread the word about him being a hot head, but on second thought he knew Wally wasn't that kind of guy.

And there was Lelia, working all hours. She didn't complain, but he knew he'd let her down by losing such a good job and thereby his benefits.

Didn't anyone understand how frustrated he felt? Try for even a minute to understand where he was coming from? It did occur to him as he drove out of town that maybe he could try to see where other people were coming from for a change. Maybe Wally was having trouble at home or something. He knew his wife hadn't been well. Maybe Wally himself was sick or something and wasn't letting on. Hadn't he given all of his employees a big Christmas bonus last year, *and* a turkey? This year he and Lelia were just trying to make grocery money. Wally had given him severance pay, but that went for bills. Even so they'd had to give up their cellphones because they could no longer afford them.

No, he couldn't go home just yet. He had to try to get himself in a better frame of mind or there'd be another fight and he'd blame himself, just like he always did. He hated to see his wife cry, and Lord knows he'd made her cry often enough these past few months. But today was different. Today he would put a smile on her beautiful face. He tried to think out the perfect plan to surprise her with the dog. Maybe he'd wait until Lelia was in bed and then come in and let the dog lick her face or something. Or turn on the light and pass her the poodle. Yeah, maybe that was the way to go about it. He just needed a little more time to put everything together in his head. So instead of turning and heading for home, he continued on out into the country.

He knew one thing; he had two cigarettes left and he needed a smoke. He had enough money in his pocket to buy a pack. So the first store they came across that's what he'd do.

Snowflakes had been lying morosely on the seat. She now sat up and looked at him pointedly, even whining a bit before giving a single bark.

"What?" he asked the dog, smiling. "We're going to be home soon enough, maybe a couple of hours. Just hang in there."

The dog whined again and then it struck him. "You need to go pee?"

Snowflakes obviously recognized the question and barked once in agreement.

"You're a smart little goober, I'll give you that," he told her affectionately. "Okay, we'll stop, but I have to find something to use for a leash. I know if I let you out, you're gone."

Brett parked on the side of the road and pulled the tie out of the bottom of his jacket pocket and fastened it to the red collar. "There, you want to do your thing? Let's go."

He walked around to the passenger side, opened the door and the tiny dog hopped out and proceeded to answer the call of nature, both numbers.

Brett laughed. "Sorry girl, for making you wait. That wasn't very nice of me, was it? I'm going to have to get better at this."

Kind of like having his own kid he thought, although he knew he wasn't exactly father material. At least that was one good thing about him, he thought. He was well aware of his shortcomings. Dr. Phil said that was called insight. He smiled. He was enjoying being with the dog. Loving it actually, so maybe there was hope for him after all.

Back in the car Snowflakes looked at him hopefully again, her mouth lolling open in that sweet canine smile. He smiled back. "What?"

She barked, then smiled as if expecting him to know what she wanted. Obviously, someone, that being the cowboy, was very good at reading her mind and she saw no reason to believe that everyone wouldn't be the same way.

And then it struck him. "You're hungry, aren't you?"

Another bark, and he clearly understood that one to be yes. Hmmm.

He had just enough money for cigarettes. A bag of dog food he imagined would cost about the same, especially at a convenience store, but looking at that little face he knew there was no contest. Snowflakes would eat. He needed to quit smoking anyway. Lelia was always after him about it. Now was just as good a time as any to get started. He wasn't a heavy smoker anyway, so cold turkey it was. That would be *his* Christmas turkey, no more smokes.

"Okay, Pooch," he told the dog, "Daddy's going to get you something to eat."

"Daddy! Come on Brett, you're losing it," he said out loud, but he couldn't help but try it on for size. Daddy. No way. He just wouldn't be a good father although he was feeling kind of fatherly at the moment, for what that was worth.

He came across a country store not far down the road and sure enough they had a small bag of dog food, for puppies it said. Considering her size, that might be a good choice. And water, the dog would need water. So he grabbed a bottle of spring water too and put it on the counter with the kibble. He didn't quite know how he was going to get the water from the bottle into the dog, but he'd figure something out as he went along.

Carrying the dog food and the water he started out of the store, looking forward to being greeted by that cute little face. However, when he rounded the corner to his vehicle, the dog was gone.

Chapter Two

Cole adjusted his Stetson and undid the buttons on his fleece jacket. The temperature in the store had risen to an uncomfortable level because of the crowd. All he had to get was a small turkey, a bag of dog food and one of those oversized TV dinners to throw into the oven for himself tonight. He was hungry, it was getting late, and he didn't much relish having to peel vegetables and thaw a steak before he could eat. He glanced at his watch as he headed to the frozen food section. He'd better hurry because that poodle hadn't been watered in a while and he wasn't thinking about the water going in.

He didn't often have the opportunity to entertain Snowflakes because she actually belonged to his ex-wife, well soon to be ex-wife, Elsa. *His* dog, Rascal, a golden lab/shepherd cross, had gone to that big dog kennel in the sky about six months ago and he missed his old friend like crazy. Snowflakes was a rescue dog, and he could remember the day she'd come home with Elsa. Too cute to leave her there was how Elsa had described her, and indeed, Snowflakes was probably the cutest thing on four legs with her fluffy white coat and almost constant smile. And it wasn't hard to figure out how she got her name either, that had been inspired by the weather the day Elsa had brought her home. It'd been snowing at the time, big soft flakes. Hollywood snow, because it was so perfect. The little poodle, elated with her new home, had dashed around the yard trying to catch snowflakes, only to have them melt on her tiny pink tongue. Snowflakes just seemed like the obvious choice of name.

Snowflakes was with him today because he was dog sitting for Elsa who'd gone to Fredericton on two-day business trip. No problem, he liked the dainty little thing, and she wasn't any trouble at all, probably the friendliest dog he'd ever seen. Very loving. He'd enjoyed snuggling down with her last night in bed, Snowflakes resting her head on the pillow like she owned the place. He smiled as he called that image to mind and remembered *she* was smiling at him when he woke up.

Having made his selections, the shortest line he could find was at the self-checkout, but even that stretched almost the length of the store. The last few days before Christmas were always chaotic, and he'd only finished his Christmas shopping yesterday. He was a typical wait 'til the last gun is fired male shopper. Really though, he only had to buy for his mother and father. When he couldn't find the perfect gift, he'd booked them on a cruise to Alaska. It was a trip they'd often talked about taking.

Out of the corner of his eye he noticed a woman standing in the line-up adjacent to his, stealing furtive glances of him. She was pretty, in a cosmetic kind of way, but since his divorce wasn't final yet he wasn't out looking. Besides, he wasn't even sure he would then. It would take him a while to get back in the dating groove seeing as how he hadn't been in it for so many years. He probably wouldn't even know how to go about it now. Dating practices had changed a lot, and the fly in the ointment for him was that the divorce hadn't been his idea. He was still deeply in love with his wife.

Feeling the woman's eyes on him he looked in her direction and could see she was now full-out watching him. He gave her a fleeting smile and the briefest nod of his head just to be polite.

"Busy, isn't it?" she asked, initiating conversation by stating the obvious. "I think we're going to be here all night."

"I think you might be right," he answered noncommittally. "I guess we can expect things to be slow at Christmas."

"You only have three items so you can go ahead of me," she offered generously.

She even stepped back a pace or two in her line to make room for him to come stand in front of her, and thereby bring him much closer.

"Nah, I'm good," he said, "but thank you. This line's starting to move."

She continued, undaunted. "Are you from around here? I shop here all the time and I haven't seen you before."

"Not far from here," he said as a customer finished paying and the line truly did begin to move.

He did not want to continue this conversation. She was probably a very nice lady but there was something predatory about her, it was in her eyes. It was always in the eyes. Too … intense. Too interested. Too … everything. He'd take a pass; continue with his unofficial vow of celibacy because that's what it had amounted to since he moved out of the marital home. Actually before that if the truth be told.

Finally it was his turn to ring through and he wasted no time bagging his items and heading back out into the chilly December evening. He set the groceries in the back of his truck and went around to get in, realizing with a start that Snowflakes was not in the cab.

He immediately hurried around to the other side of the pick-up and looked under the seat and behind the seat and then in the crew cab. No fluffy white poodle. She was nowhere to be seen, and unless in the half hour he was tied up in the supermarket she had learned to undo the door and close it again, she'd been taken. He was stunned. Never in a million years did he ever think such a thing would happen, but it apparently had. Stealing a dog right out of someone's vehicle at Christmas.

Security cameras! It had to be on camera somewhere. They could get a license number and get the dog back pronto. So back into the store he went on the trot and asked to speak to the manager.

Within minutes Cole was in the manager's office along with security, reviewing camera footage.

"There he is right there," the security guy pointed out as he leaned closer to the screen, "but the camera faces the drivers side of your truck. You can see the guy making his move though. You pulled in right beside him, one space over."

They watched what appeared to be a male wearing a dark hoodie as he took the dog out of the truck. Seconds later the vehicle left the parking lot. They could basically identify the make and model of the car, but the license plate was pretty beat up and covered with road dirt, so therefore unreadable. Great!

The manager was sincerely apologetic. "I'm sorry, Mr. Donahue. I'll call the police and have them respond if you want to report it. Was it a valuable dog?"

Cole folded his arms, disappointed there was really nothing to go on. "To us it is. It was a rescue dog, but of course it has huge sentimental value. I know the police have their hands full at the moment with what happened last night, so I won't bother them with this. The surveillance footage is of no real use, but thank you anyway. We'll have to look for her ourselves and I think we should get started on it right away."

The security officer was sympathetic. "Does it belong to one of your kids?"

The question caught Cole off guard, triggering a lingering disappointment that the big family he and Elsa planned to have had never materialized. Their marriage had failed before they could get to where children would be part of the picture. It was a sore spot with him, and she refused to discuss it, so he could only assume it was a tender issue with her as well.

"It belongs to my wife," he said, not wanting to get into the ex thing with strangers. She wasn't his ex yet anyway, but none of that was anybody's business.

The security officer folded his arms. "I don't know what your chances are of getting the dog back because there's so little to go on, but I wish you all the luck in the world. What kind of dog was it?"

Cole sighed, dreading the news he would have to break very soon. "A small white poodle."

The store manager had gotten to his feet behind his desk. "At least she's not out running around loose. The temperature is supposed to drop fast tonight. It's going to be a cold one."

Minutes later Cole was back sitting in his truck. Poor little Snowflakes, he only hoped she was safe and that whoever took her would be kind. He shoved unpleasant images from his mind with an effort. He had to call Elsa right away and tell her what happened, but then just as quickly decided he couldn't do it over the phone. She at least deserved to be told in person. She was not going to be happy, and he couldn't blame her. He wouldn't be too happy either if that had happened to his dog.

He made his way to what was now Elsa's place, alone, in Stoney Creek. He kept a sharp eye out for a tiny white dog on foot, hoping against hope, but of course there was nothing. No such luck to have the dog back safely in his care. He might as well face the music and be done with it. He could see that her car was in the drive when he pulled in and got out. He was glad she wasn't in the window watching for them because she'd know immediately that something was wrong if he was walking to the door without the dog.

She answered on the second knock and looked at him strangely when she didn't see Snowflakes. "Where's the dog?" she asked, checking the ground to see if she had walked to the door instead of being carried.

"Can I come in?"

"Certainly you can come in, but where's Snowflakes?"

He stepped in and pulled the door shut behind him. "Elsa, I'm afraid I have some really bad news and I wanted to tell you in person rather than over the phone."

She looked stricken. "What do you mean you have really bad news? I assume it's about Snowflakes since she isn't with you."

"It's about Snowflakes. She was...."

"Run over?" she demanded, tears springing to her eyes. "Snowflakes is dead?"

He reached to put his arms around her, but she deftly stepped out of his embrace, stiff as a poker so he dropped his arms. "No, she didn't get hit by a car and as far as I know she's not dead."

"What do you mean *as far as you know*? What's going on, Cole? Where's my dog?"

"She got stolen out of my truck at the supermarket. I was only inside for a short time and when I came out, she was gone. I'm so sorry. I feel terrible."

"Oh no! Was the theft caught on camera? Are they looking for whoever did it?"

"The theft was caught on surveillance camera, but the footage is poor. The camera faced the driver's side of the truck, not the passenger door. You can see that somebody went to the truck and took the dog, but it wasn't possible to get a license number because the plate was in such poor shape."

"So the police have nothing to go on, is that what you're telling me?"

"Basically."

"Well how could they have gotten the dog if your doors were locked? They broke in you mean?"

Cole let out an exasperated burst of air, loathe to confess his negligence. "That's the thing, the truck doors weren't locked."

"The doors weren't locked? What do you mean they weren't locked?"

"It means just that. I didn't think of it, I'm sorry. I never lock my doors."

She had her arms wrapped tightly around herself, but he knew she would still not be receptive to a comforting hug seeing as how he was the cause of the problem. She might be more inclined at the moment to provide the blindfold for the firing squad.

"And now my dog is gone ... because of *you*."

"Well *I* didn't steal her," he said, knowing he didn't have a leg to stand on.

"No, but somebody else was only too happy to because you didn't bother to lock your doors. You couldn't have made it any easier for her to be taken. An unlocked door is practically an invitation."

"Elsa, I'm sorry. You've got no idea how badly I feel right now. I cared for that little dog too you know."

She turned away from him, her shoulders hunched, and he knew she was crying. Talk about feeling like a first-class heel.

"Elsa, sweetheart, I really am sorry. Look, I'm going to do everything I can to find that dog. We'll make posters and put them up and surely through those as well as social media we can get her back in no time flat. Someone somewhere will see her and let us know. We're going to get her."

She kept her back turned to him. He put his arms around her, still hoping to offer some comfort, but he felt her stiffen at his touch, so he backed off. Maybe it was not so much about the dog as it was that she was distancing herself from him now that their divorce was close to being official, although she'd said all along that she wanted them to remain friends.

She turned to face him and indeed there were tears on her face. "What is that poor little thing going through right now I wonder? As you know, she was rescued from a difficult situation when I got her. Now she's been thrown right back into God knows what, and all because you didn't lock your doors. How could you be so irresponsible? I trusted you to look after her, not throw her to the wolves."

He gritted his teeth. This was going down just about the way he suspected it would, but again, how would he feel if his dog had been stolen because she had forgotten lock her car doors? He knew he'd react in the very same way. He could also understand that her imagination was likely going into overdrive, worried about the dog's wellbeing.

"Elsa, I'm sorry about the doors. I apologize but yelling at me isn't going to bring the dog back. I said I'd help you look!"

But she wasn't quite finished venting her frustration. "What if that had been our child, would you have been just as careless?" she threw at him angrily, but she was stepping into delicate territory.

He felt his gut tighten. "Hey! Let's not start down that road, Elsa. I said I was sorry, and I will do everything I can to find the dog."

"Sorry isn't going to bring Snowflakes back, Cole. I'll call Matt. Maybe he can help fix this mess."

He could feel his blood pressure jumping in double-digit increments. So there was someone else. Matt.

"Matt?"

"Yes, Matt. He's a guy from work, one of the district managers."

"A guy from work."

"That's right, a guy from work."

"Well unless Matt is a magic man, I don't see how he can do anything other than what I've already done."

"Like lose the dog you mean?"

"Elsa, I'm not going to play this game with you. What I do want to do is get busy trying to find her. We could go out and drive around; maybe we'll see her."

"I don't see why the police aren't looking too. A crime has been committed."

"That's true, but like I said earlier, there simply wasn't enough information for them to go on; no license plate, no good description of the guy who took her. Those surveillance cameras at the supermarket aren't the best. You'd really have to know what you were looking for in the first place. I mean a good description of the guy."

"Perfect!" she said folding her arms. "But I suppose the police already have their hands full with that bank robbery yesterday; they're still trying to track down the suspects. They probably wouldn't even have time to look for a missing dog, stolen or otherwise."

He sighed deeply, nodding in agreement. "We have to look ourselves. Whoever did it can't have gone far; it had to be someone here locally and the dog just might get away from him and try to come home. You never know."

"But if she was taken by car she could be almost anywhere by now. When exactly did it happen?"

"About an hour and a half ago, give or take."

Elsa was fighting back tears again as the news of Snowflakes' theft continued to sink in. "Heaven only knows where she is, or even if she's still alive."

"I don't imagine they'd take the dog with the intention of harming her."

"Was she still wearing her collar and tags when you left her?"

"Of course she was. I wouldn't take that off."

"Well that's a big plus. If someone does find her, she'd have her identification on, and I'll get a call."

"I know it sounds hopeless right now, but we have to believe we'll get her back, do everything we can to accomplish that. Do you want to make some posters? I'm sure you've got lots of pictures of Snowflakes we can use. We should get them up right away in case she's still in the area."

She still looked like she wanted to flay him alive, but common sense prevailed. "You're right, we should get some posters up as soon as we can, and I'll get her image out on social media too. We've probably already lost too much time. Maybe you could have called and let me know what happened so I could have already gotten started on that."

Cole knew he wasn't going to get off the hook without a few more shots, but whatever, he deserved them for leaving the truck door unlocked. He always figured if they were going to steal his truck, they'd find a way to do it, whether the doors were locked or not. He never kept anything of any real value in the cab anyway, so it didn't matter. That was until today of course and he kicked himself for putting poor little Snowflakes in harm's way.

"I thought I should tell you in person, not over the phone. Again, Elsa, I'm really sorry. I truly am. It was stupid of me not to lock the doors with her in the truck."

She sniffed. "Come on into my office so we can work on a poster. It shouldn't take long to put one together."

He followed her through the huge house where he'd lived until a year or so ago. He called it the mausoleum because footsteps actually echoed here in places, not to mention their voices. He knew that because their arguments had sounded like they were taking place in a stadium, not the family home. The last thing he'd wanted was to live in a mansion, and since Elsa also went for minimalist décor, he'd never felt at home in the thing. It was more like a museum, plenty of costly accoutrements and never anything out of place with Elsa presiding over the grand manor. It just wasn't his style, and that, along with a number of other things, contributed to the downfall of their marriage. Elsa was on a power trip, and he'd been one of her first victims.

Her office was still at the back of the house on the first floor, although when they got there, he thought it somehow looked larger than he remembered. The space reflected her rising star as a company executive. She needed the space he guessed because she brought more and more work home with her as she rose steadily through the ranks. This square footage was also a study in white on white with a surfeit of chrome. It just looked … cold … unwelcoming. Removed from reality somehow.

He was a good ole boy, born and raised on a ranch where he still worked as foreman, although following his separation from Elsa he'd also started his own ranch. He was in the process of growing his herd on the five hundred acres he'd bought out in Shenstone. He'd also built himself a cozy cabin and had just begun to settle nicely into that. Would he like to get remarried someday and have that family he'd always thought he'd be raising at this stage of his life? Time would tell. Right now, Elsa still occupied his mind, front and centre, rent-free.

How he and Elsa had gotten together in the first place was something of a modern mystery. The daughter of a high-profile politician, she'd become used to the finer things in life at an early age. As an only child she pretty much got whatever she wanted. And she had wanted him and got him. The marriage had soured early, but he loved his wife enough to stay the course and try to work things out. He'd signed on for better or worse. He believed that way down under all of those ambitious layers was the Elsa he'd fallen in love with.

He pulled up a chair and sat down beside her in back of the desk as she scrolled through photos of the dog. Soon they found a great likeness of Snowflakes in an adorable pose, both quickly agreeing it was a good choice.

"Okay, I think we should post a reward for her safe return."

She nodded with a slight movement of her head, still not completely thawed. "That's a good idea."

"Let's say $500.00, and I'll pay it. That much money should be a great incentive, especially at this time of year. People should take notice of that. I'll bet we have her back before morning."

She sniffed again. "We've got to, Cole, it's going to be really cold tonight. I can't bear to think about her out there … she was still wearing her little red sweater, wasn't she?"

"Yes, honey, she was," he said reaching over to touch her hand, then pulling away when she looked at it pointedly. "We'll look all night if we have to."

"Don't you have work to do? Look after your own cattle?"

"I called Jake Patterson on the way over here and he's going to do the evening chores for me, no problem. He said he'd help tomorrow too if I need him, and I might. Dad's going to step in for me at his place."

"So you really will help me look, even if it takes all night?"

"Of course!"

"But where will we start?"

"It'll be like looking for a needle in a haystack, but we'll just keep moving. Make a pile of posters and we'll cover all of Riverview and Moncton for starters."

"Should I put my telephone number on them? I'm really not comfortable having my home address out there or other personal information where I live alone."

That answered his next question to his satisfaction. Whoever this Matt person was, at least he wasn't hanging his hat here. But then again, this place was so big, he could be living in the east wing or something.

"You can use my telephone number, Elsa. In fact I think you should. And put my address, not yours. It wouldn't be a good idea to have your information out there for God knows who to see."

"So your camp is liveable? I didn't think you had it built yet."

He looked at her sharply. "My camp? Liveable?"

"You know what I mean."

"No, Elsa, I don't. It's small yes, but only by these standards. And it's not a camp, it's a cabin."

She shrugged. "If that's what you want."

"That's what I want. So, okay, put that address and my phone number and let's print these off and get on the road."

"Where are you going to put yours up? We don't want to duplicate our efforts and waste valuable time. I could start with Riverview."

He didn't like the idea of her going it alone. He still felt protective toward her, not to mention enjoying spending time with her even with her as mad as a wet hen. "Why don't you come with me, and we can cover the area together? We'll take turns putting them up."

"What about Matt?"

"What *about*, Matt? What's he got to do with any of this?"

"He wouldn't mind helping, I know."

'I'll just bet he wouldn't,' Cole wanted to say, but didn't. What he did say was: "By all means call him if you think he should know. I guess the more people involved the better chance we have to get the dog back."

"That's what I was thinking."

After she had finished posting Snowflakes' image on social media and asking that the post be shared to help find her dog, Elsa put a call through to Matt. Cole couldn't hear the other end of the conversation but listening to this side told him Elsa's request was not producing the desired results.

"I understand that you're busy, Matt. Would you have even an hour or so to spare to help look? No, I'm with my ex-husband, Cole."

He wanted to remind her that he wasn't an ex just yet, but he didn't think it was a good idea to interrupt. He did give her the *look*, and it must have been received in kind because she glanced away. Good. That was how he felt about it.

"I don't think she will find her way back home, Matt, she was stolen. She … yes, I've seen the Incredible Journey, but there are hazards out there, and it's going to be freezing cold tonight. All right, I'll let you know if she makes it back home. Bye."

She refused to meet Cole's gaze when she hung up a little too hard. He was secretly relieved that Matt wasn't as devoted as she had led him to believe.

Elsa was quiet as she stacked paper into the printer and ran off the suggested number of posters. "Do you think seventy-five will be enough, Cole? Maybe we should make a few more."

"Do a hundred just to be sure. And if you don't have a heavy-duty stapler and staples, we can drop by my place. I've got some there."

"I've got those things here so let's get going. Poor little Snowflakes is out there somewhere. I can't bear to think of her being out alone at night, especially in this weather."

He wanted to hold Elsa, reassure her, but again it didn't feel like the thing to do. She was still super angry with him, and he knew from experience that it wasn't going to go away anytime soon; at least until they found the dog. He'd been up all hours last night with a sick cow, so he'd better get some double-strength coffee into him if he was going to pull another all-nighter.

He retraced his steps to his truck, Elsa climbing into the passenger seat and snapping her seatbelt in place. It was funny how things worked out. He never believed he'd ever see her in his truck again, be this close to her, but here they were. However it wasn't the most pleasant of circumstances, and certainly not romantic in any way, shape or form.

Fortunately it was a calm night, although bitingly cold; it would have been much worse if it had been snowing and blowing. Cole was no fan of the snow, too much of it could make ranching a difficult task. He knew too that Elsa was no snow bunny herself, remembering her comical attempts at downhill skiing. Yet here they were on a cold, clear, moonlit night, looking for Snowflakes.

Chapter Three

The closer Brett got to the car, the harder his heart pounded. Had someone taken the dog from him? As he stood looking into the darkened vehicle wondering what to do next, the sweet little face popped up like a tiny friendly ghost. She scurried onto the passenger seat, front paws resting on the door vinyl. He hoped she didn't have anything left over from her potty break and made a deposit on the back floor of the car. Nah, he decided, relieved that the poodle was still with him. She was probably just exploring.

Walking around to the driver's side he climbed in quickly lest Pooch here really did decide to make a fast getaway. He liked the name Pooch better than Snowflakes, but that was just him. He'd heard that name as a kid although the hound so-named was ugly compared to this little beauty. He accepted that he wasn't very good at picking out names, Pooch being a prime example. It would be up to Lelia to come up with something better if she wanted to change it from Snowflakes. It was her Christmas gift after all.

Once settled on the car's bench seat, he opened the bag of kibble and folded back the top to create an instant dog dish, and sure enough the poodle dove in, most unladylike. Then as if remembering her manners she slowed to a more graceful pace, nibbling the kibble, although continuing to crunch through it at quite a clip. It occurred to him that it might be possible to overfeed her, but weren't dogs smart? Wouldn't they stop when they were full? On second thought, they probably weren't much worried about waistlines, so watched closely until he thought she'd had enough and closed the bag's zip top. Her stomach could only hold so much, right? It looked like she'd already taken in more than there was room for, considering her size.

Once the main course was finished, he uncapped the bottle and poured some water into one cupped hand, and it worked like a charm. The poodle quickly lapped it up with her tiny pink tongue. He repeated the process several times until it seemed she'd had her fill and backed away, leaving him with a handful of water. He opened the window, shook his hand free of the moisture, and dried it off on his jeans. There, chow time was over.

Now for the main event. He had to get the dog home to Lelia. By now he reckoned there might be people out looking for Pooch, so the first thing he had to do was get rid of the dog's bright blue identification tag that hung beside the metal heart on the collar. A pocketknife stretched the metal ring enough that he could pull it off. He heaved it out the window and it flew clean across the road and landed with a soft ping on the other side. For some reason that's when it, the gravity of what he had done really began to settle over him. He'd stolen somebody else's dog and was now hiding evidence. He'd never stolen anything in his life, hated thievery, but he'd done it on the spur of the moment. A sick feeling lodged in the pit of his stomach.

It still wasn't too late to get rid of the smoking gun as it were, but even the notion of setting this little dog loose on a cold winter night was unthinkable. Despite not being able to come up with a decent excuse for how he'd come into possession of her, he could return to the supermarket parking lot right now and put it back; take it into the supermarket and say he found it wandering around, lost, but then he remembered the surveillance cameras. Of course, they had him on camera, so his goose was cooked any way he sliced it. He truly did feel sick to his stomach now. What if they got his license plate? He climbed out and checked and was relieved to see it covered in road grime and therefore undecipherable. Also, it had been dark when he took the dog, and he had his hood up so they wouldn't have gotten a very good picture of him. Still, he couldn't take the chance of returning to the scene of the crime.

He'd committed theft. He'd broken the law. First he lost his job, and now he'd done a crime for which he could go to jail. That was a sobering thought. He'd lose Lelia for sure. He could get away free and clear if he let the dog go, maybe leave her at the country store and say he found her walking, but he still felt guilty. Besides, there'd be cameras in this store too, inside ones, and he hadn't thought to put his hood up when he bought the food and water. Damn! He was the world's worst crook. If he'd gotten lucky the first time around, they'd get him from the store surveillance footage for sure.

The smart thing to do would be to let the little poodle out of the car and make his escape from this whole thing, but he'd already decided that was not an option. No way! Snowflakes smiled at him as if reading his thoughts, her eyes clearly telling him: I know you wouldn't do that to me. You'll take care of me, Brett ... I love you too.

Confound it! How had she gotten into his heart so easily? No, he'd take her home and give her to Lelia as per the original plan, but a little voice asked reasonably: you'd give a stolen dog to your wife for Christmas? He felt even sicker but knew he couldn't sit in his car all night with the dog. Lelia was probably already wondering where he was. He had to go home. Now.

The devil on his shoulder spoke again, telling him not to make a mountain out of a molehill. He'd simply found the dog and brought it home. Oh, so now you're a liar too, he taunted himself. He looked at that tiny trusting face again and knew he'd take the dog home to someone who would do right by her.

He was obviously a loser, but at least Lelia would be worthy of the poodle's love and affection.

He could see the kitchen light on in the apartment when he drove up, so unzipping his coat he slipped the dog inside out of sight, zipped it back up and went indoors.

"Brett! Where have you been, honey? I've been worried," Lelia called out, not turning from the counter where she was peeling potatoes.

He shrugged. "Nowhere in particular. Just out."

"How did you make out at the factory? Any openings at all?"

"Not a one because they're laying a bunch of people off in a few days. Downsizing he said."

"That's too bad, although I don't think you would have liked the work."

"Hmmm. Boring."

"Did you get the stuff at the store I need for supper?"

Too late he remembered the groceries in the car. He'd have to make a second trip, dog and all. "I just forgot to bring them in. I'll go get them…."

At that point Snowflakes had enough of the heavy jacket routine and gave an insistent bark from within the depths of the garment. It was likely dog talk for let me out! I can't breathe in here!

Lelia whirled around. "What was that? It sounded like a dog barking. Brett, have you got something tucked in your coat?"

Snowflakes poked her head out, all smiles, and gave another friendly yip.

"Oh my gosh! A puppy!"

His smile was now at least a mile wide too. "Not a puppy, but she's not very big. Merry Christmas, baby!" he said lifting the fuzzy little poodle out of his coat and passing it to a wide-eyed Lelia.

A born animal lover, Lelia cradled the tiny dog in her arms, laying her face against its soft coat. She began to croon to the poodle as Snowflakes smothered Lelia's face in wet kisses.

"She's so adorable, and she's even got her own little red collar and matching sweater. But where did you get her?" she asked her husband. "We don't have any money and I know dogs like this are very expensive."

There was nothing he liked better in this world than to see his Lelia smile, it lit up her face. It also lit up the room, much better than any Christmas tree ever could. In that moment he was glad he'd taken the risk, although common sense had already erased most of the original shine.

Still holding the dog she reached out her free arm to her husband, tears in her eyes, and he stepped into her embrace.

"Thank you, Brett, this is the best Christmas present ever. I can't believe I have my own little dog. It's something I was looking forward to someday when we had our own place."

He knew Lelia wasn't making a dig. She wasn't the type to be sarcastic, but he understood that someday was still a long while off at the rate they were going. "It looks like your dream came true a little early," he told her as the three of them continued to share the hug, Snowflakes happily smack dab in the middle of it.

"What should I call her?" she asked him, touching her nose to Snowflakes' shiny button nose.

"Her name is Snowflakes, it's on that metal heart hanging from her collar," he said helpfully and knew as soon as he'd opened his mouth that he'd made a mistake. He looked away hoping his wife wouldn't notice his tell tale guilty flush.

"Snowflakes? Oh it's perfect, isn't it? But you didn't tell me where you got her. You barely had grocery money. How could you possibly end up with this dog?"

"I found her," he said, making it up as he went along and knowing he was doing a terrible job of it. "She was walking along the street looking lost. I stopped and she hopped right up into my car."

"But what are we going to feed her?"

"I bought a bag of dog food for her on the way home, so we're all set," he said, remembering how fast Snowflakes scarfed down kibble.

Lelia laughed. "With what? Where are you getting all of this money all of a sudden?"

He grinned, knowing what he had to say next would make his wife even happier because she was not a fan of tobacco use. "I spent the money I had for cigarettes on food for little Snowflakes here. She was hungry and, well, she came first. Anyway, I've decided to quit smoking."

Lelia looked at him, her mouth open in a perfect O. "Wow! Brett, I'm impressed! I mean really impressed! Thank you, honey. That makes me very happy."

"So Merry Christmas, Lelia, a bit early, for both things. I obviously couldn't wait until the big day to give the dog to you, could I? She's small but I couldn't hide her until Christmas, and it's because of her that I gave up smoking."

"I can't tell you how glad I am you did that. And it doesn't matter to me that Snowflakes came a little early, I'm just happy to get her. Wait 'til I tell Mum about this. She'll want to come right over to meet her, I know she will because she loves animals too. I can't wait to show her off."

"Ahhh, maybe don't tell anyone about little Miss Snowflakes."

Lelia looked at him, puzzled. "Why not?"

"Ahh, because if she is missing then people will come forward and she'll have to go back home. You wouldn't have her for very long if that happened."

She looked down at the dog for a long minute, before raising her head and snaring Brett with a questioning gaze. "Is there something you're not telling me, Brett?"

He could feel warmth flood his face and cursed the fact that he blushed easily. "Like what?"

"I don't know, that's why I'm asking. So is she mine to keep or not?"

"As far as I'm concerned, she's yours to keep. I can't think of a better home for her than right here with you and I, can you? You don't want her to go back to wandering the streets, especially on a cold night like this."

"Of course not. I do love that you brought her home to me, Brett; that you wanted me to have her. But if she belongs to someone else, maybe her real owners are out looking for her at this very minute. Maybe she belongs to a child who's crying their eyes out over the loss of their pet. If it was our dog, we'd want someone to bring her back."

He shrugged. "Lelia, don't go making up this big sad scenario and getting yourself all upset. It could be they didn't want her anymore; maybe it's great that she has a new warm and loving home. Maybe she's been on her own for a while and is relieved to be here with us, especially at Christmas."

Lelia chuckled, but it was without mirth, as though the truth was dawning on her. "She's in pretty good shape for a dog that's been wandering the streets. Her coat is as white as snow, her sweater is clean and she's very healthy. I'd say there's a pretty good chance she hasn't been on her own for very long. She probably wants to go home."

Brett never took his eyes off the dog. "I don't think she's missing anyone too much, look at how she's taken to you. She hasn't stopped licking your face since she's been in your arms. I don't see her crying at the back door wanting to leave. I'd say by the looks of it, this is where she wants to be."

Lelia turned her attention to the little dog. "What about it, Snowflakes? Are you missing someone tonight?"

Snowflakes barked, then cocked her head to one side watching Lelia.

Brett smiled. "See? She said no."

"I think that was a yes. I really love the gesture, Brett, but this dog has to be returned to her rightful owners. Maybe we could keep her for Christmas and then afterward we'll start looking to see if she's lost. If so, make sure she gets back to where she's supposed to be."

Brett felt something like relief start through him. Maybe there was a way out of this after all without getting in any deeper. Lelia could enjoy the dog for Christmas, and after that he'd make sure Snowflakes was returned to her real owners … somehow. He'd figure it out. Leave her anonymously somewhere, with a note, an apology, and the rest of the bag of dog food as a gift. If he went about it that way he wouldn't be arrested. The dog would be back with the cowboy, and everybody would be happy.

"But in the meantime, Lelia, say nothing, okay? You're right the dog should be back with her real family. We'll do that, but let's enjoy her for the next week or so."

"So I shouldn't tell my mother, is that what you're saying?"

"They won't be coming over here anyway, so it'll be just you and me and Snowflakes. Even though she'll only be here for a short time, I think this might be the best Christmas we've had so far."

"I just thought of something else. There's another reason why we can't keep this little Christmas elf, as adorable as she is."

"What's that?"

"Don't you remember? We're not allowed to have pets here. Our landlady, Mrs. Brownleigh, was very specific about it. That rule didn't bother us when we took the place because we didn't intend to get a pet, but it is cause for eviction."

Brett's head drooped. "Honestly, I never thought about that. I just saw the dog and thought what a great Christmas present it would be for you. Now the more I think about it, it was a stupid move from beginning to end but I couldn't leave her out in the elements."

"You did the right thing. I know this little darlin' won't be a problem, but Mrs. Brownleigh said she doesn't want her property damaged. She has the right to enforce the no pet rule."

Brett huffed, rolling his eyes. "Yeah, like this is such a palace. It's already damaged enough if you ask me. Did Mrs. Brownleigh leave yet to go to her daughter's for Christmas?"

"I assume so. Her car was gone when I got back from work and there were no lights on upstairs. She said she was going early because it's supposed to snow in the next couple of days and she wanted to make it in time for Christmas. So we'll be able to let Snowflakes out for a pee when the time comes. We'll pick up whatever else she leaves behind, so the landlady won't find it. That way she won't know we have her here, or had her here, I should say. Hopefully Snowflakes will be reunited with her owner right after Christmas. Mrs. Brownleigh usually stays with her daughter until New Years so we should be okay."

Brett smiled the smile that Lelia always said transformed his face. It looked like his Christmas gift was going to get some traction after all. Maybe everything would work out for the best. Kind of like a borrowed Christmas gift, and Lelia seemed pretty comfortable with the fact that she'd only have the dog for a short while. But when the time came to part though he was sure it was going to be a different story. She'd be attached by then; he knew it because even a few minutes with a kitten and she didn't want to give it back. He himself was already attached to Snowflakes, he could feel it, so it was going to be hard. Honestly though, he'd feel better when his mistake was corrected.

"Okay, Brett, why don't you go and get the groceries out of the car? I'll hold Snowflakes until you get back." She nuzzled the dog, burying her face against her snow-white curly top.

After they'd finished eating, and Snowflakes had emptied another small dish of kibble, Brett made her a bed from a cardboard box and a towel. Snowflakes hopped in, turned around three times then settled down as if she was lying on silk. She did appear to feel very much at home in this small basement apartment and seemed to accept the young couple without complaint.

Brett and Lelia sat on the sofa watching the little dog sleep.

"I think she's sad," said Lelia after a few minutes. "It's the look she has on her face."

"Nah, I think she's just tired. It's been quite a day for her, and who knows how long she'd been walking before I found her?"

Lelia shook her head slowly. "Not much, I would say, because she couldn't stay that white while walking the streets. Maybe she got loose from somewhere nearby and ran off."

"Yeah maybe, so we should be really careful to always have a leash on her when we take her out into the backyard. I used the tie from my jacket when I was in the car, and it worked fine. I'll bring that in and that'll be our leash."

As if on cue the poodle hopped out of the box and marched purposefully to the back door, scratched against it once, and then looked hopefully at both Lelia and Brett. She switched her gaze from one to the other as though determining which one would do the honours.

"I guess she's telling us she wants to go out," said Lelia, disengaging herself from Brett and yawning as she got up from her comfortable spot on the sofa.

Brett was on his feet before Lelia reached the closet to get her coat. "I'll take care of it," he said, starting for the door. "Come on, Pooch. Let's make tracks."

They were back in under five minutes, Brett's face already red from the bitter cold. "She only had to pee," he announced when Snowflakes trotted into the warm apartment ahead of him. "Nothing too drastic, but we've got to find some plastic bags for … later. Kibble in, kibble out."

"You know," said Lelia when Brett had rejoined her on the sofa, "I was thinking. Maybe we should put up a tree after all. Just a small one and we still have tomorrow to do it. I can get a discount at work, or even find a small one real cheap. I feel more in the Christmas mood now since you brought Snowflakes home. I feel … I don't know, happier. What do you think, should we put up a tree?"

He shrugged, smiling, loving the warmth that had sprung to life between them again, and eager to nurture it. "Sure, why not? But don't bother getting one at work, a friend of mine has a tree lot. I might go and see if he needs a hand tomorrow because there are always people who leave getting their tree to the last minute. He told me before he has trouble finding people to work in the lot, so that would bring in a few extra dollars. And since I guess I won't be smoking anymore, it will give me something to do and not sit around thinking about … smoking, I'm doing pretty good now though, what with Snowflakes to distract me. I like looking after her."

She put her arm around him. "But what about when I go to work? Who's going to look after her then?"

"Hmmm, right, that could be a problem. But she should be okay for a few hours on her own, and I'll come home a couple of times during the day and check on her. I'll take her out for a whiz and feed her. The tree lot's only a few blocks away. I'll go there first thing tomorrow morning and see what he says."

Lelia was smiling as she settled into her husband's arms once again. "It sounds like a good idea, and I was thinking, Brett, since we're in the Christmas spirit, why don't you call Wally and apologize? Wish him a Merry Christmas? Maybe he'll give you your job back, you never know. You said yourself you wish you hade done things differently that day; that you miss the job."

"I don't know. Wally can be a pain sometimes."

"We can all be a pain sometimes. Personally I like Wally, I think he's nice and he was always very good to you. Let's face it, Brett. You need the job. I know you loved it, and it doesn't pay to make enemies."

Brett pulled a humourous face. "I wouldn't say Wally's my enemy, we just had a difference of opinion."

"Enough difference of opinion that you lost your job over it. I thought you told me he'd hinted that he had been going to give you a promotion?"

"He talked about it, but even if he did take me back now, I'd be at the bottom again having to work my way up."

"So? At least you'd be back in. I think it's worth a shot. You need a job, Brett. I'm not trying to get on your back about it, but you said yourself I can't take care of everything myself. I can't bring in the money we need to realize some of our dreams, like a new house. I think Wally would be very forgiving. You never did tell me what you said to him, but it probably wasn't that bad, was it?"

"Not really. I just told him it was a nowhere job and he could shove it ... stuff like that."

"Brett! Well let's put it this way, there's no harm in trying because all he can say is no. You won't be any further behind than you are right now, would you? Can you at least try?"

He sighed. "It's not as simple as that, Lelia. It's not like we had a simple little disagreement. I was pretty forceful with what I said to him."

"Your anger again."

"Yes, my anger again, okay?"

"Please don't get upset, honey, we're just talking."

Brett's voice began to rise. "It seems like it's always about me. I'm one big screw-up, okay? You married a dud!"

The dog got up, whining and went to Brett. Placing her little feet on his leg she looked up at him imploringly.

"It looks like someone thinks we're arguing," she said.

Reaching down she picked up the dog and settled her on her lap, stroking the soft curly coat to reassure her.

"Brett," she said, returning to their conversation. "I did not marry a dud. For the millionth time I married you because I love you, and no other reason. If I was only looking for dollar bills, I would have gone out with creepy Mason Baldwin when he asked me."

"You probably should have," he muttered under his breath.

"What did you say?"

He looked at her. "I'm pretty sure you heard me. Look, Lelia, I love you with all my heart, but…"

"But what?"

"But I'm a screw-up. I never seem to get things right. I make bad decisions."

"You're not a screw-up, Brett."

"I'm more of a screw-up than you know. Things get to me, okay? I'm just one big mistake walking around waiting to happen."

"Are you not happy here with me?"

He reached for her hand. "Of course I'm happy with you, Lelia. I just feel bad that I'm not able to give you what I think you should have, what you deserve. I wish I was a better person."

"The only way a person can be better is to do better, that's all I know to say. Apologize to Wally and get your job back. I'm sure he'd give it to you, and then go on from there. We all make mistakes, you're certainly not the first. Own it and then rise above it."

He sighed again, a smile tugging at the corners of his mouth. "Someone else has been watching Dr. Phil, but okay I get what you're saying. Maybe in the new year I'll think about it. In the meantime I'll see about the tree lot. That way if I get a few dollars, I can get a turkey for our Christmas dinner, a few more groceries. Some treats."

"We could always go to the food bank you know and get a few things. A lot of people need to go there. That's why it's there, for people who are having a tough time financially. There's no shame in doing it."

"You know how I feel about that, Lelia. A man should be able to provide for his family and that's what I intend to do, try to anyway."

"Men fall on hard times just like everyone else and shouldn't be too proud to take a few groceries when they're offered. Then when we're doing better, we can help someone else."

"I'll think about it, okay? No promises though. We're not starving yet."

She sat stroking the dog, now fast asleep in her lap, quietly changing the subject into less troubled waters. "I love your Christmas surprise for me, Brett, even though I might not be able to keep it. I know you were thinking of me when you brought her home. You got her off the streets, and I love you for it. Just even being able to be with her for a few days is a nice enough gift and I thank you very much."

"I wish we could keep her."

"Me too, but someday we'll have our dream home, and we can get our own little dog, just like this one. We won't have to worry about landlady rules then."

He reached over and stroked the dog too, Snowflakes sighing contentedly under the ministrations of the two new people in her life. She even appeared to be smiling in her sleep.

"I would say Snowflakes has fallen for you, Lelia. Look how contented she is; right at home."

"Would this be the kind of dog you'd like to have when we finally get our own home? I always took you for someone who'd like something a little bigger."

He smiled. "Yeah, me too, but this ball of fluff has stolen my heart there's no doubt about it. She makes me feel protective. I mean we only met a few hours ago but right now I'd do anything for her. I love looking after her."

"Can you see yourself losing your patience with her? Being angry at her for anything?"

His reaction was kneejerk. "No way! I'm not that much of a loser. I'm saying she brings out the protective side of me. I just want to look after her and make sure she's okay." He laughed self-consciously. "I'm not overly familiar with that side of me. Maybe there's hope for me yet."

Lelia laid her head on his shoulder. "That side of you is in there all right, I know it. That's what drew me to you in the first place. You're too hard on yourself, and sometimes you're too hard on other people. Not everyone is against you, Brett. Take this little dog for instance. She's trusting and loving toward you because she knows you'll do the right thing by her. She's giving you back what you're giving her. When you're really nice to people too, they'll be nice back, just like Snowflakes here."

"Hmmm", was all he said, but he was already deep in thought.

"What I was going to say earlier is that you gave me a really nice Christmas present this year, so now I have a really nice Christmas surprise for you."

"Come on now, Lelia, I don't want you spending money on me. I don't know where you'd get it to spend anyway with the state of our finances at the moment."

"This didn't cost me anything actually."

"So do I have to wait for Christmas morning, or do I get my surprise early too?"

"You want it right now?"

"Sure," he said, "do you have it here with you, or you mean you're going to bring it home tomorrow?"

"No, I have it here with me."

"Now you've got me really curious. Are you sure you want to do this tonight, not wait for Christmas morning?"

She snuggled deeper into his embrace. "Tonight is fine. Perfect, really."

"Okay then. Here pass me the dog and I'll hold her for you while you go get it."

"I don't have to get up to tell you my surprise."

He smiled, kissing her cheek. "Okay then, what is it? Tell me."

"Well," she said softly, "I'm pregnant. You're going to be a daddy, Brett. Merry Christmas."

Chapter Four

"Have you had supper yet, Cole?" Elsa asked him as they started for the city in search of Snowflakes, colourful Christmas lights decorating homes and businesses along the way.

Cole was one of the kindest men she'd ever met, although uncommonly stubborn. She shouldn't have jumped all over him for leaving his truck doors unlocked. She knew he would never in a million years purposely do anything to harm her dog … any dog or animal. He had been nothing but gentle and patient with Snowflakes.

"Cole," she said, her voice softer when he didn't immediately answer her. "I'm sorry I was sharp with you for not locking your truck doors earlier. I've actually done the same thing, walked away, and forgotten to lock up so I'm just as bad. I'm upset that she's gone is all. I love that little dog."

It was a moment or two before he spoke, and she wondered if he would. "I couldn't be sorrier, no matter how it happened. You trusted me with the dog, and I allowed someone to walk off with her. I didn't protect her and that makes me feel like a jerk."

"You're hardly that. I would never call you a jerk."

"You've called me worse," he reminded her although there was humour in his voice.

"Yes, but you deserved it at the time," she told him, her sassy side asserting itself.

"Probably," he agreed, remembering the playful pranks they used to play on each other in the old days.

Oh how times had changed. When had the fun gone out of their marriage? She knew the divorce was her idea, and it was what she felt should happen at the time because in her opinion their differences had become irreconcilable. They were out of step; wanted different things out of life. It wasn't that she didn't still care for him, at any point in their journey together, that wasn't true at all. It was simply that perhaps taking separate paths might be in the best interests for both of them. The chemistry between them was still there though, the air fairly crackled with it when they were anywhere near each other. Was that enough to continue to build a future, given the way she looked at things now?

She'd certainly thought they were on the same page when they got married almost six years ago, or more to the point hoped they were. Maybe they'd always been too different. Was it her fault that she had grand ambitions? She'd been brought up to think like that. She had to maintain certain standards at all times, although truthfully, she did enjoy pushing against them on occasion. At the end of the day though, she found herself embracing her parents' expectations of her. It seemed she too was influenced in many ways by her mother in anything she set out to accomplish, because when Phoebe said jump, people lined up to say how high? Yet when she'd emulated her mother's assertiveness in her own marriage, Cole had balked, dug in his heels and she got nowhere, fast. After awhile that became their norm, her cracking the whip, and him refusing to take heed. It simply couldn't continue like that. And then there was her father, Senator Randolph, an indomitable force of nature and the obvious choice of partner for someone like Phoebe. Both were formidable social climbers.

Now as she sat here in the darkened truck cab, stealing furtive sideways glances at Cole's rugged profile, every nerve in her body was alive. Their lovemaking had been spectacular, and she now realized that should have counted for more than it did. That too had suffered once she began her ascent up the proverbial social ladder on her own, not as the wife of a man whose family had practically built Albert County. The Donahues were famously well to do, and that image had mattered a great deal to her, although it was just not that important to either Cole or his family. From tough, spirited pioneer stock, they were content to go their own way. They lived their lives simply as generations before them had done, unpretentious and close to the land. The last thing they were interested in was a social ladder, or God forbid, climbing it.

She'd been thinking a lot about their past lately, both hers *and* Cole's, and doing a lot of daydreaming, like this. Shaking off her reverie she wondered if he'd spoken while she hadn't been paying attention. Had he answered her about supper? She'd feel silly if she asked again, but she had to because he'd go without eating just to make things right about the dog no matter how long it took. That was the single-minded, implacable Cole Donahue with the unshakable code of honour that she still secretly admired. Maybe they weren't that different after all, both strong-willed; neither one interested in taking a step back.

"I'm sorry, I wasn't listening," she apologized. "I was too busy thinking about Snowflakes, what's happening with her right now. I asked you if you're hungry, if you've eaten supper yet, but I don't know if you answered me."

He glanced over at her. "Not yet. My supper's on the back of the truck there," he said motioning with his head in the direction of the truck bed.

What on earth could be on the back of the truck that he'd planned to eat for supper? "It'd be thawed by now wouldn't it, whatever it is? Would it still be any good?"

"Not in this cold it wouldn't be thawed out. It's a frozen TV dinner, one of those big ones that I like. Pepper steak I think it is."

She wrinkled her nose. "Ugh! Mystery meat, you mean."

"Whatever."

"Okay then, if it doesn't matter where the meat comes from, let's stop for a burger or something. I grabbed a bite earlier at home, so I'm fine, but I want you to get something for yourself."

He never took his eyes off the road. "I don't need to stop for anything, I'm fine. All I want to do is find the dog."

"You need to eat, Cole."

"No, really, I'll wait until I get home. What we do need to stop and get are some extra staples, and I think another stapler too so we'll both have something to work with. Get some heavy tape to use on metal surfaces."

It was still a few more miles to the nearest hardware store and they covered the distance quickly. He insisted on running in to take care of the purchase himself while she waited in the heated truck.

Twenty minutes later he emerged, cussing under his breath when he climbed back into the cab. "Nothing's fast this time of year. I got what I was after, but the line-up was long. Luckily a woman with a cartload of stuff took pity on me. Score one for the Christmas spirit."

They headed for the supermarket parking lot from where Snowflakes had been taken and grabbed one of the few remaining spaces near the street. "Okay, all we could see on the surveillance tape was that the car turned right when he left the parking lot. So I don't know whether he crossed the bridge or headed straight up the road toward Salisbury. Anyway, I think we should start here. Tape a poster up on that light standard right over there. You never know, someone may have seen something and call. I can't imagine you haven't gotten anything yet on social media."

She sighed. "We haven't, I just checked even though I haven't had any prompts. Maybe people are too busy with Christmas to be bothered with a missing dog. It's too bad circumstances weren't different and we could have involved the police. All those extra eyes on the road would have been a huge help."

"Right, even if it wasn't an active search, they could have kept their eyes open for her. But I heard on the news that they've brought in extra officers to help them search for the suspects in that bank robbery because they believe they're still in the area. It's hard not to think about the family of the teller who was killed. Everyone wants those guys caught. That, of course, is a law enforcement priority right now. Not good for us, but much more important, our love for that little dog notwithstanding."

She felt like crying but tamped it down. "I know they wouldn't have time to worry about a little dog with everything else that's going on, but poor Snowflakes. Nothing was in her favour today, was it?"

"We'll find her, Elsa, but in the meantime I'm sure the guy who took her is looking after her. I can't imagine that she's out walking the streets, although I know we also have to consider that as a possibility. Most dogs would have bitten whoever opened the door, you know guarding their territory, but not Snowflakes. That little poodle is so friendly she'd go with anyone, and she obviously did so without a fight."

And speaking of fights, she thought, given their pattern just before they broke up, they would have gotten into a mighty scrap over this. But tempers had long since cooled and they both understood, at least about the present situation. They had to set their differences aside. It was best to pool their energy and ideas and get on with it. The most important thing was that the tiny dog, clad only in a red sweater, could be out in the elements on a bitterly cold night. They had to consider that possibility among the several other scenarios that came to mind. So they got moving, putting up posters as they drove around town until Snowflakes' pretty little face was smiling back from just about every telephone pole and lamppost. They were probably breaking town and city ordinances that prohibited the blanketing of the area in paper notices like these, but a fine was nothing to worry about if their work produced results. Cole would in all likelihood get the clean-up bill since his name was on the posters, but she knew he wouldn't care a thing about that under the circumstances.

"I'll put one up on that telephone pole over there," she said pointing toward an incline in back of a deep ditch and was out of the truck before he could object.

"Be careful," he called out the window, "I think it's icy down there after that freezing rain we had last week." Sure enough he had no sooner gotten the words out of his mouth when down she went, taking a painful spill on the side of the road.

Cole was out of the truck in a heartbeat, covering the distance quickly to where she was sprawled on the slippery ground. He knelt beside her, grabbing hold of her hands, and helping her to her feet.

"Are you all right, Elsa?" he asked.

Holding her knee she could only grimace. She felt like a fool, or more comically, a cow on ice. If this weren't such a serious situation, her dramatic wipe out would have been pretty funny. It was a moment or two before the discomfort began to ease.

"I landed on my knee," she told him unnecessarily, "and you know what that pain feels like. I seem to recall you had the same reaction when you got bucked off your horse. You made a one-point landing on your right knee and tore your ACL."

"Do you think we should go up to the hospital and have them take a look at it? You don't seem to be able to put any weight on it."

She shook her head quickly. "I'm okay. Just give me a few minutes. The pain is already starting to ease off."

"You're sure…."

"I'm sure."

"All right then let's get you in the truck and I'll come back and put the poster up myself. Here," he said as he bent to scoop her up in his arms, "I'll help you."

"Cole, I can make it over there under my own steam."

"The way you're limping?"

"Well all we need is for you to fall carrying me, now wouldn't that be a sight!"

"I'm not going to fall, so stay still and let's go. Elsa, you've lost weight," he said as he lifted her, "and you couldn't afford to. You were already slender enough. What's going on?"

"I don't know, I might have lost a few pounds."

"Don't tell me you're on a diet!"

"No, I'm not on a diet. I don't do diets, you know that."

"Why then?" he persisted. "Are you sick?"

"Cole, I'm fine, all right? It's just a few pounds. It's been a little stressful lately is all, my appetite isn't what it usually is."

It had been stressful all right. Work was no picnic, but honestly, the closer it got to the divorce being finalized the more stressed she got. Had she made a mistake? Did she want to try to work out their differences, or was it her stubbornness all that was keeping them apart?

She'd look like a ninny if she suddenly called everything off. Besides, he had obviously moved on, he hadn't even contested the divorce! She must have really meant a lot to him if he'd let her go without even so much as a fight. No, let the divorce go the way it was headed. It was for the best all the way around. It would be final in the new year and then they could both move on with their lives. It seemed Cole had little trouble in that department having already bought land, built a house, and started his own ranch. Talk about a mismatched pair!

But my, oh my! How wonderful it felt to be in those strong arms of his. It stirred something deep inside her, something that didn't need much rekindling. It was all she could do to keep from putting her arms around his neck and nuzzling him. How many times had he done just this same thing, carried her up the stairs to their bedroom and laid her down before his weight joined hers? Too many to count in the early days, she reminded herself. There hadn't been much carrying up the stairs as time had gone on; she'd found her own way there and turned out the light before he eventually came up to bed. She also knew she had forced that distance between them. Yes, the divorce stood. Leave things as they were. Nevertheless it was a good job he couldn't hear her heart beating double time through her heavy jacket or he might start to question her true feelings toward him.

Once they reached the truck, he easily opened the passenger door and sat her carefully onto the seat, then laid his hand on her left knee. "Is it still hurting?"

"Other knee."

He switched knees. "Right, is it still hurting?"

"Not really, you know how a banged knee feels. It hurts like anything when it happens, but it goes away in a few minutes. Except in your case I guess, with the torn ACL. I'll live; so will my knee."

"That's good to know. Now, if you wait here, I'll go staple that poster on the pole."

"I think I dropped the stapler when I fell, and the poster flew away. Darn! And we only have a couple left."

Returning to the pole where she'd gone down, Cole was able to find the stapler where it had skittered into the ditch. He also caught up with the poster where it had fetched up against the skeletal remains of a winter bush. Within a minute or two he had the poster in place, Snowflakes smiling from the telephone pole as if to say thank you.

She thought about the poodle, missing her keenly. Hopefully it was like Cole had said, the dog warm and safe and being cared for by the thief. As ridiculous as that sounded, they had to believe it was true. Snowflakes had a way of bringing out the best in people, and when she really drilled down and thought about it, Cole could be right. Anyone who would steal a dog must have had intentions of looking after her. Over the next few minutes she tried on a variety of scenarios and found some comfort there. Such as, someone who was so lonely, they'd been driven to steal a pet because they couldn't afford to buy one of their own.

At the next stop her leg was back to normal, except for the colourful bruises she figured would have bloomed there by tomorrow. She insisted on putting up the last three posters herself, just to prove that she could. Now their supply was exhausted although they'd only yet covered a relatively small portion of the tri-community area.

"At least we have most of Riverview done and some up in Moncton. I thought a hundred posters would go a lot further, but we soon used them up."

Just then Cole's cellphone rang, and Elsa shrieked in reaction. "Quick! Answer it! It might be about Snowflakes. Maybe the social media post or our posters are starting to get results."

Cole activated his hands free service. "Hello? Oh really? When? No, the dog is white, a little white poodle. No, not brown and white, she's all white. Yes, even her feet. Yes, a red sweater, all red. Okay, thank you. That's okay. No worries. Merry Christmas to you too."

"What was that all about? Please tell me there was a sighting."

"A sighting of a brown dog wearing a blue coat."

"What! How could they get that mixed up? I'm trying not to get upset, but it's been hours now and nothing, other than a sighting of the wrong dog."

"But at least it means people are looking, keeping an eye out for her. We have to be patient. Someone will have seen her and call us. We were able to give a very exact description, white dog with a red sweater and the picture shows exactly that."

"Very helpful, that's why we get a call about a brown dog with a blue coat. What kind of dog was it, a Great Dane?"

Cole laughed which helped to dispel some of the tension. "She didn't say how big the dog was. Anyway, do you want to go home and make more posters?"

The wind had come up considerably, creating the wind chill factor as the temperature continued to plummet.

"Yes, I do. I know you're tired because you worked hard all day, so I'll come back in town myself, go over to Moncton and put up more around the north end."

"No way you're coming back in here alone to do that at this time of night."

"It's no problem, Cole. I'm a big girl."

"It's not going to happen. I'll come with you, and we can continue to look, together. It's still my job to take care of you."

"Like you took care of my dog?"

The moment the words left her lips she wished she could have bitten them back. Not only was that a mean and hurtful thing to say, he didn't deserve it. Why was she so angry with him? Not just about the dog, but in general? That was something she was still trying to figure out.

He went still.

"I'm sorry, Cole. I shouldn't have said that. I'm tired and on edge and I'm taking it out on you. I'm sorry. Okay?"

"How many times would you like me to say I'm sorry about the dog? Don't you think I feel bad about what happened? I'm doing everything I can to help."

"I know, it was a terrible thing to say and I'm sorry I said it. There, we're even, we both messed up today. Let's hit rewind, please?"

Starting the truck he slipped it into gear and made the turn that would start them on the road for home.

"I said I was sorry, Cole. Say something, please."

"Okay, let's go to your place and make those posters and then we can get back on the road again. It's almost midnight, but I see no reason why we should stop. We have to keep looking."

"First of all I think I should make you a sandwich. You have to eat, Cole. I know your appetite, you must be starving."

He shrugged. "I could maybe grab something quick while you're printing the posters."

"Good idea. You know your way around. Just raid the fridge while I finish up in the office, and I'll check my social media pages to see if anything's come in, in the past few minutes. I haven't had any prompts but sometimes this phone doesn't work like it's supposed to, which drives me crazy. I keep meaning to go and replace it, but I haven't gotten around to it yet."

When they were back at the mansion Elsa continued on to her office, leaving Cole to hit the fridge. She knew there wasn't much to find except for a loaf of whole wheat bread in the freezer compartment. There was butter and peanut butter in the cupboard along with the toaster, so he'd have to go that route. She remembered that he hated whole wheat bread with a passion, the only thing it was good for in his opinion was to use as sandpaper. It would take the edge off though.

"This should do it," she said minutes later, meeting him back in the kitchen with a fresh pile of posters.

It was difficult to remain positive as the hours ticked past. It didn't bear thinking about that Snowflakes might have met with misadventure, well worse than being stolen from the truck. True she had been rescued when she was about a year old, they guessed at the time, and it had been obvious she'd seen her share of misery. However she'd lived a pretty comfy life since then and probably wasn't tough enough anymore to withstand being on the lam.

"I hope you found something to eat," she said.

"I can see why you've lost weight. There's nothing in the fridge to eat except bread, so I made toast. Are you hungry? I can toast some for you if you want."

"Thank you but no, I'm not hungry in the slightest. Sorry about the fridge. I cleaned it out on garbage day and got rid of most of what I had in there. I obviously have to go grocery shopping before Christmas."

"Just curious, what are you doing for Christmas this year?"

"Mother and Daddy are expecting me to go to their place, so that's what I'll do. You know how they love to entertain. I won't be wanting for company. They're having their first annual Christmas Eve open house, so I'll probably be visiting with a lot of people I haven't seen in a while. It's going to be a catered event for a hundred."

"A hundred! I'd have thought most people would want to be home for Christmas Eve."

"They will be, of course. This will start at five o'clock and be over by eight-thirty. It's a family thing, complete with a really great Santa impersonator; a local man my mother heard about. She asked me to meet with him and if I liked what I saw, to book him. I thought he was great. You know my mother, she's been planning this thing all year and every detail has to be perfect. People RSVP'd very quickly, mostly families, so there'll be lots of little ones running around too. What are you doing?"

It felt awkward to ask, almost like they should be spending it together, although it would be their second Christmas apart. Their first Christmas, just weeks after they'd separated, had not been fun although she told herself the loneliness would lesson as time went on. A break up of any kind was difficult, especially a marriage.

"Mum and Dad have asked me over, but I'll probably just stay home."

"Stay home! Alone?"

If so, that answered her question as to whether or not he was seeing anyone. If he were, they'd likely be spending it together for at least part of the time. But why should she care she asked herself yet again. She didn't, so there. It was just that, well, Cole was a nice guy, and she wanted the best for him.

"I like my own company, so yes. It's just another night."

"It's not just another night, Cole, it's … Christmas Eve."

He chuckled. "I won't exactly be hanging my stocking by the fireplace."

"You have a fireplace?"

"As a matter of fact I do. I built it myself from fieldstones. It's not huge, but it fits the room and I enjoy it very much."

"Wow! Sounds great. But come on, Christmas Eve is a big deal. And what's the point of having a fireplace if not to hang stockings from the mantle? Seriously, don't be a

Scrooge. You never were, don't tell me you've turned into one all of a sudden."

He laughed. "This fireplace is just for sitting in front of, warming the room. No stockings will be hung anywhere near it. Sounds like a fire hazard to me anyway."

"Come on, Cole, where's your Christmas spirit?"

"I'm not four years old, Elsa. I found out a long time ago there wasn't a Santa and I've made peace with it."

"Very funny. Spending it with your Mum and Dad would be nice. I always liked them."

"Then how come you never stayed in touch? Mum said she called you for lunch, but you told her you weren't able to make it."

The truth was she wouldn't feel comfortable facing his mother, or father for that matter. She could only imagine how upset they were about her asking Cole to leave, having him served with divorce papers. Looking back, it did seem cruel the way it happened. She also knew he couldn't have been all that happy living with her because he hadn't put up much of a fuss about going. That spoke volumes, although it had worked in her favour.

"I can't imagine your mother wanting me to go to lunch with her, just to be friendly. I would imagine I'm not her favourite person now. You are her son, after all."

"My mother is not vindictive. She likes you Elsa, the two of you got along fine when we were married."

"We're still married, Cole."

Now why had she found it necessary to point that out? He'd start thinking the wrong thing if she wasn't careful, but he seemed to let it go so she didn't bother to correct herself.

"I'm just saying Mum wouldn't hold a grudge. She might not have agreed with the way you went about things, but it went the way it did, and you can't change history. My mother is very forgiving. It's probably time we all moved on."

"Anyway, enough about that. If you think she won't be upset with me maybe I should give her a call and ask her out to lunch sometime. Actually, it would be nice to see her again."

"They're good parents. Even if I don't go for the entire evening tomorrow night I'll drop by for a visit on Christmas Day. With Chip and his wife living in BC now and not able to get home for the holidays, they'd like to at least see some of their family."

"I think you mentioned that Jory was pregnant. Did she have the baby? Is that why they can't come?"

"She did. The baby was born prematurely a month ago and is still in the hospital so they're sticking close to home. It's a girl, Ada, and she only weighed like three and a half pounds or something at birth. She's a trooper though and doing fine."

"Thank God! Ada is a cute name; I like that. So that makes two grandchildren for your parents now, I imagine they're happy about that."

She knew she was wandering into dangerous territory again. Children had become a major sore spot between them. Elsa had put off getting pregnant in favour of her career, with Cole running out of patience as time went by.

She should try to think about something more cheerful. She pictured Cole's fireplace and what she imagined it looked like. If he built it, it had to be done well because he was a perfectionist when it came to home projects. And then of course her imagination carried her one step further to a rug in front of the fireplace and her on it with Cole, enjoying the heat of the fire; both of them naked…. She shook herself, mentally. Maybe it had just been too long because there hadn't been anyone else since Cole. The break-up of their marriage hadn't meant that she wanted to leap into bed with the first man she met. She ended it because it probably shouldn't have been allowed to start in the first place.

She'd mentioned Matt from work earlier. He was a friend, or more to the point friendly. He was somewhat interested but not at all interesting. She thought of him as a pal, a sociable colleague and they hung out a bit, went to a movie together from time to time. He'd helped her move some furniture around, things like that, but nothing more. The very notion of being in bed with him was so off-putting it was laughable. Despite the fact that she and Cole were practically divorced, no one had even begun to compare with what they'd had together. She shook off those unsettling thoughts.

"Okay," he said, snapping the silence, "let's put some posters up on this street, like every fifth telephone pole. It's a long street so we'll spread them out, and then do the next street over, same thing."

"If the police come along, they'll probably wonder what we're doing out here at almost two o'clock in the morning."

"I hope they do and if they want to keep an eye out, that'd be great too."

"Aren't you getting tired, Cole? I'm starting to fall asleep because this truck is so nice and warm."

"As soon as you step out in the deep freeze, you'll wake up fast enough. Elsa! Where are your gloves?"

She dropped her head forward in frustration. "I forgot them at home when we went back to get more posters. They're on the table by the door. I know that's where I left them. Darn!"

"You stay inside then. I'll do the posters."

"I'll be all right. I want to help. It only takes a couple of minutes for each poster, and it is my dog after all."

"And I lost it, remember? I don't mind doing the leg work."

They turned the corner onto West main and Elsa let out a shriek. "There she is! There's Snowflakes!"

Chapter Five

Lelia held her breath as she watched a range of emotions parade across Brett's handsome face.

"What do you mean?" he finally said, once her news appeared to sink in.

"What do I mean?" She smiled; eyebrows raised. "I mean I'm pregnant. I've done the test and it was positive. I'm going to have a baby."

He stared at her in disbelief. "You're absolutely positive about this? Aren't those things wrong sometimes?"

She could feel tears start in her eyes. She'd felt strongly when he'd come home in a festive mood, gift in hand, that it was the right time to break the news. She sincerely hoped she wasn't mistaken, but he seemed anything but pleased.

"I'm absolutely positive."

Brett got up and went into the kitchen, leaving her sitting alone on the sofa, holding the dog. She decided not to go after him, knowing him well enough by now to realize that he needed a few minutes alone to sort things out. He'd be back, and sure enough he was, but he wasn't smiling.

"How did this happen, Lelia?"

She couldn't help but laugh out loud. "*How* did it happen? I think you already know the answer to that."

"Don't play games, okay? We were really careful, that much I know."

"I guess we weren't careful enough, were we? You know I stopped the pills because we couldn't afford the extra expense of the prescription every month. We talked about that before I did so, and if you recall there was that one night.... Anyway, I am definitely pregnant."

"But the timing is all wrong, Lelia. I'm not saying I don't want us to have a child, just not yet. We can barely afford to provide for ourselves as it is, how do you think we're going to make out once the baby arrives? Have you given that any thought at all?"

"Brett, you're making it sound like this is all my doing, and obviously it isn't. You know about the birds and bees, it takes two. I know the timing isn't good, sometimes it just isn't, but we'll make it through somehow. We have so far. And as I've told you, I've got a very good feeling that Wally will take you back if you just give him a call and make things right. I think he would be very understanding and respect you for coming to him like that."

"Eat humble pie, you mean."

She looked at him solemnly. "If that's what it takes, yes. It might not be as bad as you think."

He flopped back against the sofa, doing a careful study of the ceiling. His breathing had sped up just a tad and it looked as though he was trying to calm himself. It was an encouraging sign that he was learning to control his temper.

She continued to stroke the dog's silky coat. Snowflakes was watching their faces intently, picking up on the tension between them. Lelia glanced back at her husband, but it didn't seem as if he was interested in making eye contact at the moment. Actually he was doing pretty well, all things considered. She thought there'd be a blow-up when she told him and was greatly relieved when there wasn't. She'd wait for him to speak first, give him the time he needed to adjust to the news. It was another few minutes before he found his voice.

"You know why it's a bad idea to get pregnant, beside the money part. How far along are you?"

"About a month I'd say."

"Why didn't you tell me before now?"

"Because I might have only been late, and I didn't want to say anything until I was sure. I used my lunch money to buy the test and then I knew for certain that I am."

"So in about eight months, thirty-two short weeks or so, we're going to be parents."

She reached and took hold of his hand. "I'm just as scared as you are, Brett, but I'm excited too."

She thought about their financial situation, but also knew that her family would help in any way they could. Her mother was already excited about the prospect of being a grandmother. Brett's family was another matter altogether. His father had left ten years ago and never returned, and she couldn't help but think that he should have left much sooner. She'd heard the stories her husband had told her, the verbal abuse and rough treatment he'd suffered at the hands of his father. He'd hung around just long enough to screw up his son's life, cutting the child down on a regular basis. All of that had left Brett angry and confused.

Brett's mother, having suffered years of persecution herself, both growing up and while married, was a cold and distant woman. She'd left for parts unknown when her only child was seventeen. He hadn't heard from her since. Not much wonder parenting terrified him so much, he'd been exposed to the worst of it since he was old enough to remember.

Lelia thought back to when she and Brett first met. She'd been attracted to the good-looking, dark-eyed teenager with the James Dean vibe who kept mostly to himself. It wasn't that he was unfriendly, wary would be the better description. It didn't take her long to discover that he had a chip on his shoulder the size of a tour bus. Unwisely, experts would say, he had become her project and she'd thrown herself into the effort to knock that chip off by loving him enough so he could realize his own self worth.

At the heart of it all, Brett was a good man. There was a kindness in him that she responded to. She firmly believed that over time he would let go of that old hurt and realize what a wonderful human being he was. He just needed to be given half a chance; someone to believe in him.

And now he was facing a crisis. He was going to be a father and he had to find it within himself to accept that he could be a good one. He knew he had a temper, became angry easily, and that's what still worried him despite her encouragement to the contrary. But she knew if she could crack through that heavy wall of self-preservation he'd built so high around himself, that fear could be healed. It was just a matter of patience.

"Brett," she began, settling back so that their eyes met, "you don't have to be afraid that we're going to have a baby. You are a kind and loving man and that's how you'll be toward our child. I know it."

She knew she was stepping into the lion's den. Not physically, because he had never showed any inclination toward violence, but emotionally. Nevertheless they had to have this conversation sooner or later and now was as good a time as any.

'I told you before, Lelia, I'm going to let you down. I'll let the baby down because I'm not father material. I don't know how to be a father. I couldn't even get the son thing right. I was certainly told that often enough."

"You're getting the husband thing right. I tell you *that* often enough. But really, Brett, you know as much as any man does about being a father before they learn the job; actually get the chance to prove how good they are. Everyone's scared at first; it's natural. Like I said, *I'm* scared."

"You'll make a good mother, no contest. Our baby could not want for a better mother."

"And you'll make a great father. You know how I know?"

"How?"

"Because of how you are with little Snowflakes here. You are attentive, kind, gentle and loving. You even gave up your cigarette money to buy her food and that was *huge*! If that isn't good father material, I don't know what is. No one's a saint, we're just people trying to do a good job with things. If you're loving and kind, that's what you will teach our child."

"But a baby will be different than a dog."

She laughed. "Obviously, but what I mean is I've seen a different side of you since you brought this poodle home. Think about it, Brett, you're going to be a natural. My mother always told me parenting is the hardest job in the world, and it doesn't come with a how-to manual. Everybody just does the best job they can and learn as they go."

He snorted. "Yeah, like my father did."

"I never met your father, but I think he must have been a very troubled man to treat you the way he did."

"Troubled like I am. My mother told me I was the very same as my father, even though I tried not to be. She said there was no escaping it, I am my father's son."

"Your mother was wrong to say that to you. You are not your father, Brett, and the sooner you realize that the better off you're going to be. He had a wonderful son, and he didn't even know it, which is so sad. I know you, Brett, there's no way you're going to be the way he was."

"But what if you're wrong? What if I turn out to be exactly like my dad?"

"That's like saying what if the moon turns pink tonight? You just know it's not going to happen, like I know you don't have it in you to be the way your father was. If you were really like that, I'd know it by now and I haven't seen any sign of that at all. Why would you all of a sudden turn into a horrible person? Does that make sense? No! You're going to treat our child with as much love and affection as you treat me and have done since I've known you. Let's face it, Brett, you're a nice guy whether you want to admit that to yourself or not."

As if on cue Snowflakes disengaged herself from Lelia's lap and made the short trip to Brett's lap. He reached for the little dog, not content to just stroke her fur. Picking her up in his arms he cuddled her close to his face.

What Lelia saw heartened her, and she knew without a shadow of a doubt that she was right. A child would bring out the best in her husband, and the last of her fears were swept away. Brett simply had a few rough edges, but didn't we all?

"See Brett? Look how you are with that dog. You're so loving and gentle, just pretend for a moment that you're holding a baby."

He laughed. "Right, our baby. Now that you mention it, she does look a lot like your mother."

"Very funny! My mother really likes you."

"Just kidding! I like your mother too."

"Brett, we're going to do just fine with this child. I want both of us to take parenting classes and they offer them for free over at the community centre. A baby is a big adjustment, although we still have lots of time to get used to it and iron out the details. This is a new road ahead of us and we have to prepare for it together. I just have to know you love me and want to stay married to me. Maybe you have something you'd like to say about that, and now would be the time to do it. Are you happy with me?"

His reaction was immediate. "Of course I'm happy with you! I love you! You're everything to me; I'd be lost without you. You always know just the right thing to say to help me understand things. It's like you give me hope. You tell me what a good person I am, especially when I don't deserve it because of something I've done."

She looked at him curiously, if ever there was a loaded statement that was it. "Maybe you better tell me what you mean by that."

His eyes clouded over. "I'm not as nice as you seem to think I am." He shifted the dog when Snowflakes kisses came a little too close to landing on his mouth. "Sometimes I really screw up, Lelia, big time."

A cold feeling went through her and suddenly everything fell into place. No way was a snowy white dog found wandering the streets without a speck of dirt on her. The poodle would have been frightened … guarded, and she was neither. She had obviously been loved and cared for and now likely missed very much. "Why don't you tell me about it."

Snowflakes now dozed contentedly in Brett's arms, Brett not raising his eyes from the dog.

"Brett, you didn't just find the dog, did you?"

His face reddened as he shook his head, not meeting her eyes.

She sighed. "I didn't think you did, not the way you explained it to me. Why did you lie?"

"Like I said I'm a screw up."

"Brett, that's a cop-out. You're no more of a screw up than anybody else, you're just used to hiding behind that. We all make bad decisions from time to time. I know I do. The thing is to own it, do what you can to make it right, and not repeat it. Where did you get the dog?"

"I told you I did something terrible, and I won't be able to be much of a father because I'll probably be going to jail. There, how's that for that wonderful stand-up guy you're so in love with?"

Lelia felt as though she had swallowed a cold rock and it lodged painfully in the pit of her stomach. Brett could go to jail? He had obviously stolen the dog, but why would he ever do such a thing?

"Tell me, Brett. Who owns the dog?"

Silence stretched between them until he finally spoke. He sounded as though he was on the verge of tears, something she had never really seen from him. He was always into his tough guy *nobody can get me* image.

"I stole her. I can't believe I made such a stupid move, but I did."

Lelia was next to tears herself. "Why would you do such a thing, Brett? And right before Christmas?"

He turned to look at her then and true enough, his eyes were bright with unshed tears. "Because I couldn't afford to buy you anything. I was at the supermarket, getting ready to leave and this big shiny expensive truck drives up and parks one space away from me. There was Snowflakes riding shotgun. She was so cute I knew you'd love her and before I could talk myself out it, I was at the truck after the guy went into the store. I couldn't believe it wasn't even locked! So I took the dog, put her in the car and started driving. They probably got me on surveillance tape, although the license plate on my car is so grimed over I don't think they'd be able to make it out. The further I drove the worse I felt because I have never done anything like this in my life. It was a spur of the moment thing, but I've always hated people who steal and then I did the very same thing. I'm sorry, Lelia. I let you down. Now do you believe me when I say I'm a screw-up? Who does something like this? I wanted to get you something nice for Christmas and I end up giving you a stolen dog. I've got no class, that's my problem. Zero!"

Now Lelia was the one trying to stay calm as anger surged through her. "You know what, Brett? It's not that you have no class, you've got plenty of that if you'd just stop putting yourself down. Your problem is that you enjoy feeling sorry for yourself. It's become a habit with you. I'm not saying you didn't have a rough time growing up, I know you did, but that's over now. You were a boy then, you're a man now, and you don't do boyish things anymore. I love you with all my heart. I'm deeply touched that you wanted to get me something so nice, but this was wrong. It was a terrible thing to take that man's dog. He must be frantic trying to find her."

He stared at her. "First of all I do not feel sorry for myself."

"Oh yes you do! You can only blame so much on your past and then you have to do better. Now is the time to move on and make things right. You have to fix this, Brett."

"Thank you, Doctor. Lelia."

"Seriously, we have to give the dog back."

"To whom? I would have no idea who to call, and if I took it back to the supermarket and tell them what I did, I'd be arrested. I can't imagine you'd be thrilled about that, your husband in jail for Christmas."

"You said your license plate is covered with dirt, so the police probably aren't even involved, especially with what happened at the bank yesterday. I don't imagine they've got much time to go chasing after a stolen poodle. But the dog has to get back to her owners as soon as possible, however you go about it."

"Lelia, I just want to apologize for doing this, for putting us in this position. I'm so sorry, baby. I'll tell you one thing, I will *never* do something so stupid again, something so boneheaded. Never! I've had this sick feeling in my stomach ever since I did it, like I couldn't believe I would do such a thing. Trying to undo what I did isn't easy either. It's like trying to put the genie back in the bottle. As far as finding the owner goes, I would imagine there are lost dog posters up all over the place by now. Isn't that how they usually go about it?"

"That wouldn't surprise me."

"There could also be a reward."

"Brett Murdoch! Don't you even think about it!"

"Are you serious? Take a reward after I stole the dog? No way! I'm not that much of a screw up, but I'm just thinking how bad these people probably want their dog back."

Lelia breathed a sigh of relief. It was a very bad thing that he did, no matter how noble the reason, but she was reassured by his behaviour now; how he felt about the deed. All they had to do was make sure the dog was returned to its rightful owner, and they would do what they could to see that it happened in time for Christmas. Snowflakes was not theirs and it was not possible for them to keep her, but it was already obvious the positive difference she'd made in their lives during her all-too-short visit. The little poodle had succeeded in bringing out the side of her husband that she needed to see, at just the right time. It was certainly wrong to have taken the dog, but it was almost as if Snowflakes coming into their lives when she did was nothing short of serendipitous.

She reached over and stroked Snowflakes' curly fur, the poodle seeming reluctant to leave the comfort of Brett's arms. Lelia knew she and Brett were already attached to the dog, and it would appear that Snowflakes felt the same about them. It would hurt to see her go, but she couldn't stay anyway because of Mrs. Brownleigh's no pet rule. She would be theirs to love for only a few hours.

Lelia sighed as she continued to look at Snowflakes. "I don't have to go into work until noon tomorrow, so first thing in the morning let's go out and see if we can see a poster or something. I can't check social media because I don't have a phone right now and my laptop died last month, so we'll do the next best thing. Okay?"

"Sounds like a plan, and again, Lelia, I'm so sorry about all of this. I *am* too down on myself, you're right, and it's not fair to put you through that. And another thing, I'm calling Wally tomorrow. I'm not waiting until next year. If I'm going to try to do better, that's a good place to start. Besides, we've got a baby on the way; I really need to find a job more than ever."

* * *

Brett did not sleep well that night as he continued to come to grips with the magnitude of what he'd done. He'd essentially broken into a vehicle and stolen something valuable; that dog likely cost several hundred dollars. It still shocked him that he was even capable of such a thing. He would definitely qualify for the stupid prize of the day! But, he also reasoned, maybe this was as bad as it was going to get because not only would he never do it again, he vowed right then and there to turn everything around. Lelia was right, although he might not tell her so. He was feeling sorry for himself because of his past, but enough of the poor me routine.

He could hardly wait until morning to start to set things right. But what if they couldn't find a poster? They just had to get the information they needed somehow. That would be his penance, he reasoned, finding a way to get it done.

He'd also get back on track with his plans for owning their own home, although he knew raising a child was extremely expensive and there'd be challenges along the way. He'd hopefully get back on with Wally, but if Wally said no, he'd find another job, a better job. Once they had their house, one of the first things he'd do would be to get a little dog just like Snowflakes. It would be theirs to keep; they wouldn't have to worry about Mrs. Brownleigh telling them what they could and could not do. No, someday they would have freedom, and he as man of the house, would be the one to get it for his family.

He drifted off to sleep just after three that morning, resolved to be a better man.

At five o'clock he was wide-awake again, eager to go in search of a poster. Lelia got up when he did and dressed quickly. She had her coat out of the closet and about to put on, but he stopped her.

"You stay here where it's nice and warm," he told her. "I'll go look to see if I can find a poster. All of this is my fault so I should be the one who goes out and freezes their butt off. Matter of fact, I'm looking forward to it."

Lelia smiled. It was wonderful to see the new, more positive Brett emerging and she never loved him more than at that moment. "I'd call my mother and ask her to check to see if there was anything on social media. She'd wonder why I was asking though and we don't want anyone to know we have the dog, so I guess this is the only way now."

He sighed. "I'll be very surprised if I don't find a poster. You see them all the time about lost pets. Snowflakes is sort of lost, thanks to me."

It was a bone-chilling morning, but since it was the day before Christmas there was already plenty of traffic on the streets. There were already cars in the parking lot of the big box store down the street waiting for it to open at six a.m. He walked a four-block radius but found no poster. Freezing, he went into an all-night convenience store and asked the middle-aged clerk if she'd seen a missing dog poster. She had not but offered to check on social media and sure enough, there was the information he was looking for. It made him feel even worse when she read that the dog had been stolen from a vehicle, and how despicable she thought that was, especially at Christmas. Little did she know he was the one who had done the deed. Yeah, well now he was about to undo it if he could.

The clerk was kind enough to copy the pertinent information for him when he told her he might have seen the dog. Thanking her, he stuffed the paper into his pocket. Within minutes he was back home, and a tearful Lelia met him at the door.

His heart leapt into his chest. "Are you okay?" he asked, watching her face anxiously. "What happened?"

"I'm fine, but I opened the back door for a minute and the dog shot right out past me. I had just finished putting her sweater on and maybe she thought she was going for a walk or something. It all happened so fast, and I can't find her anywhere. Snowflakes is gone!"

Chapter Six

"You see Snowflakes, Elsa? Where?" Cole whipped his head in the direction of her gaze and sure enough there was a small white poodle a short distance down the street with a man walking beside it. Cole hit the gas, but it became obvious the closer they got it was not Snowflakes. The poodle on the end of the leash being walked by an older man was much rounder than svelte little Snowflakes and could also do with a good trim. False start.

Elsa turned away, her gaze suddenly focused out the side window and he guessed she was crying. He reached over and laid his hand on her arm. "It's okay, honey, we'll find her."

She sniffed. Elsa always fought away tears as though it was a sign of weakness if she shed them. He was elated that she didn't repel his touch this time around.

"I'm all right," she insisted. "It's just that I got my hopes up when I saw that dog, but the likelihood of us finding her that easily is remote. Maybe we'll have to make peace with the fact that she's found a new family. I only hope and pray that whoever took her is a dog lover and they're not being abusive toward her. That would kill me if they were being unkind."

Cole's cellphone rang and he immediately pulled over to the curb and yanked it out of his pocket.

"I'm the one who stole your dog," a young man's voice told him. "I'm really sorry. I've never done anything like that before in my life and I never will again."

"Why did you take her?" he asked, aware of Elsa's eyes boring into him, an intensely hopeful expression on her beautiful face.

"I did it because I didn't have a present for my wife. When you pulled in beside me at the market, I got the idea I could give her a dog because she really loves animals. It was the stupidest thing I've ever done. I'm not that kind of person at all and I just want to say I'm sorry."

"Where is the dog now?" Cole interrupted, not meaning to sound harsh or dismissive of the young man's confession, but first and foremost he wanted the dog back. At this point he didn't even care that a crime had been committed. The most important thing was that the dog was safe and in good shape and they'd soon have her back with them. After that he was prepared to look the other way. At least the guy had gumption enough to call him. That took courage considering the seriousness of what he'd done.

"She was home with us and in perfect shape, then my wife found out I stole her. She wasn't very happy with me, and we both knew she had to go home right away. She slept with us all night and we kept her fed and everything. This morning I went out to see if I could find a poster with a number to call, and when I got back my wife said the dog ran away. I'm very sorry but the poodle is gone. We've both been out looking for an hour and we don't see any sign of her."

"So you're saying you don't have her now?"

Elsa groaned loudly from the passenger seat, tears threatening again.

"That's what I'm saying. I'm really sorry, mister."

"I don't need your name, but I want to know the area where the dog was last seen so we can start looking there … call her and see if she'll come. Will you tell me that?"

"Are the police looking for me?"

"The police aren't involved. It was a dumbass thing to do, going into my truck and stealing that dog, but all we want right now is to get her back. That's it. No questions asked. Just tell me the part of town where we should look."

"We live over Lewisville way. My wife tried to catch her, but the last she saw of her was at the end of the street. The poodle ran down an alley and then just seemed to disappear. That was down on Spring Street. I'll still keep looking on foot because I don't have a lot of gas in the car to drive around with. My wife would help too but she's pregnant and I don't want her out in this cold any longer."

"We're on our way over there right now. We'll go to the Spring Street area and call the dog. If we're lucky she'll hear our voices and come to us, and we can get her. Thank you for the call."

"Again, I'm sorry about all of this. You have no idea how sorry."

Cole was silent for a moment. "I've got a pretty good idea how sorry you are, but the most important thing is that we get the animal back. Now, I'm pretty sure you know my truck. If you'd be so kind as to watch for me in that area, I want to have a word with you, face to face."

There was only a moment's hesitation on the other end of the line. "I will definitely do that," the man assured him, although he also sounded scared.

Within minutes they were driving down Wheeler Boulevard headed toward Lewisville, Elsa regarding him with a sidelong glance. "You went pretty easy on that guy don't you think? He stole my dog out of your truck. Snowflakes is out on the street somewhere, in this cold, because of him."

Cole sighed tiredly. "I know that, but he sounds like he's just a kid. He's not more than twenty or so, and he had guts enough to call me and own up to it. Thanks to him we have some idea of where to continue our search and it's nowhere near where we were looking. He also agreed to meet me which surprises me."

"But why would he do such a thing in the first place? Did he explain that?"

"He made a mistake. I think it was just a spur of the moment thing. He didn't have anything for his wife for Christmas and he saw the poodle and decided she'd make the perfect gift. He apologized over and over."

"And I take it he doesn't have the dog anymore. Where is Snowflakes now, does he have any idea?"

"It seems she got away on them earlier this morning."

She groaned. "I don't believe this. Is he still driving around looking for her?"

"He's looking on foot, in this deep freeze, because he doesn't have enough gas in his car to do it that way. It doesn't sound like they have any money, and his wife is pregnant. I can't judge him. I might have done the same thing under similar circumstances. It was wrong of course, there's no question about that, but like I say, he's just a kid."

"Maybe he thinks if he finds the dog we'll give him the five hundred dollar reward."

Cole thought for a moment. "He never asked for the reward, and he said he had a copy of the poster, so he knows about it. No, I think he's a decent kid who got carried away and made a poor decision. He was afraid the police were after him."

"They could well have been, him pulling a stunt like that. But I can see how someone could make that mistake. He must love his wife a lot to take that kind of a chance. He could have gotten himself into a whole lot of trouble. He actually agreed to meet you?"

"Yes, face to face, and that takes guts. He did something stupid and he's sorry; like me. I left the door unlocked, which was stupid, and I'm sorry too. All we can do when we mess up is try to make things right."

"You can hardly compare the two, Cole. You didn't steal anything or break the law. Besides, I told you, I've done the same thing myself not thinking that anyone would ever go into my vehicle and steal her, so you see you're not so bad after all."

He turned and smiled at her before returning his eyes to the road. "Does that mean I'm forgiven?"

She smiled too, although it was sad. "Of course you're forgiven. The most important thing in all of this is Snowflakes, and I'm hugely relieved to know she wasn't out in the elements all night long. At least she was warm and dry with people who treated her well. Fed her, I assume. However now she *is* out on the streets in this bitter cold, so we have to find her right away."

They made the left hand turn at the lights and continued on, taking another left under the hill. Sure enough, there stood a young man on the side of the street looking as though he was waiting for someone. He raised his hand to flag Cole down once it appeared he recognized the truck.

Cole pulled into the curb and got out, the young man bravely walking up to him. He did look terrified yet determined at the same time. He reached for Cole's hand, and they shook, giving brief introductions.

Cole rested his dark-eyed gaze on the young man. He'd been told often enough that his eyes were unnerving. There wasn't anything he could do about that except look at a person, and he did look on this young man with respect. Yes, he'd done a crime against him, but by having the courage to face him, he showed an unusually strong sense of character for one so young.

"No sign of her I take it," Cole said to him.

Brett shook his head slowly. "I've been all over this area at least twice, and nothing."

Cole studied him after glancing at his watch. "I appreciate that you kept looking, but it's after seven o'clock now. Don't you have to get to work?"

Brett held Cole's gaze. "I don't have a job right now, or I would be at work."

Cole was direct. He hated it when people beat around the bush, hedging. "Why don't you have a job?"

Brett coloured, Cole could see it in the growing daylight, aided by the overhead streetlamp.

"I was in construction, but I got fired a few months ago because I got in an argument with my boss. He owns the company, and he wanted me to do it his way."

111

Cole folded his arms, aware that a smile was tugging at the corners of his mouth, but he successfully kept it at bay. "Of course he'd want it done his way, he's the boss. That's usually the way it works, whether you like it or not."

Brett dropped his eyes. "Yeah, I know; again, stupid."

Cole nodded. "Stupid is right. What did your boss say when you apologized?"

"I didn't."

"Why not? That's usually what you do when you're wrong. You did it for me, why wouldn't you do it for your boss?"

Brett was suddenly overly interested in the toe of his sneaker. "I'm going to, soon. I only found out last night my wife was pregnant, so everything has to change."

"Why not apologize now, today? You're going to need a good steady job if you've got a baby on the way. I see good in you, Brett. It took a real man to call me and own up to what you did. Not everyone would have the nerve to do that."

Brett looked up, meeting Cole's penetrating gaze again. "My job's probably gone now anyway, but me and my boss used to get along good. He said before that I was one of his best workers. I wish I could hit rewind, undo what I did. I was having a bad day and I took it out on him and ruined everything."

"You can always his rewind, Brett. How old are you?"

"Twenty."

"How long have you been married?"

"About two years."

"So why make the call to me when you figured I could turn you over to the police, or in the very least be mad enough to teach you a lesson?"

Brett squared his shoulders. "Because I don't want to see anything happen to the little dog. I did the wrong thing. Now I'm doing the right thing, but I will admit I was scared I would go to jail when I called you. Or that you'd rearrange my face."

"I'm not much for rearranging people's faces, yet you still took the chance. I like that. I know it was a boneheaded thing you did with the dog, but you called me and tried to make it right. So do me a favour. Call your old boss and do the same thing. Look at it as what you can do for me to help fix this. Apologize, and mean it. Maybe you're right, maybe your job is gone but there's a big construction project scheduled for Riverview soon and you might want to get in on it. They're crying for people, so I'd say there's a pretty good chance he'll rehire you. And if you want to use me for a reference, go ahead. I won't go into detail as to how we met, just that we did, and I was impressed with you. Okay?"

Brett was all smiles as Cole produced a business card and passed it to him.

"And another thing, rein in that temper of yours and listen to your boss if he takes you back. If he owns the company, then he has a right to do things his way. He's the one paying the bills. Is he a good guy?"

Brett nodded. "He's a good guy. Actually I really like him, and I felt bad ever since then that I said some of the things I did. What if he blows me off when I call him? Hangs up?"

Cole laughed. "He might, but he might not. One thing I can guarantee you though, he'll have more respect for you when you finish apologizing then he did before you started."

"You think so?"

"I know so, that's the way it usually goes. That's what a real man does, stands up and tries to do the right thing. And another thing, I want to help you out."

Brett shook his head. "No, I can't take anything from you. I'm just lucky you didn't have me arrested. Anyone else would have."

"Never mind how this thing started. I'm looking at where we are now and you're doing everything you can to help. That's what I'm thinking about. So please, take what I'm offering."

Brett shook his head again. "I can't do it, man. There's no point in taking a loan from you because I don't know when I'll be able to pay it back. It'll be a while and I don't need that hanging over my head with everything else. I'm grateful though and thank you for wanting to do that for me."

Cole smiled. "I can be just as stubborn. This isn't a loan. This is some Christmas money, our appreciation for you helping. Buy your wife something nice, get a turkey, some groceries." He reached into his jacket pocket and pulled out the roll of bills he'd put there on the way over for just that purpose. "Here, put this in your coat. Merry Christmas."

Brett had tears in his eyes. "I don't know what to say."

"You don't have to say anything. Just maybe hang around for a while and help us look for the dog." He glanced down and saw that Brett was wearing ragged sneakers, which were no real defence against the biting cold. "On second thought I think my wife and I can handle it from here. The dog might not come to you anyway, but we'll call for her and see if she hears us. We'll also put up posters in this area and I'm sure we'll get some results. Thank you for your help, Brett, and make that call to your old boss. Today. Okay?"

Brett nodded, his teeth chattering. "I'll call him as soon as I get home. Thank you for this. I won't forget you."

After Brett walked off down the street, Cole climbed back into the heated truck and turned up the fan.

"Well?" asked Elsa, "is he going to help us look?"

"He wanted to, but I sent him home. He's only half dressed, and he was freezing."

"I'm relieved he took the money though."

"He didn't want to at first, but I talked him into it. Maybe now they'll have a better Christmas. He's a good kid. I can see that. I think he got a rough start in life or something. He just has to believe in himself a little bit more, that's all. Anyway, I gave him some advice and it seemed like he's going to take it. I hope so anyway. I've got a good feeling about him. He's going to be all right."

She looked over at him. Her expression was unreadable, and he met her eyes. "What?" he asked, wondering what she could be thinking.

"You," she said, not taking her eyes off him. "I could hear what you were saying to him, and I could see his face in the mirror. He was hanging on every word you said. You really helped him, and I liked that he refused the money. I'm glad you finally got him to take it. You're just unbelievable...."

"Unbelievable in what way?"

He hoped it was good but figured there was no way he could improve himself in her eyes anymore. She hadn't exactly said she didn't want to get divorced. It was still full speed ahead with that as far as she was concerned, so he wouldn't try to read anything into her reaction right now.

"Just unbelievable."

"Thank you, I think."

"No need to thank me, but it's a good *unbelievable*."

He didn't really know what to say next, one of life's awkward moments. So he handled it the only way he knew how, by taking charge.

"Okay," he said gruffly to disguise his emotions, "we've got a dog to find, so are you ready to get out in the cold? Believe me, it isn't any warmer over here than it was on the other side of town. I just remembered you still don't have any gloves! Look in the glove box. I keep an extra pair in there. They'll be lots too large, but they'll still work."

She smiled. "You're the only person I know who actually keeps gloves in the glove box."

"You'll find lots of other stuff in there too, so come on. Grab them and let's hit the streets."

And hit the streets they did, but because of the early hour tried to keep their calls for Snowflakes at a lower decibel so as not to wake anyone. They spent two hours walking the entire neighbourhood, doubling back, but still no Snowflakes. When that search seemed fruitless, they stapled the rest of their posters up, stopping to talk to anyone they met. They described the dog and that there was a reward offered. Finally realizing there was nothing more to be gained by going over the same territory again, reluctantly decided they would leave for the time being.

"We'll go home, get some rest, and then come back later," he told her as they started down the street. "We haven't given up yet. The temperature is supposed to go way up today, so at least we'll get a break from this deep freeze."

"That's good because my toes are paining so bad I don't think I can stand it much longer. I can only imagine how little Snowflakes is feeling, and her feet are bare. She might be dead by now anyway for all we know," she finished glumly.

"You can't think that way, Elsa. That dog is not going to stand in one place and freeze. I would say she's already found shelter; any animal would if they're trying to survive. Besides, she could be miles from here by now depending on which direction she went once she got to the end of the street. You know how fast she moves. She could cover a lot of ground with those little legs of hers."

"What if she's going to try to make it back home? If she went overland, she'd end up on that ice in the marsh and maybe drown. The poor little thing wouldn't stand a chance."

"Here, come here," he said going to where she stood and pulling her into his arms. "We will find the dog, maybe not as quickly as we'd like, but someone somewhere will see her and call us. Then we'll come back and search *that* area. They might even catch hold of her and then we'd come and pick her up. We've got the word out as much as we can because I've already called the radio stations. Remember? We've got a lot of people looking and Snowflakes is going to come out of this just fine."

She laid her head against his chest, and it felt like the most wonderful feeling to have her in his arms again. It felt like they were alone instead of standing on a windy, freezing street corner the day before Christmas. Considering he never thought he'd get to touch her again this was nothing short of a miracle. Actually *holding* her and boy did she smell good; sexy.

She stirred against him. "Cole you must be exhausted, you have to be. You worked hard all day yesterday and you've been up now, what, about thirty hours?"

He nodded. "Pretty much. I'm sorry, Elsa, but I have to go home and get some sleep. I called Dad again and he's going to fill in for me for a couple of days. We've done all we can do at the moment. I know you need sleep too, so come on. Let's go and do that. I don't imagine it'll be long before the phone starts ringing anyway."

"That's all I want for Christmas. I wasn't planning on anything special anyway but having her home again would be the best Christmas present ever."

"What, no lavish gift from *Matt*?"

She laughed, but it was tired and lacking amusement. "Hardly," she snorted derisively. "We're just … friends."

"Okay then, friend, let's get back to the country and get some shuteye and hope for the best."

They retraced their steps to the truck, which as it turned out was parked ten blocks away and every step was torture as they walked into the biting north wind. Once inside he started the vehicle, the air still frigid until the motor warmed up.

"Here, Elsa, take off those high-heeled toe pinchers and let me warm up your feet in my hands. I can't imagine how you walk in those things anyway. How come you don't have winter boots on?" he asked.

She winced as the chill blains started, but he continued the warming massage in order to restore circulation to her toes.

"Sorry," he told her, as she howled in pain, "they should stop hurting in a minute or so."

He reached behind the seat and pulled out a plaid woollen blanket. "Here, wrap them up in this if you don't want me to rub them. Are they starting to come around at all?"

"Cole, they're hurting so bad I can hardly stand it."

"Why wouldn't you wear something more sensible on your feet in weather like this? Those are not winter boots."

"They are so, they're lined."

"With what, satin? They wouldn't keep anything warm. I wouldn't wear them."

"No, I don't think they'd be a good look for you." She laughed despite herself. "I think my feet are starting to warm up a little bit now. At least they're not paining quite so bad."

"Good, just keep them wrapped up in the blanket and maybe they'll warm up faster." Fastening his seatbelt he slipped the truck in gear. "Do you want anything to eat on the way home? We could stop at a convenience store and get a breakfast sandwich or a pastry or something. A cup of coffee."

"No thanks."

"Elsa, you have to eat. There's not enough to feed a flea at your house. All right, if you don't want me to stop for anything, why don't you come home with me? I have food."

"I have food too."

"Bread and peanut butter won't hold anyone for very long."

"What do you have that's better than that?"

"I'll cook you some eggs and ham, toast, and there's also orange juice and coffee...a real breakfast. How does that sound? Am I tempting you at all?"

"You know you are, but why are you cooking me breakfast? I'm divorcing you, remember?"

"How could I forget? So are you coming home with me or what?"

"You make it sound ... intimate. It's not. I'll just go there to eat and then I'll go home and maybe catch a nap."

"What, you think I'm so desperate I'll jump you the minute you're inside the door? Come on, Elsa, you know that's not my style."

"I didn't say that."

He slowed the truck. "We're almost to your place. Do I drop you off there or do you want to come and let me feed you? You know I'm a good cook, and I don't think you're going to get a better offer than what I just told you. What's it going to be?"

She was quiet for a moment. At least she was considering his offer, and he really hoped she'd accept. There was no one he loved spending time with more than Elsa, hell, he loved her. Always had, well since he met her when she was a sassy eighteen-year-old. He'd been twenty-three and had dated a lot, but there'd never been anyone else for him after that. He honestly wondered if there ever would. It felt like more than a year since she'd filed for divorce, but he hadn't considered moving on. A couple of pretty women had caught his attention, but that's all it amounted to, nothing more. No, he wasn't even close to being ready to look elsewhere despite the fact there'd been bona fide problems in the marriage. But it also seemed that the head of steam she'd had up over the divorce had fizzled somewhat. That was good, because he could always hope that maybe there was a chance for them yet. That's why he'd been content to bide his time. He knew Elsa, she didn't like to be pushed and so he wouldn't. He'd just keep his fingers crossed that she'd eventually change her mind and ideally before the thing became final. Now wouldn't that be some Christmas present!

"All right," she told him. "I'm so tired right now I could eat anything."

He chuckled. "Thanks! That's a ringing endorsement for my cooking."

"I'm sorry, I would love a nice home-cooked breakfast. You know I'm not much in the kitchen. You were the cook of the family and I always enjoyed what you made. That's what I really meant to say."

"Thank you, compliment appreciated. Besides, this will give you a chance to see my place since it's finished."

"Your little cabin."

"You make it sound like a phone booth."

"Well how big is it? You said you wanted a smaller place."

"A five bedroom bungalow would be smaller than the mausoleum you live in."

"I happen to like a nice big home, not be cramped up in some hunting camp."

He laughed. "I hardly live in a hunting camp, but why don't you reserve judgement until you've had a chance to see it? It's nice and cozy and I love it there. It's got everything I need."

"Just big enough for two."

"Maybe, who knows?"

"You assumed that Matt was my boyfriend," she said, conveniently changing the subject. "Won't I be making somebody jealous if I show up there with you? Or word gets out that we've been seen together? People have eyes you know, they'll talk. I won't be getting you into hot water, will I?"

"If that's your way of asking do I have a girlfriend, the answer is no. Not yet."

"Not yet?"

"Not yet. Now, here we are, we're coming up to the house."

Cole stopped in front of a handsome cedar log home, and while not huge by Elsa's standards, it was not miniscule either. It was … cozy.

"It's really nice, Cole. It suits you. We could fit it inside my home though."

"Exactly. It's just the right size. Come on in and I'll get breakfast started. Before I do, I'll light a fire in the fireplace, and you can cuddle up in the armchair and close your eyes for a few minutes while everything's cooking."

He opened the back door, and she followed him in. "Cole, this is really nice; very homey. I like it."

* * *

He woke her when breakfast was ready and they both ate hungrily, tucking into the hearty meal. When they were finished, he cleared the dishes away.

"I'm going to lie down for an hour or so, Elsa, and I think you should too. That little catnap in front of the fire wouldn't get you very far."

""You know, maybe I will. My eyes are still falling shut. Where is your guest room?"

"The next door down from my bedroom, but there's no furniture in it. I haven't got that far yet. Come on and stretch out beside me and I'll throw the comforter over both of us."

"I'm not getting into bed with you!"

"I don't bite. Don't worry it's a good-sized bed. You take your half and I'll take the other. As tired as I am, you're quite safe. I'm going to be asleep in five minutes anyway, so don't get any ideas about me either."

"You wish!"

Yes, he did wish, but he wasn't going to tell her that. "Come on, Elsa, you're not afraid to sleep with me, are you?"

Chapter Seven

Snowflakes raced down the street and turned right at the corner, a very large dog hot on her heels. She shifted into overdrive and began to put some serious distance between them. However in her headlong dash to escape she found herself cornered in a small fenced-in backyard, the gate standing ajar. She barked furiously at her approaching pursuer, explaining her predicament to anyone who would listen. A woman who happened to be in said backyard saw the whole thing and hurried for the gate, dropping the latch into place in a nick of time.

"You go home, Brutus," she admonished the lab/shepherd cross whose deep bass bark made him sound much more ferocious than he actually was. "Don't you be scaring this poor little thing."

Brutus obeyed, loping away, glancing back once or twice at the neighbour who'd ruined his fun. He wasn't a bad dog, overgrown was all, and he liked to chase anything that was smaller, from squirrels to cats to tiny dogs. If it ran, something was awakened from his species' ancient past, and he couldn't resist pursuit. If the smaller critter held its ground and stared him down, as some actually found the fortitude to do, Brutus lost interest almost immediately. On occasion, he'd been challenged in just that way by the odd cat, well … there may have also been a claw or two involved. When that happened there was no end to his *poor me* yelps. At home, when he needed exercise, he was let out into a backyard enclosed with a chain link fence. But he had become very adept at leaping over it. Likely, when he saw the little poodle walking down the street it was game on.

"There now, little one, don't be afraid," the grey-haired woman soothed the poodle who kept her distance in the far corner of the yard.

She slowly approached the small dog so as not to further alarm it, and was relieved to see that it didn't growl, bark, or even show its tiny white teeth. She seemed to understand the woman meant her no harm. She would have no way to know that it was because she was so adorable that people reacted to her in such a positive way. They wanted to be close to her, hold her, and she responded in kind. Snowflakes was a very loveable dog.

Marjorie Clements went back inside out of the cold, cradling Snowflakes against her chest. The dog's little red sweater would not entirely keep out the bitter north wind that punched against the old wooden house and rattled nearby trees.

"You knew it was a good day to come by for a visit, didn't you?" she asked Snowflakes, striking up an immediate rapport as though the poodle was a long lost friend come to call. "Walter and I are alone here together now, and we get lonely. We lost our own dog a little over a month ago and we still miss him something fierce. You're just in time to cheer up two old people for Christmas."

"Who are you talking to, Marj?" called the voice of an elderly man from the bedroom down the hall. "Do we have company?"

Still cradling the dog she headed for the bedroom where her husband was propped up in bed, leaning heavily against several pillows. He'd lost his eyesight nearly a year ago, but when she placed the poodle in his hands his face broke out into a smile that shone as brightly as the Christmas tree lights in the corner of their small living room.

"I was talking to this little scamp," she told her husband cheerfully. "She came running right into our yard a few minutes ago. I had just finished putting garbage out in the shed or I would have missed her. She's very small, isn't she?"

"How did she happen to come running into our yard?"

"You might have guessed it. Brutus was after her. He can be such a bully sometimes, but she won the race by a mile. It was just that she ran out of places to hide."

Walter fluffed the dog's curly coat. "She feels like a poodle, but I don't think she's overly thin, just small."

"Indeed she looks as though she's been well enough cared for. I can't imagine where she came from; I mean which direction. I just saw her come sailing into the yard and I got the gate closed before Brutus could get in and harass her any further. I was afraid for a moment he might try to jump this fence too, and he might have if I hadn't been there."

"I'll bet that someone is looking for her, they have to be. Is she wearing dog tags or anything?"

Marjorie searched the dog's collar but other than the red metal heart with her name inscribed on it, there was no identification tag.

"I don't see anything other than her name tag. I daresay there are people searching for her although no one's come to the door. It's very cold outside so we have to keep her here until we determine where she belongs. It would be cruel to let her back out on the street in this weather or put her in the SPCA as a stray. That's what I'll have to do though if we can't find out who owns her. In the meantime I think we have a furry companion to spend Christmas with."

Walter smoothed the mass of white curls on the top of Snowflakes' head. "She's smaller than Fritzer, but if there was just a bit more to her, I'd swear it was our own little dog."

"I wish you could see how white she is. Her name is Snowflakes and she's well named because she's as white as the driven snow. She's also cute as a button and appears to be very well mannered."

"I daresay she belongs to some children, and I'll bet they're a bunch of sad kiddies that she's gone, especially at this time of year. She can't live far away either because you say she's in such good shape. If she was out on her own for very long, she wouldn't be white as snow, no matter what time of year it is."

Marjorie couldn't resist fluffing Snowflakes' silky white curls with her fingers. "I would guess that this critter has not travelled any great distance, and I doubt she'd get too far in this frigid weather anyway, it would be too cold for her. For one thing she'd freeze her feet. Feel how tiny they are!"

Walter chuckled when he took hold of one white curly paw. "They're tiny all right, but then by the feel of it they don't have a whole lot to carry around."

Snowflakes, enormously content to be the centre of attention, settled down onto the bed with Walter. "I think she likes it here," he said, happiness apparent on his softly wrinkled face.

He then turned his full attention on the dog. "Do you like it here, Snowflakes? Is it nice and warm? You can stay as long as you like you know. We don't mind a bit, in fact we'd really enjoy the company."

Marjorie couldn't help smiling as she watched the two of them together. "I think she might be hungry too, Walter. That chase alone would have worked up her appetite."

"We must have some food left in the cupboard from Fritzer, don't we? That should work just fine because it's for small dogs."

"I have half a bag and I can get more if we need it. I'll fill a bowl for her in the kitchen. I imagine she's also thirsty after that run."

Walter was still smiling broadly, something he hadn't done in a while, especially since his old friend, Fritzer, passed away. The passing of the darling miniature schnauzer left a huge empty hole in their lives.

"Why don't you bring the food in here and feed her on the bed?"

"Feed a dog on the bed? Whoever heard tell of such a thing! No, the dog will be fed in the kitchen where she's supposed to be, Mr. Clements. Stop trying to break the rules," scolded Marjorie, but she did so in the customary playfulness between them.

Walter was far from intimidated. He simply played his part in their friendly banter. It was all just so much good-natured fussing. "Oh come on, Marjorie. It's Christmas. This little doll won't be with us for very long because someone will come looking for her. Let's break the rules just this once. I love to hear a hungry dog eat."

There was laughter in Marjorie's voice. "Okay, you old tyrant, you win. I'll bring in a dish of kibble, but no water on the bed. That will be taken care of in the kitchen where it should be. Deal?"

Walter was still grinning. "Okay, Mother. Water in the kitchen."

Snowflakes seemed blissfully unaware of the genial tug of war between the elderly couple. Their loving tone of their voices told her she had nothing to fear. She smiled too, tilting her head as she looked from one to the other. She was content to receive the gentle pats on her head as she settled down again with a sigh on Walter's lap. Marjorie removed the little sweater and set it aside so the dog would be comfortable indoors.

She stroked the silky little head herself as she stood up to leave. "You stay here any length of time you're going to be spoiled rotten. You know that don't you? You wait right here, and I'll bring back a nice dish of kibble. I guess it's breakfast in bed for you both today, although Walter, you've already had yours."

Within minutes she had returned with a small blue ceramic dish half full with beef flavoured kibble, the name Fritzer lettered on the side. She set the dish beside Snowflakes so she would not have to leave Walter's lap.

"There you go, Snowflakes. If you can get all of that into you, you'll be doing well. And if you're hungry enough to eat the whole thing, I've got more."

Snowflakes rose lazily to her feet, stretched dramatically and took the two necessary steps to reach the food bowl. What began as dainty nibbling became an enthusiastic crunch-fest, emptying the bowl quickly.

Walter laughed. "Well the little thing can eat, can't she? It sounds like she's really going to town on that kibble."

"She must have been hungry, although you'd think for the size of her, she wouldn't be able to put that much away. She's eating the whole thing, and I put a fair bit in that dish. I think I'll leave it at that though, don't want to overload her stomach. Now, missy," she said, directing her attention to the dog, "if you want a drink, you'll have to get down off that bed and follow me to the kitchen."

Both Marjorie and Walter were astonished when Snowflakes jumped off the bed obediently and looked expectantly at Marjorie as if to say, show me where the kitchen is. I do need water.

"She's some smart, isn't she?" asked Walter, chuckling.

Snowflakes followed Marjorie to the kitchen where the woman fetched Fritzer's old water bowl from the cupboard. She filled it with cold water and Snowflakes lapped it blissfully. She'd downed a good portion before trotting past Marjorie without so much as a by your leave. Heading back to the bedroom she jumped onto the bed and curled up on Walter's lap once again. Marjorie followed her and by the time she arrived, there was the poodle, eyes already shut tight and settled down to sleep.

"That poor dog must have been walking for a long time to be so tired. We'll just let her have her rest and digest that big breakfast of hers."

Walter nodded. "Good idea, we'll leave her right where she is for the time being. If she's comfortable here, then that's where she needs to be."

"Well she's taken to you, that's for sure."

Sightless eyes filled with tears. "I'm happy to have her as a guest for however long she wants to stay."

Marjorie pulled the door shut on the unlikely pair and made her way back to the kitchen. After pouring herself a cup of coffee she sat down in the living room with a magazine. She was preoccupied, so the magazine lay unopened on her lap. This was the first time she'd seen her husband smile in weeks. Diabetes had cost him his vision, and his memory was also getting a bit dodgy at times. However he certainly didn't need to be bedridden because of that. It was as though he'd decided to give up, becoming even more despondent after the loss of their little Fritzer. It had just about killed her to have to take the dog to the vet for his final goodbye. The job had fallen to her, as did most things now, because she had become her husband's caregiver. She'd suggested getting another puppy from the same kennel where they'd gotten Fritzer, but Walter had adamantly refused. "No more dogs!" he'd declared. She knew it was because he felt no other dog could take the place of his beloved schnauzer. Nevertheless this tiny poodle had succeeded in winning her husband over almost immediately. It did her heart good to see them together and gave her much needed hope.

She thought of Walter's beaming face again. Oh how she had missed his handsome smile, the things they used to do together. It frightened her that he was actually giving up on life because at his age it was a slippery slope to the end if he didn't try to turn things around. Plenty of people led active lives despite being blind and she'd tried everything to bring her husband out of his depression. So far nothing seemed to work. She had a very strong feeling that a new puppy would help do the trick, but Walter had warned her not to try to bring another dog into the house because he wouldn't have anything to do with it. They could well afford one. It was Walter's reluctance to accept it that stopped her. She certainly didn't want to make things any more difficult than they already were. It was clear he wasn't over Fritzer's death yet. After all it had only been a relatively short time. Nonetheless she knew something needed to happen soon. She could well lose her husband if he continued to squander what was left of his health. Lost ground could be difficult to recover at his age.

Walter had taken his diabetes in stride when he was originally diagnosed many years ago, vowing it would never get the better of him. And then his disease had begun to worsen as the doctor had warned him could happen. No matter what he did, he couldn't seem to get his sugars under control. He'd been a very youthful, active eighty-two when he'd lost his eyesight. He tried not to let it get him down, but it did. He and Fritzer had been inseparable after that happened, the schnauzer seeming to realize the extent of Walter's medical dilemma. Then Fritzer began *his* decline, given his age, and the end was inevitable.

She thought of the look on Walter's face when he and Snowflakes had been lying together on the bed and that strengthened her resolve. After Christmas and New Year's were over, she was definitely going to call the kennel and make an inquiry about obtaining a new pup. She was taking a chance of raising the famous Walter Clements ire to go against his wishes, but she was seriously thinking now of doing just that. The love of a puppy could melt away even the strongest of reservations. Hadn't she just seen that with her own eyes today?

With that decision made she actually began to feel lighter and started to leaf through the magazine. She heard people's voices down the street, calling, but it was likely kids out playing. She got up and glanced out the window, but didn't see anyone, so went back to reading a particularly interesting article on African violets. It did occur to her, idly, that it was a darned cold morning for children to be out playing. With it being the day before Christmas maybe it was giving busy mothers a break to finish wrapping or baking, or any one of a hundred other pre-Christmas chores.

At noontime she looked in on Walter and Snowflakes. The dog was still sound asleep, although Walter was awake. Now lying on his side, Snowflakes was cuddled in the circle of his arms. Walter, having heard the door open, slowly lifted a finger to his lips in a silent message to Marjorie to not wake the dog. Her husband was not one to miss a meal, or be late for one come to that, and here he was telling her he was willing to wait for his lunch so as not to disturb Snowflakes. There was her answer. It couldn't be any more clear if it was written in big bold letters across the sky. Walter was ready for a new companion. She still disliked the idea of contacting the kennel behind his back, but she loved her husband more than she was worried about upsetting him. She now knew without a doubt she'd be doing the right thing.

A few minutes later she heard a sharp little bark at the bedroom door. She got to her feet quickly because that could only mean one thing, Snowflakes had to relieve herself.

Hurrying to the bedroom she opened the door to let the poodle out. Walter appeared to be asleep, so she closed the door quietly behind her so as not to wake him.

"You have to go outside do you, sweetie?" Marjorie asked the dog in a stage whisper. Sure enough the poodle trotted down the hall ahead of her and headed for the back door. Marjorie wasn't naïve enough to open the back door and let her go out on her own. They might never see her again. If Snowflakes did head for the gate, it would most likely mean that she wanted to be on her way, but she couldn't deprive her husband of the little dog's company just yet. More time was needed. So finding Fritzer's old leash, she snapped it into place on the poodle's collar and went outside.

Sure enough there was some watering to be done and following that a more substantial deposit was made on the frozen ground. Kibble in, kibble out, and Snowflakes tore up a bit of dried grass in a vain attempt to cover the evidence.

"Don't worry about that, Snowflakes," she told the dog. "I'll take care of it. Now if you're finished, I think we should go back inside because it's still a bit nippy out."

Snowflakes seemed to be in complete agreement as she headed for the back door and waited for Marjorie to open it.

Once back indoors, Snowflakes wasted no time heading for the bedroom and Marjorie eventually caught up, unfastened the leash, and opened the door. The dog trotted inside and hopping up on the bed beside Walter. She looked back at Marjorie and smiled as if to say: I like you too, but I know you understand. She really was the cutest little thing. Maybe they'd consider a poodle this time around.

Marjorie padded back down the hall to the living room and plunked herself in her easy chair, this time her attention going to the pretty fibre optic tree their daughter Rhonda had given them last year for Christmas. It was beautiful the way the lights sparkled on it, and Marjorie had enjoyed hanging her heirloom blubs as the finishing touch. She'd decorated the house too, but it had been a half-hearted attempt this year because Walter would not be able to see her handiwork. Also, and the timing was terrible. They'd known since September that Rhonda would not be able make it home for the holiday season. It was only fair that she and her husband, Davis, should split their Christmas time between their two families. The couple had moved to Ontario for Davis' job last March, so they would spend Christmas with his parents this time around.

Rhonda's absence was likely why Walter was also so down in the dumps. She was the apple of his eye, and he looked forward to seeing his daughter, but of course he understood the arrangement. It wasn't fair to always have their Christmas visit, because Davis' family looked forward to having them too. There was to be a call on Christmas Day though and that was something to look forward to.

It was a shame too that there were no grandchildren, but they'd long ago made peace with that fact of life. Rhonda and Davis had decided before they ever got married not to have children. Walter had bombarded them with hints in the early days until Rhonda asked Marjorie to speak to her father about it. His campaign wasn't going to change anything. Eventually he'd given up on that tact and never mentioned it again. It was just about that time that Fritzer had entered the picture and there was no need to question the timing. It was perfect.

And of course there'd be no Fritzer for her and Walter this Christmas either. She remembered how excited the schnauzer got about the Christmas tree, racing round and round and barking up a storm. He never damaged it in any way, just made a lot of noise, acting as though the tree was a colourful intruder and it was his job to announce the invasion.

Marjorie dozed in her chair. After all, she'd earned a rest, but she awoke with a start, and saw that twenty minutes had passed. Walter needed a bathroom break and since she was now his eyes, and happily so, she hurried to help guide him down the hall.

"You know, Walter, you and Snowflakes seem to be a pretty good team," she said from the other side of the bathroom door.

"You're right," he agreed. "How did she come to run into our yard?"

Marjorie was becoming accustomed to repeating things from time to time, but it didn't bother her as she recounted the story of Snowflakes' flight from Brutus.

Minutes later he came out of the bathroom. "I love having her here, but we have to find out who owns her."

"Of course we do, I thought maybe we'd keep her inside for a day or so just to be sure she stays warm. After Christmas I'll check around to see if there's a dog missing that fits her

140

description. I'll hate to see her go, but I would imagine she has a family, and they must be frantic, worrying about her, wondering where she's gone."

Walter held out his arms and Marjorie stepped into his embrace, something that hadn't happened between them in much too long. She laid her head on his shoulder, sinking into the warmth of his arms. How wonderful it felt to be held like this again.

"You know, Marj," he whispered against her ear, "maybe we should look at getting another dog. She'd be great company for you."

She chuckled, relief flooding through her. "And you too, you old tyrant. Don't kid me, I think getting a dog would be exactly what both of us need. We've been so lonely since Fritzer died. But I thought you were adamant about not getting another pup."

He sighed. "I know I was, and I shouldn't have been. If that little dog has accomplished anything by being here with us, even for so short a time, it's to show me how foolish I've been to take to my bed. I tell you, Marj, she has opened my eyes."

"We'll call her our little Christmas angel, but you're absolutely right. We'll have to try to find out who she belongs to. In the meantime she's safe and warm and well fed. I think it's supposed to snow later today anyway. They say not much, but who knows, so she's better off here than out there somewhere. And speak of the devil he's sure to appear. Hello, Snowflakes, don't tell me you're hungry again?"

Snowflakes sounded her insistent, I need attention right now bark, standing on her back legs and pawing the air with her front feet.

They stepped apart as Marjorie laughed, still holding Walter's arm. "Remember that little dance that Fritzer used to do when he wanted something? Well Snowflakes just did the very same thing. I can't believe it. Anyway, I'm going to go and feed her, I think in the kitchen this time. Why don't you come on into the living room, dear, and sit with me? I'll bring your sandwich in on a tray. I think it would do you good to get out of that bed for awhile."

He shrugged amiably. "Sure, I can do that. Let me get dressed first and then I'll spend some time with you."

She guided Walter back to the bedroom, laid out his clothes. She then set off to feed Snowflakes, who proceeded to empty the half-full dog dish with great gusto followed by fresh cool water to wash it down.

Soon Walter was sitting in his chair, Snowflakes in his lap, curled up again although she didn't seem to want to sleep. She looked up adoringly at him and then over at Marjorie, her soft pink tongue lolling in that darling smile that would melt even the hardest of hearts.

"She's not going to stay, Marjorie. I reckon she'll be gone before Christmas morning."

Marjorie looked at him, puzzled. "What makes you say that? She seems pretty comfortable here with us."

"You rescued her and now the danger has passed. Besides, I'll bet she only lives about a block or so from here and she was on her way home. We're probably keeping her from being with her family and there's only a few hours left before Christmas Eve."

"But how do we know who that family is so I can take her back?"

"We don't, but she does. I expect it won't be long before she wants to leave and go be with them. We've had a nice visit with her, kept her here longer than we probably should have. When she wants to go, we have to let her. I believe the weather has warmed considerably, and the wind has died down completely. She'll have a nice jaunt home and be curled up in her own warm bed within five minutes. You said she didn't look as though she'd been on the streets because she was so nice and clean. That means she lives very close to here. Maybe she was chased out of her own yard by Brutus."

"I wish I knew where to take her though instead of letting her just walk off."

"Don't worry, Mother. She knows where she lives. And she'll go there when she's good and ready."

"You really think she'll leave?"

"I know she will. It's just a question of time. Snowflakes has a mind of her own."

"I know she's only been here for two or three hours, but I'm going to miss her."

Walter stroked the little poodle. "Me too, but at least she got me out of bed. I owe her that."

Suddenly the dog raised her head, cocked it to one side then hopped to the floor and headed for the door.

"I think she needs to pee again."

"Probably," said Walter, looking straight ahead, "but remember, Marj. If she wants to go, don't try to stop her. We shouldn't keep her here against her will. There are probably people looking for her and we have no right to hold her back."

Marjorie slipped Snowflakes into her sweater, opened the door, and let the dog out. True enough Snowflakes did have to use the facilities as it were, but when finished, turned toward the gate, and waited patiently as though knowing full well Marjorie would come and open it for her. She did, and Snowflakes passed through, pausing to glance back at the woman who'd been so kind to give her safety, warmth, and love, then she trotted daintily away.

Marjorie went back inside with an unexpectedly heavy heart. "She's gone, Walter. Our little Christmas angel is gone."

Walter's eyes were misty, and he cleared his throat noisily before attempting to speak. "Why don't you make that call to the kennel today, Marj, and see if they have any puppies?"

Chapter Eight

"Afraid to sleep with you, what kind of a question is that?" she demanded but knew in her heart that it was a darned good one.

He smiled tiredly. "A question that needs an answer I guess."

The thought of lying down next to her soon-to-be ex-husband was indeed frightening, especially when she thought she'd tucked all those old feelings safely away where she didn't have to deal with them anymore. The last thing she wanted to do was make a fool of herself, but here he was, those dark, fathomless eyes of his boring into her soul. She knew she had to sound callous, no matter how much he still affected her.

"Cole, I'm divorcing you. It has nothing to do with fear, but everything to do with proper conduct. There's no sense going back, we have to keep moving forward."

"Divorcing," he underlined unnecessarily, "not divorced. You are still my legal wife, Elsa, and that makes me your legal husband. I don't need to go any further, do I?"

"What does that mean? Do you intend to lay claim to what you feel is still rightfully yours? Exercise your conjugal rights? Is that it?"

He laughed out loud this time. "I just told you I want to go to sleep, obviously it's you who can't handle all this closeness. Relax, nobody's going to force anybody to do anything they don't want to do, Elsa. We're not some randy teenagers alone for the first time."

"My reasons for wanting the divorce are still the same as they were when I filed the papers. So yes, I can lie down beside you and not go to pieces. I think of you as a friend now, Cole, and that's all. Maybe I always did. Anything there might have been between us was over a long time ago, and I for one, intend to keep what belongs in the past, in the past. So goodnight, or good day or whatever."

"Good morning I believe would be correct."

"Okay then, good morning," she said, relying on bluster to get through this thing.

She never expected to have to deal with something like this while she was at his place. It hadn't crossed her mind, or she likely wouldn't have come; being practically forced to lie on the same bed with him. She'd nearly choked on the words telling Cole that maybe all she ever thought of him was as a friend. Ha! It's a wonder her nose didn't grow six inches from telling such a terrible lie. She guessed that Cole knew it was all just so much artifice. He'd remember as well as she did that there was a time if they went anywhere near a bed, look out. If truth be told, there were times when they didn't make it to the bed. So why, after all of the water that had passed under the bridge between them, were all these feelings rising up to stare her in the eye now? Well she'd show him how strong she was. She knew her own mind and if lying down with him was what was necessary under the circumstances; that's what she'd do. No problem. The most important thing at the moment was getting her dog back, and she required, and *appreciated* his help in doing so. That didn't mean there was anything other than her gratitude up for grabs, literally.

Needing sleep badly herself she laid down and pulled the comforter over her, then stopped short as she was about to stretch out. "Cole, I don't have a pillow. Is there an extra one in the linen closet I can use? And also, where is the linen closet?"

His voice already sounded drowsy, as if she'd awakened him as he was drifting off. "Just one pillow," he said, half asleep.

"One pillow? Who buys just one pillow? This is a double bed for crying out loud."

He did sound more alert this time, if not a teensy bit annoyed. "I ordered a bunch of bedding, pillows included, but some items were missing from the shipment when it arrived a couple of days ago. I only received one pillow. When the rest of the shipment arrives, I'll have four pillows." He moved his head to the left. "Here, share mine. I don't mind. My back will be to you anyway, so you won't have to worry about me breathing on you or getting too close."

She growled. "I give up," she muttered, then positioned her head carefully on the oversized pillow. It wasn't so bad, nice and soft, but she didn't care for the fact that her back was smack dab up against his, and not just his back, their butts too. She shivered involuntarily in response to his closeness, her body the worst kind of traitor.

There was a smile in his voice, the previous drowsiness seeming to have evaporated. "Are you cold, Elsa? We can get under the covers if you are."

Oh perfect, the two of them under the covers. Now that could be downright disastrous in the face of what she was determined to accomplish with the divorce. "No, I'm fine," she said, then promptly shivered again. It was as much from awareness of him as the chill she'd gotten earlier this morning.

"Elsa, come closer and let me warm you up."

"Keep your hands to yourself, buster. I told you I'm fine, I don't need any warming up, thank you very much."

He chuckled. "Liar!" he taunted her, "don't you think I can feel you shivering?"

"Says you," she shot back.

He sighed, swinging his feet to the floor. Getting up he pulled back the covers and she was forced to disembark as well or be rolled off onto the floor. Both remained fully clothed. He knew if he went anywhere near his buckle and zipper she'd be out of here like a scalded cat, so they'd do it this way.

"Here," he said, taking her hand and urging her toward his side of the bed, "get in under the covers then scoot over and take the pillow with you. Okay? I'm going to get a throw cushion off the sofa and use that. There, problem solved. Whatever we do, we only have a couple of hours and then I think we need to get back to the city and start looking again. Can you live with this arrangement until then? Scouts honour that I won't come anywhere near you while you're asleep."

She felt a little silly. "That's good, Cole. Sorry for the schoolgirl stuff. I obviously still haven't worked everything out, but I'm getting there. Thank you for being a gentleman. At least we can still be friends."

"Yeah, right," he grumbled under his breath, but she pretended not to hear.

It was almost one o'clock in the afternoon when she opened her eyes, now face to face with Cole and his even breathing told her he was still in a deep sleep. She watched him from under lowered lashes. Oh how she missed him, especially at night. Sleeping together was something they always did particularly well, the snuggling part. When the marriage was working that is. It seemed their subconscious had taken over today when they'd drifted off, because here they were, legs entangled and her in his arms, their faces inches apart. He smelled so good, a mixture of saddle leather and country air and she drank it in knowing it might be the last chance to be with him like this. The divorce would be final soon enough, and then she could move on and begin to heal.

They'd become warm under the blankets, since they were both still fully dressed, so the covers had been tossed off in sleep. Her eyes were drawn to his red plaid flannel shirt, or more to the point where the first two buttons were undone. She could see flesh, still bronzed from the summer sun when he stripped to the waist while working outside. The urge to undo the rest of those buttons was most overpowering. Her fingers twitched at her side, but to what end? They were going to be divorced and probably the worst thing they could do was rekindle their relationship. If they did, they'd be right back where they started with nothing resolved. The reason she had called a halt to the marriage still existed, that was true, but her body ached for him. She literally ached for the fulfillment she knew instinctively only he could provide.

She suddenly became aware that his deep even breathing had softened into wakefulness, and to her mortification he was watching her watch him. She started to pull out of his arms, but he was stronger, faster, and before she knew it his lips were on hers. Her body betrayed her yet again as she felt herself giving itself up to his caresses. And her fingers did what they had been longing to do too, undoing several buttons on his shirt, and sliding her hand inside against toasty warm skin and those glorious rock-hard muscles.

And since turnabout was fair play, his hand crept under her sweater and was now teasing the clasp on her bra, a front fastener that let go entirely too easily she decided. But it felt wonderful it felt to have his hands on her, proprietary, demanding, yet gentle, sensual as they heightened her desire to a fever pitch.

She was enjoying the kiss as much as he obviously was, but it just couldn't be! Hadn't she explained as much not an hour or two ago, if not several more times before that? What was the point of getting a divorce if they were still going to play at being married? She could see ground, hard won, slipping away as easily as if no divorce proceedings had ever been started. There was going to be a divorce for a reason, she reminded herself, a very good reason, and so there could be no more of this. She succeeded in disentangling herself from him and sliding out the other side of the bed, righting her clothes in preparation to leave.

He sighed, and she cringed at the exasperated sound. Like here's Elsa, playing with me again, but he obviously dealt with it without rancour. That was one thing about Cole, he shook stuff off that would upend most people. He just didn't get excited about things that should be gotten excited about. Oh he could get angry, if pushed hard enough. She'd seen it on several occasions when his buttons had been well and truly pushed.

She hoped he didn't think that's what was happening now. It was just that things got out of hand if they got too close, but there was more to what she was now looking for in a marriage other than red-hot sex.

A few moments later it was as if the kiss had never happened. In the end, it came down to which one of them was the better actor as both tried to pretend this was just a normal interlude when there was actually so much that needed to be said.

"Are you hungry, Elsa?" he asked, more gruffly than was necessary she thought, although she knew he had to be frustrated by her slamming on the brakes.

She tried to keep her voice light, unaffected. "After that big breakfast you fed me earlier?"

"I could use something and wondered if you might too. Nothing too big."

"Do you have any yogurt by any chance?"

"No, I don't have any yogurt."

"Croissants?"

"No," running his hands through his hair. "I've got eggs, ham, orange juice, or I could cook you some pancakes."

"Man food."

"Good food."

She smiled, remembering the easy way they used to have between them once upon a time. They fell right into it as though they'd never stopped being playful with each other, although the strong undertow couldn't be ignored.

"I'll settle for a banana if you have any of those," she said as they walked into the kitchen, "or an apple."

"I have both actually, over to your right on the counter," he said, pointing in the direction of the fruit. "That's what I'm going to have, a banana."

Elsa's cellphone jumped to life in her purse and changing direction she headed for where her pocketbook was still sitting by the door. She remembered as she tore it free that it wasn't her telephone number on the posters, it was Cole's, so this wouldn't be a call about Snowflakes. She could see by the screen that it was her mother.

Phoebe Randolph, the senator's wife, to whom everything was about appearances. Happiness and contentment always took a backseat to how the prominent couple would be perceived by others. She was glamourous to a fault; impeccably turned out at all times with never a hair out of place, or God forbid, a chipped nail.

"Elsa, dear, I'm just touching base about tonight. I think you should plan to arrive about three-thirty this afternoon, that way you can get settled and be changed into what you're planning to wear for the evening. Our guests should start arriving around four-thirty and I'd like you to be on hand to help us greet them. I think it would be only proper that we meet everyone as a family."

"I won't be able to make it tonight, Mother. I'm sorry."

There was a pregnant pause on the other end of the line, a slight cooling of Pheobe's warm melodious tone. "I beg your pardon?"

"I won't be able to attend the gathering tonight, something has come up and I just wouldn't feel right about being there. Besides, I haven't had much sleep in the past twenty-four hours so I wouldn't be much fun anyway. You're going to have to carry on without me. Please make my apologies to your guests."

"Elsa, you can't change your mind at the last minute! The invitations all have your name on them as well as ours, and our guests were told we three would all be here to greet them, just as we always have. There will be no exception this time, dear."

Elsa drew a deep steadying breath. Her mother could be an intimidating opponent, not to mention her father. They were both used to having things their way.

"Mother, Snowflakes is missing. She was stolen out of Cole's truck last night. We've been looking for her all night. I'm just sick about it."

The silence on the other end stretched out a bit too long. "Snowflakes is your dog, correct?"

"You remember the little white poodle we call Snowflakes? Because…."

"Right, and you say someone took her?"

"Someone took her right out of Cole's truck at the super…."

There was some serious frostbite coming over the line now. "That's what I thought you said, Cole's truck."

"He was looking after the dog while I was away in Fredericton on business."

"We would have been happy to look after your pet for you, so you wouldn't have to ask *him*," Phoebe pointed out disapprovingly.

"Cole didn't mind, he...."

"I thought you two were getting a divorce?"

Her mother and father had never approved of Cole as her choice of husband. They'd had someone more suitable in mind in the person of Tompkins Fraser, an up and coming young politician. A few years her senior, he was today, the highly respected speaker of the house. Now happily married with three lovely children, Tom was obviously no longer a candidate for son-in-law. It wouldn't matter if he were. She hadn't been interested then and certainly wouldn't be now either even if he was available, completely smitten and strumming love songs under her bedroom window.

Her parents were aware that Cole came from money, but were disgruntled that he didn't act the part. His dreams were more modest in nature; work as foreman for his father and run a good-sized herd of his own, build a nice comfy house and drive a good truck. He didn't need to own half the county to be happy. He'd already found contentment within. But even if he had achieved his father's level of success, he wouldn't have appealed to Elsa's parents. After the word cattle, they hadn't heard much else. It was the rural aspect of it all, and given their urban sophistication and lifestyle, Cole simply did not fit in.

It had been teenaged rebellion, pure and simple, that had seen Elsa go to the western bar with her girlfriend, Vesta. They'd been out for a little fun on the wild side of town, as her friend had put it. It had hardly been wild, but when the tall lanky cowboy had asked her to dance, she'd been all too happy to say yes. They'd quickly hit it off with for real stars in their eyes, and before she knew it, she was head over heels in love with him. And the fact that she knew her parents would not approve was the ideal catalyst that saw the relationship take root and quickly grow into something longer term than she'd originally intended. She had not got the brakes on in time but felt sure she could eventually bring him around to Randolph suitability. She had been dead wrong about that though because she hadn't taken his cussed stubbornness into consideration. Still she'd gone through with the wedding, and it would likely have been fodder for a movie to see the bride's socially conscious family mix with the groom's family who didn't give a whit about such things. More to the point, they didn't mix very well at all. It would probably go down as one of the more awkward social occasions of the year, but it had indeed gone down.

When she'd announced their impending divorce, her parents tried to hide their relief, their behind-the-scenes mechanizations notwithstanding.

Zoning back in, she remembered her mother on the other end of the line. "We are getting a divorce, Mother." She pretended not to see the look Cole gave her, whether he intended to or not. Then just to be contrary she added: "Perhaps I should bring him along to say hello, you know, catch up."

Now she could not ignore Cole's hiked eyebrows. She knew if she did ask him, he wouldn't go, so she felt fairly safe to make the comment.

"I don't think that would be a good idea, Elsa. For one thing there'd be no place setting for him, and everything would be … you know…."

"Awkward," Elsa finished for her. "Don't worry, Cole won't be coming, and neither will I. We'll both be out looking for Snowflakes. We simply have to find her. She's been gone since suppertime last night and I'm frantic to know she's all right."

"Elsa, you can't let a … dog … ruin our plans. As you're well aware we have family friends coming from away, and they're looking forward to seeing you again, dear. Cam and Maureen, and Moe and Judy will be there. So you see, you have to come. It would be rude not to. I simply won't take no for an answer."

Elsa sighed. She knew her mother would not make this easy. A dedicated hostess, she insisted that everything run smoothly and on cue, her cue. No general demanded more of his troops than Phoebe did of her team, family included, when there was a social engagement to be either organized or honoured.

"Give them my regards, please, Mother, but I won't be able to attend."

There was a *very* long pause on the other end of the line, then muffled voices and she wasn't at all surprised when her father came on the line. They were the ultimate tag team. She felt like a nine-year-old who'd misbehaved at summer camp. Phoebe was calling in the big guns, certain that would produce the desired results because *nobody* argued with Senator Randolph.

"What seems to be the trouble, Elsa?" he began, his voice as smooth as warm honey on a summer afternoon. "You are expected here tonight and there's no excuse that your mother and I will accept to the contrary."

Elsa gripped the phone, her head thrown back, eyes closed. If she dared to look in Cole's direction, she knew he'd be enjoying this. He was probably relieved that he was no longer expected to toe the line, not that he ever did try, much to the consternation of her parents … and herself.

"Daddy, my dog was stolen out of Cole's truck. He was dog sitting for me, and someone took her. Isn't that terrible? We looked for her all night. We're just about to go back out and start again."

"You're still maintaining a relationship with Cole?"

Now why did that trump the fact that her precious dog had been stolen and was now missing?

"Yes," she said simply, then added wickedly, "we actually just woke up."

There was a weighty pause on the other end of the line, her father no doubt working out the proper tact to win the day and bring his daughter into compliance. Why was her appearance so crucial to the success of their Christmas Eve celebration anyway? The senator and his beautiful wife would be the centrepiece for the whole thing, as usual, and she'd just be window-dressing. The dutiful adult daughter shoring up the ranks.

"Elsa, I'm very disappointed by some of the things I'm hearing right now. Your mother and I thought you had come to your senses, and now … this. But let me be very clear about one thing, you committed to this Christmas Eve event, and we expect you to be here, dog or no dog. I want to see you here no later than three-thirty, as previously discussed."

"Daddy, I'm not a child…." but the line had gone dead. The nerve of that man, she fumed to herself as she slammed the receiver into the cradle.

"Hey! Don't break my phone! I just bought it."

"Sorry," she said, flopping into the nearby armchair. "You'd think I was seven years old,

159

not a grown woman. My father practically ordered me to be there, they don't care a thing about poor little Snowflakes being out there alone in the city."

"Are you going to do it?"

"Do what?"

"Go to their party?"

"No I'm not going to their party. You and I are going to look for Snowflakes. That's what I'm going to do."

"Well, well, well … I'm impressed. Other than your teenaged rebellion that saw you and I get together in the first place, I do believe this is the first time you've actually said no to your parents. Let me get my phone because this is a moment worth capturing."

She turned red; she could feel it. She also knew why he'd said it, but she wasn't going to mine that particular acre at the moment. That was a conversation best left for another time, if they ever had it at all.

"Not funny! They'll be upset … they're already upset with me, but it can't be helped. I know they love me and want me to spend Christmas with them, but this party tonight is all about appearances. There'll even be media there for the Santa portion. Sometimes I feel like a trick pony that's just trotted out for special occasions, like having my picture stuck on the annual Christmas card. It hurts that they don't even care about my dog. Their party is more important. Anyway, it is what it is, and I can't change how they look at the world."

"I know from experience that an angry Senator Randolph is a worthy opponent."

She couldn't help but smile. "So are you, Cole. I'll never forget the argument you two had at Daddy's big fundraiser barbecue. It was just lucky none of the guests had arrived yet, but it was a good one."

Cole sighed, peeling the banana. "He took great exception to my boots and jeans, but Senator Randolph does not tell me how to dress. Period. I don't think he'll try that again. But I seem to recall that you sided with him," he said, taking a bite, his eyes not leaving her face.

"He's my father, what do you expect?"

"And I'm your husband. You should have stood with me, Elsa. That's what I expect."

She nodded, glumly. "You're right. I should have apologized about that a long time ago, so I'm apologizing now. Looking back though, would it have killed you to change clothes just even that once? You knew you were dressed inappropriately."

"Change what I was wearing to keep Senator Randolph happy? Not a chance, sweetheart. I'm my own man. Besides, it was a barbecue, not a state dinner. And one thing I can say for sure, I'll never be talked into wearing a pink cardigan, and white loafers just aren't my style."

She laughed at the ridiculous image of Cole in white loafers. Or a pink cardigan for that matter which just happened to be a routine choice for her father, always worn with white

161

slacks and polo shirt of course. It would look just as funny to see her father in jeans and western boots. Those two worlds were never meant to blend, collide would be the more apt description.

"Well anyway" she said, still chuckling, "it's over now, but it was the first time I ever saw anyone stand toe to toe with my father and not back down. I might not have agreed with you, but you were great, actually."

"And you were great just now. Your dad might get the idea after a while and relax a bit. Not everyone has to bend to his will. I'm surprised that your mother does because she's a pretty strong-minded lady in her own right."

"That's why they get along so well, they think the very same way. They agree with each other on everything. I never had to wonder where I stood as a kid. Whether I was talking to my mother or talking to my father, it was the same. At least in that way they were consistent, and still are."

Cole finished his banana, put the peeling in the compost bin and went for their coats. "We should get back on the road. The wind's gone down and I think it's warmed up considerably so that'll be good for the dog. If she gets tired, she can hole up somewhere and get rested up. She's a smart little thing too and I'm sure she knows the sound of my truck. Ready?"

Elsa slipped her arms into her coat. "At least we've got a lot of posters up in the area where she was last seen, but we haven't had even one single call and that surprises me. I wonder why nobody has seen her? A little white dog running loose is sure to be noticed by *somebody*. With a poster on practically every telephone pole I can't imagine that someone hasn't got something to tell us. They must know we'd be frantic by now and would want to help. And there's even a generous reward. That alone should be a good incentive."

They got to the truck, Cole going around to open her door for her out of habit. She'd loved the chivalrous side of him too.

"Like I said, the dog could be holed up somewhere taking a rest and therefore people wouldn't see her. She could have gotten into someone's baby barn or shed, you never know. We'll give the area another going over and then I've got to get back here. Jake helped me out last night, but I told him I'd take care of things from there. He should be with his family on Christmas Eve, not over here doing my chores. So I hate to say it, but if we don't come up with something by this afternoon, I'm tied here for a few hours. The work has to get done."

"I can take my car and go around myself and look."

"No, I don't want you to go on your own, Elsa. I think it's better if we go together."

"Why, are you worried about me, Cole?"

"I don't want you walking the streets alone, that's all. I'm not saying I'm not free to go back at all. It just won't be until later this evening.

It'll take me a few hours to do the barn chores … unless you want to help."

She figured that Cole was calling her bluff. Well, so be it. How hard could it be? Good, hard, honest labour. And she didn't mind getting dirty. She wasn't one of those girls who wanted to be treated like a porcelain doll that was only good for sitting on a shelf. She'd ridden horses before on his father's ranch. She knew what manure smelled like, but there was no way she was doing barn chores in this get-up. They'd have to drop by her place and pick up something suitable for her to work in. She also had a pair of old hiking boots she could wear instead of these stylish contraptions she was wearing now. Why hadn't she ever noticed before how uncomfortable they were? It was probably because she hadn't tried to walk any real distance in them.

"Sure I'll help you. You know I don't mind getting a little dirt under my nails."

"You'll be using a shovel, but you'll need a pair of gloves to protect your manicure, and those I can supply. That'd be great though. Thank you. That's very nice of you considering I was the one who cost you your dog."

"I've already forgotten about that part of it. Everyone makes mistakes. I've made my share of them too; some real whoppers."

"What, like marrying me?" he asked, his voice tinged with bitterness.

She couldn't miss it, and something tugged at her heart as if realizing for the first time how much she'd hurt him. She was surprised he was still willing to give her the time of day.

"Don't say stuff like that, Cole. It won't get us anywhere."

"Right," he said tightly as he shoved the truck in gear, using more force than she knew was necessary.

Soon they had made their way back to Lewisville on the other side of the city, and practically the first thing they noticed were the missing dog posters. When they'd left earlier, the area had been blanketed with them. Now there wasn't one to be seen.

"Where are all our posters?" she wailed, hardly daring to believe her eyes. "Look, you can see the bits of white paper still stuck under the staples."

They cruised the entire area, up and down the streets, and it was the same everywhere they went. The posters were gone.

"Kids must have torn them off," he said, puffing an exasperated sigh. "I see scraps of torn paper in the gutter. Looks like our posters have been vandalized. I'm sorry, Elsa, I never expected this."

Seeing the ruined posters was the last straw for her stoicism of the past few hours. Dropping her head into her hands she gave way to tears she'd been holding in since she'd been let down by the mistaken sighting of Snowflakes early this morning.

Cole quickly found a vacant parking lot in front of an old convenience store, parked, and pulled her gently into his arms. Once there, the storm broke for good as she sobbed against his chest.

He reached up and stroked her hair in an effort to comfort her. "We'll find her, sweetheart, don't worry. This is a setback yes, but we will get Snowflakes. You just wait and see."

It felt so wonderful to be in his arms again that she could have stayed there forever but reminded herself that there wouldn't be a forever for them. Not now, because she'd seen to that. With an effort she got hold of her emotions but stayed in his arms.

"Why are you being so nice to me after what I did to you; to us?" she asked him when she trusted herself to speak again. "I don't understand."

"I think you do understand, Elsa. It's because I still love you."

Chapter Nine

Brutus, the over-zealous lab/shepherd mix, was on backyard guard duty as Snowflakes trotted happily past and a cacophony of barking immediately erupted behind the fence. The fence, merely symbolic, was cleared in one gigantic leap and the chase was on. However, while Brutus had brawn on his side, Snowflakes had wiry cunning on hers, and because of her size was able to duck into small spaces to escape her pursuer.

Onward she sped, under a low gate meant to block the alley. Brutus was left far in the distance barking furiously at being denied his prize a second time. Given his track record he would not have hurt the little puff of fur, although Snowflakes wasn't taking any chances. She put as much distance as possible between them and didn't even begin to slow down until she had accomplished that.

Winded, Snowflakes hid in the overhang of an abandoned building to catch her breath. It was actually comfy here on a bed of dried leaves that had drifted in during the fall. Since the temperature had risen considerably over the past few hours it wasn't at all unpleasant to be outdoors on what had turned out to be a lovely December day. In fact, she was overheated from running and this spot served as a most delightful rest stop.

There were now more people out and about, but she could not be seen where she was hiding. She had an unobstructed view and could clearly hear what passers by were saying. Their smatterings of conversation as they went by were entertaining, and she listened until they were out of earshot, which for a dog was a considerable distance. It was like having a front row seat to mini movies, each small snapshot of chitchat a brief peek into the lives of those involved. You could learn a lot about people in a very short period of time Snowflakes decided.

The first to walk by were a woman and a young red-haired boy in a navy-blue stocking hat.

"But Mummy, you said Santa Claus was going to bring me a water pistol, and now you say maybe not. How come he's not going to bring it? That's what I asked for."

"Now Caleb, what I told you was that you could *ask* Santa, but the answer isn't always yes. Sometimes he finds the next best thing to take its place. A water pistol is something you ask for in the summer, dear, not the winter. It's too cold in the winter to play with it outside. The water would freeze and then it wouldn't shoot, would it? It wouldn't be a water pistol anymore. It would be an ice pistol."

"But I could play with it in the house," the child whined, determined to have his way. "In my room. Me and Jordon could have water fights in there."

"Shoot water in the house? I don't think so, honey. Don't worry. Santa will have something nice for you on Christmas morning. Something that's good for winter and you'll have lots of fun with it. It'll be a surprise, and I know you like surprises."

"I don't want a stupid surprise. I want a water pistol."

"Caleb, that's enough!"

"It's not enough! Santa should bring me what I asked for, not try to surprise me with some stupid junk!"

"Caleb! You'll take what you get and be happy with it. When I was a little girl, I didn't have…."

That was it, they were out of range, and it was a few minutes before a young couple walked by, holding hands.

"Tyson, I hope you got me something better this year. Something that's for me to enjoy, not you."

"What do you mean? I get you a good present every year!"

"Yes, good for you; something for me to wear to bed, and every year it gets smaller and smaller. And I know where you go to get that stuff and what you pay. Why don't you give me the money and I can buy what I want?"

"Because I like to see you in those things. You're so sexy, Maggie."

"Tyson, honey, I'm glad you think I'm sexy, but those things are for you, not me. I want something for me, not some scrap of lace that I only have on for a second anyway. Let me pick out something on my own, something I'd like for a change."

He snorted. "I can just imagine what you'd pick out, probably a flannelette nightdress like an old grandma would wear. You're always cold."

"Bed is all you think about, I'd like…."

A few minutes later two young men came striding along, both with their hands shoved deep into the pockets of their dark jackets.

"So did you get it?" the man closet to Snowflakes asked.

"The ring? Yep! Right here in my pocket."

"Are you going to wait for Christmas morning to give it to her, or are you going to ask her tonight?"

There was a long sigh. "I don't know, I want to get it right. Maybe I should do it tonight, make it stand out more than just a present she opens tomorrow morning. I was thinking about doing one of those crazy proposals like you see on TV or online, but I'm not very creative and I don't want to copy someone else."

"Do you think she'll say yes?"

"I'm pretty sure she will, she's been dropping hints for a while, but I pretend not to notice."

"So maybe she's mad at you 'cause you don't notice...."

"Nah, she's cool."

"So one woman for the rest of your life. Be very sure, my man."

"Yeah, I have thought about that, but Samantha's the one. If only she wasn't so...."

Snowflakes strained to hear, but a truck rumbled past just then, drowning out the rest of the sentence. By the time the street was clear, they were gone. Oh well, time to get going anyway if she was going to make it back home in time for Christmas.

She looked down the street. There was no one in sight so maybe now would be a good time to get moving again because the hideaway was starting to get chilly. Slipping out into the open, off she went, until the sound of children's laughter led her to the fence surrounding a playground. There several children were playing on the swings, taking advantage of the much-improved weather and the fact that school was obviously out for the holidays. Swings, slides, and teeter-totters were filled with youngsters bundled in winter wear, their animated voices like beautiful music in the mild December air. The excitement was building as they waited for Santa to begin his nighttime rounds.

Snowflakes settled down in a clump of bushes, undetected, and watched the motion of the swing. It was mesmerizing, as was the rhythmic up and down of the teeter-totters. Of course, the mini disputes that sprang up among the children were quickly resolved as play continued, everyone in high spirits with Christmas Eve just around the corner.

The minutes passed as she watched the kids and it was time well spent, Snowflakes suppressing the urge to join the little ones in a bit of Christmas fun. But onward she knew she must go and not far away she spied a veterinary shop. The large sign in front was generously framed in lush evergreen boughs. As seasonally pretty as it was, there was no love lost for Snowflakes when it came to check-ups with the vet. She bore her darling Dr. Heidi no ill will for the routine needles and teeth checking she had to undergo on an annual basis. But this veterinary office looked a great deal different than the one Elsa carried her to in Snowflakes' red plastic pet taxi. This clinic was very festive, all decorated up for the season, and wow, what a presentation.

On the front lawn of the building was a beautiful Christmas display, the centrepiece of which featured a small mechanical white poodle with a topknot featuring an abundance of snowy curls. It was a dead ringer for Snowflakes. It was like looking in a mirror, only this was a boy poodle, and not just any boy poodle. This one sat up and begged, barked a chirpy little bark, then wiggled his hind end. It was a trick that Snowflakes had tried to do on occasion but as yet had not been able to master. If ever there was love at first sight, baby this was it. But the conundrum was determining if this very handsome boy poodle was real, or was he just a toy? Well she was called a toy poodle, wasn't she? Creeping closer to make that very important distinction she could hear the motorized mechanism, which enabled him to move. But never mind, she still felt a quickening of her heartbeat just imagining that he could be real as he performed his tricks for her, over and over again. He never seemed to tire of the performance. And that smile! Snowflakes was spellbound. She'd never seen another dog quite like him, so handsome, *and* so talented. She sat back and watched him in awe.

"Look at that baby dog, Mummy!" cried a small girl walking past with her mother. "It's real."

"They're only make-believe dogs, Sarah, but they're cute, aren't they! Dr. Remington puts that display up every year, but I agree, they certainly do look real."

"How come one of them is doing stuff and the other one is just sitting there and watching? Is he tired?"

"It's all part of the Christmas scene, dear. That's what he's supposed to be doing, looking at the other dog."

"The one that's sitting looks more real. Can I go and pat him, Mummy?"

"Sure, but not too hard. We don't want to break anything in Dr. Remington's display.

Some of those pieces are very old and probably fragile. He used to put up this display when I was a little girl. He's obviously added something new this year though, but please be very careful."

The child, having received permission, raced as fast as her legs would carry her, straight for Snowflakes. A small, gloved hand patted the poodle ever so gently on the top of her curly head and Snowflakes just couldn't help herself. She turned and licked the girl's glove. She wished it was the child's bare hand because wool didn't taste very good and tended to get stuck in her teeth. Nevertheless, it was important to show appreciation.

The little girl shrieked and dashed back across the yard to her mother. "It moved, Mummy. It was going to bite my hand."

The mother laughed. "No, honey, it's not real. That's just a mechanical display."

"But he looked at me and his eyes were sad. He's so cute."

"I know dear, come along now. We have to get home because Mummy still has a lot of work to get done before Santa comes tonight."

"I changed my mind about what I want for Christmas."

There was an understandable pause from her mother. "Sarah, it's too late to change your mind now, dear. You've already asked Santa for a Betsy-Ann doll and that's what he and his elves have been busy making at the North Pole all year. Don't you think they'd be very disappointed if they made the doll for you and then you said you didn't want it?"

"Okay, well I could still take the doll, but I want a baby dog like the one back there to go with it and then I'd have two children. We'd have to tell it not to bite though."

"Okay, maybe next year you can ask Santa for a dog, how would that be? He'd have to bring it before Christmas though because it would get awfully hot in that big sack of toys that Santa carries around in his sleigh. What do you think?"

"He could put it at the top of his sack so that it'd get air."

"Ahhh, it still wouldn't work out very well. If he was at the top he might fall out and we wouldn't want that, would we?"

"I know Santa wants me to have a baby dog, maybe even the one back there. I know he does!"

"What makes you say that, honey? We've already been to see Santa and he…."

"Because the baby dog is right behind us, Mummy. See? He wants to come home with us, just like Santa told him to."

Mrs. Barker spun around in surprise to see the white poodle trotting a few paces behind.

"So you are real, you little goober," she laughed as Snowflakes covered the distance between them, hurrying up to the child.

"Now don't you bite me," Sarah warned in her best pretend-mother voice. She extended her now gloveless hand out to Snowflakes and was rewarded with a vigorous licking of her fingers.

"He doesn't want to bite you, dear. See? He wants to lick you. And I can see it's not a little boy, it's a little girl, and her name is Snowflakes. See it right here on her name tag?"

"Oh, Mummy, Santa heard me because when I was patting the dog. I asked him to bring me a baby dog like this one for Christmas."

"Oh my goodness! Well I would say Snowflakes already belongs to another little girl or boy and she's probably lost and wants to get back home because she misses her family very much. We'll have to take her back to the veterinary shop, Sarah."

"No!" the child screamed. "She's mine! I asked Santa for her and now she's mine. You saw her, she came right to me, Mummy. Oh you're so cute," she told Snowflakes, ruffling her silky curls. "You're going to be my very own doggie now."

"Sarah, this little dog belongs to someone else, I'm certain of it, dear. We won't be able to keep her."

"No," the child argued stubbornly, "Santa Claus sent her to me so I'm going to keep her. He gave me what I asked for."

Mrs. Barker knelt down beside the dog, putting her arm around her daughter's shoulders. "Sweetie, maybe Santa sent this little dog along for you to see what you can have next year. To let you know that he heard you and to show you how cute she's going to be. But I know that he wouldn't give you somebody else's dog, and I know you wouldn't want to keep a pet that belonged to somebody else. Sometimes pets get lost, and when that happens, we have to make sure they find their way home so they can be with the people who love them."

There were tears on Sarah's cheeks. "But I already love her, and she loves me." Right on cue, Snowflakes began an enthusiastic licking of her daughter's face, much to Sarah's squealing delight.

"Let me put it this way, if you had a little dog and somehow that dog got lost, would you want someone to bring it home to you? Or do you think it would be right for them to keep your dog and maybe you would never see it again? How would you feel about that?"

"I would want someone to bring my doggie home where I lived. I would be very sad until she came back."

"So do you see what I'm trying to tell you? I truly believe this little dog belongs to someone else because she already has a name."

Sarah laughed. "I like that name."

"But you see when Santa does bring you your very own dog, she won't ever have to leave. The best part is that you'll be able to give him a name that you make up yourself. This little dog is going to be your friend for a very short while, as long as it takes to make a few phone calls and then she'll have to say good-bye. So tell me, what will you call your own dog when you get one?"

"Poopoo."

Mrs. Barker was slightly taken aback, but she had said the child could name the dog when she got one. "Do you have a second choice?"

"No, Poopoo because she will be nice and soft like Snowflakes."

She knew how stubborn her little girl could be, so Poopoo it was, double entendre overlooked. "All right then, dear. When you eventually get your own dog that's what you can name it, unless you change your mind in the meantime. You're allowed to do that you know, but once it's final that's the one we have to keep. All right?"

"All right, Mummy. So Snowflakes can come home with us now though, right?"

"First I want to check at the clinic to see if they're aware of a missing dog in the area, or maybe it got out of the clinic somehow without them knowing it."

There were no cars in the clinic's parking lot. That was not an encouraging sign, but she knew that Dr. Remington lived nearby and usually walked to work, so hopefully he might still be there. Nevertheless when she tried the front door it was locked solid. She noticed the small hand-lettered sign indicating that the clinic was now closed for the holidays and the number to call in case of an emergency.

"Well Sarah, it looks like Snowflakes will be coming home with us for a little while, but only until we try to find out who owns her. I want you to understand that. Remember, when we do, she has to go back to her real home, okay? She'll be visiting for as long as that takes, and hopefully she can go home for Christmas."

"Can I still have my Betsy-Ann doll?"

"That's what you asked Santa for isn't it?"

"Yes."

"Then I think Santa will bring your Betsy-Ann doll because you've been a very good girl this year."

Sarah and her mother started on their way again with Snowflakes following them all the way to their home five blocks away. She scampered up the front steps as if she owned the place, or in the very least, was glad to be there. She was Sarah's willing playmate and the child proceeded to take the dog through the house and show her the Christmas tree, her bedroom, and her toys. Last of all she introduced her to her as yet unborn little brother still living in Mummy's tummy. Snowflakes took the whole tour in stride before padding pointedly into the kitchen. She sat up on her back paws and did her front paw prancing that clearly said feed me, (a) because I'm adorable, and (b) because I'm hungry, in that order.

"Oh my gosh I have nothing to give you," Danielle Barker moaned aloud as she looked apologetically at Snowflakes. "Why didn't I think to stop at the corner store and buy something since I knew you'd be with us for a while?"

Just then the back door opened, and Luke Barker snuck in. He slipped a small package onto the top shelf of the closet before announcing he was home early because the office had closed.

Snowflakes was the first one to the back door to greet him, her tiny pink tongue lolling in a dazzling Christmas smile. And since there was no food in the kitchen, maybe this good-looking young gentleman might have a treat or two up his sleeve. So she sat back on her paws and giving it everything she had, pranced with her front feet. To her bewilderment her performance didn't seem to impress him, the man just stared at her as though he couldn't believe his eyes.

Next to arrive was Sarah. "Daddy!" she yelled as he picked her up and swung her around before setting her back on the floor. "Look at my new baby dog! Her name is Snowflakes."

Danielle Barker had now come to the back door as well, walking into the unblinking stare of her husband, the look that said *why is there a dog here? We didn't discuss this!*

He first stared at the dog and then at his daughter, before his gaze swung back to his wife. "Danielle, have you got a minute?"

"Sure," she said, heading for the kitchen where most mummy/daddy conferences took place, at least on the bottom floor of their modest two-storey home.

When they were in the kitchen Danielle closed the door behind her with a click. "Before you say anything, Luke, I didn't buy Sarah a dog. I wouldn't do that without discussing it with you first, and if you have a moment could you run over to Shop Now and pick up a small bag of kibble? We don't have anything to feed Her Majesty."

"Ahhh, you left out some details. You didn't buy her, but she's here and we're feeding her and that tells me she's planning to stay. That's the part I want to know about."

"Okay, dear, the dog was following us home, so we let her. It's Christmas for crying out loud and the poor little thing has to go somewhere. She has an owner, I'm sure of it because she's in such good condition. However, the chances of finding that person before Christmas are probably not very good. So she's here, yes, but not for very long."

"Does Sarah understand that?"

"Of course, she does."

"And now I suppose she wants her very own little dog," his face pulled into an expression that clearly said: *I know what's coming next.*

"Of course she does, but I managed to convince her that Santa might bring one next year, and that Snowflakes belongs to someone else who really misses her. She's okay with everything. She understands the dog is only here for a short while."

"All right then, I'll run over and get her a bag of kibble, unless you want to do it."

"I would, but then I'd miss the fun of doing all the other million and one things that still need to get done. If you want to finish the housework, wrap the rest of Sarah's gifts, and get the stuffing ready for tomorrow's turkey, I don't mind at all if we switch."

"Should I get beef or chicken, do you think? And what about treats? Should I get a bag of those too? Maybe I could run over to the mall and get something for her to chew on so we might have a shoe or two left when she goes?"

"I don't imagine she'll be here more than a day or so, so no, you don't need to buy everything in the store. I tell you, Luke, you're going to fall in love with that poodle. She is absolutely the sweetest thing. My Aunt Melba had a little poodle one time, and it had the worst temperament you could imagine. It snapped at everyone. I think that was because Uncle Chuck teased the poor dog. That man ought not to be allowed around animals because he has no clue how to treat them. Sarah has more sense then he does when it comes to handling animals. But this poodle is a dream, the best personality you could imagine. I'm just afraid Sarah is going to get too attached before Snowflakes has to go, she already *is* attached, and it's been less than an hour."

"Well at least the dog is off the streets where God knows what could happen to her. There's no registration tag on her collar?"

"It looks like there might have been but it's not there now."

"Well whoever it is they'll be mighty happy that the dog came into good hands, that she's being looked after until they can be reunited. It would be great to have her back home before Christmas, but how would we know where to begin to look? Maybe she just wandered away from her home right in this immediate area."

Danielle shrugged. "We found her standing by the Vet clinic down the road. She was watching Dr. Remington's mechanical dog display. Sarah went over to pat her, and Snowflakes just followed us home. Sarah was so happy she was beside herself. I've quite fallen in love with her myself. Maybe we shouldn't make Sarah wait until next Christmas to get her a poodle, because she says she wants one just like Snowflakes. Maybe we could do a Santa came late kind of thing."

He nodded, snitching a sugar cookie from the cooling rack. "Maybe say he forgot her in his bag of toys, something like that."

She slapped playfully at his hand when he tried to take a second cookie. "Nah, I already told her it would be too hot in his toy bag and the dog might suffocate."

He winked. "Great parenting technique, Danielle. Traumatize the child."

"Well I might not have used the word suffocate, I said it would be hot, or the dog might fall out, something like that. We have to be realistic, not let her believe when something's not possible."

"Oh like Santa and his elves worked all year at the North Pole to make her doll?"

She did a pretty pout. "The next thing you're going to tell me is that there's no Santa.

You're not going to do that, are you, Luke? I would feel very let down if you did."

He laughed, gathering her in his arms and kissing her soundly, a kiss that tasted like frosted sugar cookies. "Not only does Santa exist, but if you've been a very good girl he's going to come and visit you later tonight; after we turn out the lights and Sarah's asleep. What do you say to that?"

"I say great idea, Santa. I'll be waiting."

Luke returned from the corner store a few minutes later with a bag of beef blend dog kibble, and a small bag of buffalo style jerky for small dogs. It wasn't long before the poodle had him bedazzled too. He was quite happy to help entertain Snowflakes and Sarah while Danielle continued with her pre-Christmas chores.

It was now mid-afternoon and although Snowflakes had been at their home for only a short while, she had the entire family at her beck and call. Having chowed down spiritedly on her kibble lunch and nibbling on the buffalo-style jerky just to be polite, Snowflakes knew the next item on her comfort list was to answer nature's call, both ends again. Since she'd eaten so much, it quickly became a matter of considerable urgency. She took up her customary stance at the back door, tapping with tiny toenails. When that did not produce results, gave a sharp little bark that was reserved for more immediate action. Help wasn't long arriving.

"I'm coming, Snowflakes," called Danielle, leaving her turkey dressing preparation and wiping her hands on paper towelling before opening the back door, remembering to slip the dog into her sweater. Once properly attired, Snowflakes stepped daintily outside and found her way into the backyard that she'd entered with the same unerring accuracy earlier. When you know you just know, and Snowflakes knew.

A few minutes later Danielle went to check on Snowflakes to monitor the progress of her bathroom break, but the yard was empty. Stepping out she walked around to the street at the front of the house, but the little dog was nowhere to be seen. She called her, but although she gave the effort a full five minutes, there was no response. She knew as well as she knew her own name that the little white poodle had left as quickly as she'd come.

With a heavy heart Danielle went back inside to tell her husband and daughter that Snowflakes was gone and had hopefully returned to her home somewhere in the neighbourhood. That she probably lived close by was the only thing that gave her any comfort. Snowflakes would finally be home for Christmas.

* * *

Snowflakes kept close to the alleys, as before, but there loomed ahead a wide street with vehicles zooming in both directions at damaging speeds. There was no way around it, the street would have to be crossed because she easily identified it as an obstacle that stood between herself and home with Elsa, and Cole of course, because she loved them both.

Making her way to the edge of the sidewalk she waited as unobtrusively as possible to cross the busy thoroughfare. There didn't seem to be a traffic light to guide her, nothing to slow the vehicles, so it was obviously something she had to take care of on her own. Preparing herself she waited for what looked to be a promising break in traffic and went for it, but she'd no sooner left the sidewalk and negotiated the right-hand lane safely than she realized a car was now directly in her path. Its horn blared loud enough to terrify even the bravest heart, but she got stopped in time. The car sped past, and Snowflakes almost made it to the sidewalk on the other side of the street, and safety. However, an SUV travelling next to the curb bore down on her and there was a loud screech of brakes and under the vehicle she went. She bounced out the other side shaken up but otherwise unharmed as she sprinted away at breakneck speed, never more frightened in her life than at this moment.

She ran until there was no more air in her lungs, and then panting heavily she dipped into a narrow dark alleyway and flattened herself against the wall. Her legs were like rubber, but she was otherwise unharmed. That was a close call, closer than she'd ever encountered in her previous experience on the streets before she became a rescued stray and went to live in Elsa's big house. She swore to return nevermore to that hand-to-mouth existence, but fate had determined otherwise and so she was once again forced to survive by her wits.

When she'd finally recovered herself and shaken off the unnerving close call, she continued on down the alley and then across an open lot to what looked like a schoolyard. There were no classes in session today with Santa warming up the reindeer for his annual night ride.

She saw two teenagers sitting on the steps, and wondered why, if there were no school, would kids choose to hang out there? Go figure. She gave them a wide berth, chalking it up to canine intuition. As she was trotting past the alcove that led to the service entrance, she realized too late that it had been a mistake to come in this direction at all. One minute she could see the sky, albeit now dove grey with heavy snow clouds, and the next her world went black as something was thrown over her and a great weight came to hold her body in place.

Chapter Ten

"You still love me?" she asked Cole through watery eyes. "How could you still love me? I've always heard it said you can kill love, and I thought I had. Yours *and* mine."

He continued to hold her. "Not yet," was all he said. She guessed there was an ocean of unexpressed emotions behind those sexy dark eyes of his.

Cole had never been one to talk about feelings, but was any guy really comfortable doing that? If there was, she'd never heard about it, but then again, she had no firsthand experience with men, outside of Cole.

It's not that she couldn't have met more men. Her girlfriends had offered to fix her up with their brother, cousin, friend et cetera after she and Cole had split up, but she'd turned them all down. Her asking for a divorce was not about finding another man, never that, it was about it not working between them as a couple. You're both just too different her mother had stressed to her the one time she'd cried on her shoulder; it was never meant to be in the first place. People should stick with their own kind. She'd known what her mother had really meant. Cole wasn't good enough for her, and although that was the first time she'd ever heard her mother say as much to her face, she'd known it had been there all along lurking in the shadows. Her relationship with Cole had been fun at the outset but after a while it had set hard, like a pebble in a shoe that slowly begins to feel like a boulder.

And now, on the day before Christmas, which she had expected to spend in a much different way, all she could do was hang onto him. Words failed her at this point. There were any number of people who would think that was pretty funny, the chatty Elsa Randolph at a loss for words. That was not usually the case, but it was now, in this moment. She was content just to be held by him and forget about the outside world for a little while.

Finally she lifted her head, and he held her at arm's length, drying her tears with the pads of his thumbs. She managed a weak smile. She was sure he was going to kiss her, but sniffing loudly, she moved to her side of the truck before it could happen. She had made up her mind about the divorce, albeit wavering now and again. Nowhere in the bargain did it include being kissed to distraction by her soon-to-be ex-husband. That could very well be her undoing, so she couldn't allow a repeat of such a thing, although it seemed to be happening whether she was prepared for it or not. Remaining friends with him was one thing, slipping back into the bands of matrimony in the fullest sense of the word, was quite another.

She knew Cole would know he'd been given the brush-off yet again, but he seemed to let it go with his usual equanimity. He didn't say anything about it as was typical of him. Instead he got down to the matter at hand although it bothered her to keep slapping him away because that's what it felt like. It made her feel like a controlling bitch, but that was about the furthest thing from her mind. But in truth, how many men would put up with the way she'd behaved and still tell her he loved her? Someone who really did love her, that's who, and she didn't deserve him. It stung, but that was the truth. Cole Donahue deserved much better in a wife than she'd ever been able to provide.

That too played into it at the back of her mind. As much as she choked on the thought of Cole marrying someone else, being in bed with another woman and loving her the way he had always loved her, that's probably what was best for him. Set him free to be with someone who wouldn't try to corral him within any silly social strictures. That's the type of woman he should be with, and she had no right to stand in his way. It was almost a relief that she was giving him the chance to find someone like that, let go of all the phoniness and BS that had characterized their relationship almost from the start. But he had loved her through it all, still did, he said. Wow!

"So, what do you say we go back to your place and make more posters?" he asked, watching her face as though he could read the thoughts stumbling over themselves in her head. "There's time yet before dark to get a few more up, and if we hurry we can have them in place with a couple of hours of daylight left for people to see them."

"I say yes, let's do it," she said, eager to break the mood. "There's no time to be lost. Realistically it looks like it's going to start snowing anytime and that could ruin our posters, but all it takes is one person to see one poster and be able to help us."

He nodded, pulling into traffic and soon they were on their way back to Stoney Creek. She put on a brave face but in truth her emotions were in total disarray. All this closeness was more than she had bargained for when they began the poster blitz, but what else was she to do? His help was needed, and it was of course inevitable that there'd be a few leftover feelings waiting to be dealt with.

Driving up to her house it struck her how huge the thing was, sitting all alone at the top of the hill. There was not even a tree to relieve the starkness of the neatly landscaped yard. Now that she'd seen Cole's new home it struck her how ridiculous hers looked by comparison; completely too big and overdone. It was like she was seeing it for the first time, and it did seem impossibly large for just one person, no matter how many airs she'd been trying to put on. Not

191

that there'd always been one person living there, but after she and Cole broke up, she could have ditched the place and moved to something more suitable and affordable. Who was she trying to impress anyway? The answer jumped up in front of her with a leering grin: everyone. She'd considered relocating to Riverview at one point, but somehow town life never really appealed to her despite the fact that's where she'd grown up. Her mother and father still made their home there in a restored nineteenth-century mansion whose pompous design looked decidedly out of place in the community. Her parents' home imposed itself on the side of wide circular drive, a sizeable guesthouse just beyond, and a four-car garage at the back. They felt it was a residence befitting a senator and his wife, but she'd never been truly comfortable there as a child. In reality, hadn't she simply switched one mausoleum for another? She struggled momentarily to understand why she would recreate an almost identical setting to a place where she'd kicked so hard against the restraints that held her there until she was of age. Perhaps she was more like her parents that she was comfortable to admit. After all, wasn't she trying to emulate their lifestyle?

But this troubling introspection would have to wait for another time as all other thoughts except Snowflakes were temporarily shoved aside. Time was creeping by, and Snowflakes had now been missing for almost twenty-four hours, give or take; much too long in any case.

But she was grateful to the young man who'd come forward, setting aside for the moment that he was the one who'd stolen her. It had been a relief to know that Snowflakes had been sheltered, fed, and watered as late as this morning. The little monkey liked to eat, and even though she knew the dog was relying on the kindness of strangers, she wanted her back home again, especially for Christmas. This whole thing had gone on long enough.

"How many should we make?" she asked Cole as they walked into her office and flipped the light switch.

"I would say given the lateness of the day and the fact that not many people are likely to be out and about on Christmas Eve, fifteen ought to be enough. If we don't get her tonight, we'll go at it again tomorrow and put more posters up if need be. I don't think the snow is supposed to last for very long. Maybe just a dusting, and if it stays mild, it'll be gone by tomorrow. The warmer temperatures are definitely in our favour."

Elsa keyed in her request for fifteen copies of the Snowflakes poster and then set the printer in motion. "You know, Cole, I just had a horrible thought. What if I never get her back, I mean what if something happens to her and we don't find her? I know that sounds overly dramatic, but I'm serious. I'll always imagine that something terrible happened. That she...."

He shook his head. "Come on now, Elsa, thinking like that is not going to accomplish anything. We have to believe we'll get her back, and even if we do consider the worst possible scenario, we have to trust that someone gave her a good home. Just like that young fella and his wife did."

"I wish I could be as optimistic as you are, but unfortunately I have a much more active imagination."

"I know, sweetheart, it's hard sometimes, but it doesn't accomplish anything to think bad thoughts. If the worst happens, then we'll deal with that when the time comes. It won't change the outcome one bit to borrow trouble now."

"We?"

"Okay *you*, whatever. You know you can always come to me. We might not be married anymore, soon, but we can remain friends, can't we? You've been saying all along that's the way you'd like it to be."

"I've been thinking about the staying friends thing. I guess what I meant, or I should say the better way might be, is to stay *friendly*. Not try to hang out together or anything as though there'd been nothing between us. You can't un-ring a bell. Wouldn't it be just a tad awkward if say you remarried and you're still best friends with your ex-wife, or vice versa? I mean think about it. We have to be realistic."

"I've got no one tucked away waiting to walk down the aisle to me, Elsa."

"Maybe not right now but we're still young so I'm saying it's a possibility, someday." The very thought of it felt like a physical pain in her midsection.

The sooner they found Snowflakes the better it would be for a lot of reasons. First of all, for the love and safety of the dog, but also she could get back to her status quo, which was … exactly what? The harsh truth was that she was a lonely young woman living in a big empty house all by herself. The future didn't look as sparkling bright at this point in her life as she had imagined it would once she'd freed herself up to have things the way she thought they should be. She pushed that bleak picture away.

All right, Elsa, she told herself sternly, refocus. Get your mind off Cole, yourself, and anything else that doesn't need to be thought about at the moment. All that mattered was finding her dog. She wished for that with all her heart, but of course that meant if they found Snowflakes within the next hour or so, she'd have to get all gussied up and drive to her parents' home for the Christmas Eve event. She loved her father, but deeply resented the notion that he'd be pleased with himself that she'd been brought to heel; made to mind. No one refused a Senator Randolph command.

She made a decision right then and there that even if Snowflakes did miraculously reappear when they went back to the city, she would not attend her parents' Christmas Eve bash. She and Snowflakes would spend a lovely Christmas Eve together at home … watching

TV. She thought of Cole, sitting alone in front of a crackling fire in his fieldstone fireplace, and felt a keen yearning to be there instead.

"Okay, they're printed," she said, snapping back to the present, wishing Cole was closer than the opposite side of the room. "I really have to replace that poor old printer it's been on its last legs for a while now. I've just not taken the time to buy a new one and get it programmed. I'm not a techy person, as you know, so anything to do with set-ups and stuff like that I tend to procrastinate or avoid all together."

Cole smiled. "I've got a young guy who takes care of all that for me, so I don't have to mess with any of that stuff anymore and I don't I miss it. That was also part of what I did at Dad's ranch until they brought in a dedicated IT guy and he took over all of that. He does a fine job. As for my own ranch, I don't have a big operation, but computers are still part of everything nowadays."

At least we agree on something, she thought to herself with a smile too as they collected the posters and headed for the door. The snow was still holding off as they drove into Riverview then picked up Wheeler Boulevard and headed to Lewisville where Snowflakes was last seen. Once there Cole found a parking space and they hopped out armed with their latest batch of posters. Elsa held them in place and Cole did the stapling.

When they were finished, they were starting for the truck when a middle-aged man approached them.

"Lost your dog, did you?"

Both Cole and Elsa were immediately alert. "Yes," she said, "have you seen her?"

"I believe I have. It was just before noon I saw that same small white dog that's on the poster. She was wearing a red sweater and running down the street at quite a clip with a larger dog not far behind."

"Oh no!" Elsa cried. "He didn't catch her, did he?"

"No, that little poodle is as fast as lightning and managed to get away. She went into a yard not far from here and I saw a woman close the gate to keep the other dog out."

Elsa was vibrating with excitement. "Can you show us where that yard is by any chance?"

"Sure can, come with me and I'll take you there. An older couple live in that house, and I think you might find your dog there. I know who those people are, and your dog would be very well taken care of, if she's there. I think they had a dog of their own because I used to see either him or her out walking it, but that was a while ago. I haven't seen the dog in a couple of months, so I expect it's probably gone by now. Anyway, come with me, let's go and pay these people a visit."

Elsa looked up at Cole, beaming and he smiled back reassuringly.

The three walked the four blocks to the picket-fence yard, although the gate now stood ajar which was not an encouraging sign. Surely if Snowflakes was still there the gate would be securely closed.

"There you go, if you want to talk to them," the man said. "I'll be on my way now. Merry Christmas to both of you, and good luck with your dog."

Cole knocked on the white wooden door of the single-storey shingled house. Within the minute a short woman with sparkling blue eyes beneath a cloud of soft grey curls appeared, smiling at them. "Is there something I can help you with?" she asked pleasantly.

"We were told you might have seen a little white poodle earlier today, in your yard. She was being chased by a larger dog and you saved her."

The woman's smile was even broader. "You must mean Snowflakes."

"Yes!" Elsa cried excitedly. "Is she here?"

The woman shook her head. "No, I'm sorry but Snowflakes left about two hours ago."

"Who is it, Marj?" called a man's voice from within.

"Are you Snowflakes' owner?" she asked Cole and Elsa, to which Elsa readily agreed that indeed that's who they were.

The woman turned her attention back into the room. "It's Snowflakes' owners, dear."

The man called out again. "Well invite them in."

198

The older woman moved aside. "Won't you come in for a few minutes? We'll tell you all about our visit with Snowflakes."

Cole and Elsa stepped into the small living room, decorated gaily for the season, complete with a beautiful fibre optic tree. An older man who appeared to be blind was sitting in a chair in the corner and offered his hand while introductions were made.

Marjorie vibrated with enthusiasm; a smile never seemed to leave her face. "You're the only ones who have seen our Christmas tree. Our daughter gave it to us for Christmas last year."

Elsa turned her full attention on the tree in the corner. "It's really very nice; just beautiful. I love the heirloom ornaments. I don't mean to change the subject, but did you say that Snowflakes is gone now? You don't have her here anymore? Do you know where she went by any chance?"

Marjorie shook her head sadly. "She stayed for a couple of hours, had a nice nap with Walter, ate a good big dish of kibble and then a while later said good-bye. We just assumed she lived handy here or I never would have let her go, but she had it in her mind to leave. She was anxious to be on her way."

There were tears in Elsa's eyes. "We put up a lot of posters offering a reward for her safe return."

Marjorie looked stricken. "I'm so sorry, dear, but I haven't been out of the house all day.

I've had all my shopping done for a while and with it being so cold this morning I had no interest in going anywhere. I just happened to be out in the back yard when I heard the commotion of that awful Brutus chasing poor little Snowflakes, so I got between them and closed the gate. She was like a little Christmas miracle I can tell you. We were so lonely and a visit from your dog really perked us both up, but I feel dreadful that she's still lost. As I said, I never would have let her out if I had known. I can come and help you look if you like."

Cole shook his head. "No, but thank you. It's good to know that she's still in this area and if it's only been a couple of hours, she can't have gone too far."

Walter spoke up from the corner. "Ask them if they'd like to stay for a cup of tea, Marjorie. I imagine they're tired and hungry if they've been searching since last night."

Marjorie's smile burst forth again, although she was clearly upset at the misunderstanding over the dog. "I'm forgetting my manners. I have some nice Christmas cake, and I can make a pot of tea very quickly."

Elsa looked worried. "I think we should keep searching, we only have a couple of hours left before dark, but…."

Cole could tell she was hungry, probably as hungry as he was, the bacon and eggs having worn off hours ago. He caught Elsa's eye, and he could see she'd changed her mind and thought they should accept. He'd never known

200

his wife to turn down a piece of cake, not with her sweet tooth.

Taking off his hat, Cole returned the older woman's warm smile. "We'd like that. You're right, we've been at this awhile."

The older couple were clearly delighted to be able to entertain these unexpected guests, Marjorie starting for the kitchen. "Wonderful, it won't take but a few minutes and after you've finished don't feel as though you have to linger. We know you're anxious to find your little dog before dark, and we pray that you do."

The Christmas cake was deliciously sweet and moist. Generous slices accompanied the tea served in herringbone china cups with saucers. Cole and Elsa thanked their kind hosts and were soon back on the street searching for the elusive poodle. But after an hour of beating the streets and calling for Snowflakes, they had to accept that she would not be going home with them tonight. They were silent as they walked back to the truck, Elsa limping in her designer boots that she hadn't bothered taking the time to change.

"Elsa, it's probably another five blocks back to where I parked. Why don't you wait here, and I'll go get the truck and pick you up. You can't walk in those things."

Not having to walk anymore today sounded divine, especially in these boots. She didn't even have it in her at the moment to argue about the boots, how expensive they were, how much she loved the Sergio Volcane design. At the moment, she'd love nothing better than to pitch them in the nearest garbage can as she figured Cole was dying to suggest.

"That would be great, Cole. I'd really appreciate it. I'm about done in."

He covered the distance to the truck in long strides, and in no time, he was at the curb beside her. She climbed in, grateful to get off her feet. The heater was already starting to kick in and despite the fact that it wasn't cold outside, the cab of the truck still felt warm and inviting. The only thing that would have made it any better would be to have sweet little Snowflakes curled up on her lap. She wondered if she'd ever see her pet again.

As they slowly made their way out of the area, she pointed to a side street. "We didn't walk down that way, maybe we could take a look."

"Certainly, I was going to suggest that very thing."

Snapping on his signal light he made the right-hand turn and drove along slowly, both he and Elsa with their eyes trained on their respective sides of the street.

"Look, Cole, at that cute decoration on the lawn of that veterinary clinic. Oh my gosh! Is that Snowflakes in the middle of it? It looks just like her, stop the truck!"

He stopped adjacent to the elaborate display, and it took a moment or two to realize the white poodle at the heart of the décor was indeed a very good mechanical replica of a dog. Elsa sat and gazed at it, her mind feasting on the image they'd been seeking for so many hours. It looked just like her precious Snowflakes, but alas, it was not the real thing.

"It's a remarkable likeness, isn't it?" he mused.

"Oh how I wish it were really her."

It was with heavy hearts that they started for home. It was now late afternoon and the barn work that waited at Cole's ranch simply could not be put off any longer. The animals needed tending and the completely justifiable reason for delay wouldn't make any difference to the hungry livestock.

They stopped at Elsa's home in Stoney Creek so that she could get a change of clothes and something more comfortable for her feet. She longed for a soothing hot shower but there wouldn't be time for that at the moment. Cole waited in the truck while she rushed in and changed into a pair of stressed denims, a warm sweater and jacket, heavy socks and her well broken in hiking boots. She also threw toiletries and a few other essentials into an overnight bag. She could take a shower at his place, and she guessed it seemed fairly obvious at this point that she'd be spending the night. That is, she'd accept if he were to issue an invitation, and she realized with growing awareness that the last thing she wanted to do was spend Christmas Eve alone here in this big house.

When she finally reappeared and climbed into the truck he looked pointedly at his watch.

"Sorry, I took a little longer than I planned because I decided to pack an overnight bag," she explained. "I put it in the back. There's groceries back there you know."

He grinned. "Yeah, remember? It's my turkey and some other stuff and it doesn't matter if it gets frozen. I'd actually forgotten about all that, what with this thing about the dog. It should still be okay. I'll put it in the fridge when I get home. Ahhh ... you brought an overnight bag? I guess that means you're going to do a sleepover."

"That's if you don't mind. I just thought...."

"Of course I don't mind, Elsa. I like the idea actually, but ... I still only have the one bed unless you threw another one on the back with the overnight bag."

"No," she chuckled, "just the overnight bag, but I think we can make do with only one bed. The most important thing right now is finding Snowflakes, everything else can be worked out as we go along."

"Yes," was all he said. But there was a world of emotion in that one word, and it touched her heart. It felt like she was holding his heart hostage, playing come and get me games, but hadn't she actually blindsided him? Yes! She had! She couldn't shake the awful feeling that had been eating away at her for over a year now. Once again, she tamped down her feelings and tried to push them away to where they wouldn't keep popping up to taunt her.

"You came ready to work in the barns?" he asked her.

"I said I would help, and I will. I don't mind at all."

"What about your boots, tramping around in manure is not going to do anything for that fine Italian leather."

She laughed despite her mood. "My fine Italian leather boots are safely back at my place. I'm wearing something much more practical now. My feet are still hurting, but they should be fine."

"You sound like a lady who needs a foot rub."

She remembered Cole's foot rubs; they were pure heaven. Would she dare accept such a gift from him now? She knew darned well they would be entering dangerous territory because his foot rubs were so sensual they had always led to more. She gripped the door handle when she thought about the *more*.

"I think I'll be fine without a foot rub," she lied.

He chuckled. "Chicken."

"Whatever," she shrugged, studying the late afternoon countryside out the side window with unnecessary scrutiny. "You know it really is lovely here. I always thought Shenstone was very pretty. How are you liking it?"

"I love it. I was very happy when I found land for sale out this way. It's just far enough back that you can have neighbours, but they're not right up in your face. I was lucky enough to find enough open acreage that I could start fencing right away, and should I ever want to expand, I've got lots of room to do so. Right now I've got a winter wood supply for as long as I want it. This place has everything I need."

"I think you're probably a lot happier here than you were in Stoney Creek."

"I had nothing against Stoney Creek. I guess it's a nice enough place to live."

"It was just the house…."

"Elsa, let's not go there right now … talk about that. We're both tired…."

"Sorry, you're right. It's just that I don't see…."

He gave her a levelling stare that left no doubt that he meant what he said.

"All right, fine," she sighed noisily, giving in. "I guess there's no need to talk about that … right now."

It was true, they were both tired and the size of the house they'd shared in Stoney Creek had indeed been the source of most of their arguments. It had been a flashpoint between them although there was much more just under the surface that should have been dealt with. When they fought, he was usually the one who walked away although his resentment had built, as had hers. Cole would only go so far and then he'd shut down. What he needed was to blow his stack, as did she, relieve some of the pressure of unsaid feelings that she knew all too well still festered inside. They'd argued, yes, but about superficial things, both seeming to know not to get to the heart of what was really wrong in their marriage. They both knew she'd always held all the cards, so they'd had a neat and tidy ending. Not that they'd ended things altogether, yet, but they'd found common ground to at least be on a friendly basis up until now. And then Cole made that stunning announcement in the truck this afternoon that he still loved her. That had come out of left field, and she….

Cole's cellphone rang just as he was pulling into his yard, and he quickly answered it. She could hear every terrible word.

"We've got your dog, but we want a thousand dollars before we'll give her back. If you don't give us the money, we'll kill her."

Chapter Eleven

Elsa's eyes were as big as saucers, nodding a vigorous *yes* to the thousand-dollar demand.

Cole ignored her as he spoke to the caller. "The reward is five hundred dollars for the safe return of the dog, but how do I know you actually have her?"

The caller obviously put the phone next to the poodle and that did sound like Snowflakes' sharp little bark. It also could have been any small dog, but he was pretty sure it was her.

Elsa covered her mouth with her hand, her eyes wide and fearful, still nodding.

"Okay, you say you have the dog, the reward is still five hundred dollars; can't do the thousand. No way."

Cole knew a shakedown when he heard one, he also knew the caller couldn't be any older than fifteen or sixteen. He was bluffing to try to make a fast buck. He could smell it a mile away. If the teenager really did have the dog, he'd give her up for a lot less. He wasn't trying to knock the price down; he was still prepared to pay the reward money in full to get her back.

"Aren't you listening? I said I want one thousand dollars, so pony up, or I swear I'll kill the dog."

"Really?"

"Really!"

"A dead dog isn't worth very much now, is it? You kill that dog, and you get nothing."

Elsa was practically going out of her mind a few feet away, but wisely decided it would be best not to interrupt him. He was a much better poker player than she was.

"If you want to see it alive that's how much it's going to cost you. I know you've got the money."

Cole laughed without mirth. "What makes you so sure about that?"

"Because if you've got five hundred dollars you've got a thousand."

"Not always true. So if it's a thousand dollars or nothing, it's going to have to be nothing. Keep the dog. It's not worth a thousand dollars to us. It's worth five hundred dollars, but definitely not any more than that. Thanks for calling. Merry Christmas."

"Wait! Don't hang up, man. You say you've only got five hundred dollars?"

"That's it, that's all you're going to get for the safe return of the dog. But, if that dog is harmed in any way, if I even think she's been hurt, you get nothing. Do you understand what I'm telling you … man?"

Cole knew he could easily pay a hundred times what they were demanding. He had no patience with someone who was trying to extort money from him, even if it was just a greedy kid, especially if it was a greedy kid. The only time he'd even consider something like that was if there was a human life on the line, and then of course it would be put in the hands of professionals. He knew in this case the caller would probably take five dollars if that was all he could get.

"Okay then five hundred it is."

"Where can I find you?"

"Come to the corner of Priestman Street and Sullivan Avenue in ten minutes."

"No can do. I have a half hour drive to get there, so you'll have to be patient and wait for me."

"Have you got the five hundred for sure?"

"I do, but only after the dog is safely in my hands. That's non-negotiable. I get the dog, in perfect condition and you get the money."

"No way, I want the money first."

This kid was something else. He'd definitely watched his fair share of crime shows, and taken notes, but Cole was not in the mood for nonsense. "Listen to me, I want the dog in my hands, unharmed, and then I pay up. Those are the terms of this deal. Period."

"What if I decide I want the money first?"

"Look, you're starting to get on my nerves. Don't be stupid. I have your cell number now and I think you have a pretty good idea where my next call is going to go if you screw this up in any way. We want the dog back, that's all.

We offered a reward for her safe return, and we intend to pay up. So I'll see you in a half hour on the corner of Priestman and Sullivan."

Cole closed his phone and slid it into his jacket pocket then realized Elsa was looking at him with murder in her eyes. "How dare you, Cole!"

"How dare I what?"

"Play fast and loose with the life of my poor little dog! She's not worth a thousand dollars? Thanks for calling! Merry Christmas! Are you crazy?"

He couldn't help but laugh at her outrage. "What are you getting so upset about? He was trying to shake us down. I doubt he even has the dog."

"He could very well have Snowflakes and you know it. You heard her bark as well as I did."

"He might and he might not. It could be any dog, but right now we're going to assume he does and meet him back on the other side of the city to get this thing sorted out. We'll know very soon which way it's going to go."

"What if he kills the dog?"

"He's not going to kill it unless he's completely stupid. He's just a kid trying to be a lot cooler than he actually is, and in my opinion, he's been to the movies once too often. If he does have the dog, then we're good. Happy ending. We have Snowflakes back for Christmas, but I'm not going to pass over a thousand dollars to everybody who calls. I'm generous, sweetheart, but not that generous."

"Would you pay a thousand dollars if it meant I could get Snowflakes back?"

He gave her a sidelong look. "You know I would, Elsa, but it's not that easy. You have to expect calls like this because dishonest people are out there. If it was a legitimate thing and that was the only way I could bring her home, you know I'd do it in a heartbeat."

"Thank you."

"You're welcome."

She looked at him sheepishly. "I guess I should be the one who pays, it's my dog."

"And it was me who lost her. My pay. No question there."

"Do you have the five hundred dollars, or do we need to stop at the bank?"

"I'm good, and when we do get there, if they show up at all, stay out of it okay? Let me handle it."

She was silent for a moment. "That's not going to be a problem, you're a lot better at this negotiating stuff than I am. All I want is to get Snowflakes back, in one piece."

"That's what both of us want, so we'll see how this plays out. It could go well, and I'm praying it does, but you have to prepare yourself too for whatever else is going to happen. Maybe you don't even want to be there in case things don't go so well. Would you rather stay here, and I'll do it alone? It won't bother me if that's what you'd rather do. It's your choice."

"No! I want to go with you. I have to be there, Cole."

"All right then, but I'm warning you not to get your hopes up, Elsa. This could all be a ruse; probably is."

"We have to hope it's the real thing. I'd like to think he wouldn't have called unless he had Snowflakes. It is Christmas after all."

Cole kept his thoughts to himself. Elsa was always like a little girl when it came to Christmas. No one would do anything wrong, everyone would be happy, the world took on a special glow and so on and so forth. He was much more of a realist, but who knew? She could absolutely be right about the caller, and he hoped she was. It would be great to finally get the poodle and head home. By the way things were shaping up though, it looked like he was going to have a guest for the night, well two if Snowflakes was back with them. But then again who knew? If she had her dog there would be no reason to stay, she might remind him for the millionth time that they're about to be divorced, or get changed and head off to the command performance at the Senator's residence. He had no idea in which direction things were going to go at this point. One thing was for sure though, whichever way it went he was going to have a good night's sleep. He was going to cook a great turkey dinner tomorrow and have a nice quiet Christmas on the ranch.

* * *

The ringleader shut his phone down and slid it into his back pocket. "He's coming, but he says he's only got five hundred."

"Five hundred is good," said the second boy.

The ringleader was not mollified, as he stretched his legs out in front of him on the school steps. "Yeah, but a thousand would have been a lot better. But he didn't even want the dog if it wasn't five hundred. I thought he'd be like *oh don't hurt the dog we'll give you whatever you want*. Our luck he turned out to be a hard nose."

"Maybe you should give the dog some air or we won't even be getting the five."

"Yeah, here ya stupid mutt. Take a lungful," the first boy said as he opened the coat so that Snowflakes could breathe a little better.

Snowflakes knew a good escape plan when she saw one. With a mighty lunge she leapt out of the coat and tore across the schoolyard, the angry boys running after her, shouting and swearing, the air rife with heartfelt F bombs. One even hurled rocks at the fleeing dog, but mercifully his aim was as terrible as his manners and very soon Snowflakes left them far behind. When it was safe to slow to a comfortable trot she did so, taking refuge in a patch of woods where there were no houses. Some snow would have been a big help to blend in, because as it was, she stuck out like a sore thumb against the dry brown vegetation. But at least she was free!

Never was there a more incredible feeling than getting away from those awful boys. And then she heard a sound to her right and froze.

* * *

The half-hour deadline was just approaching when Cole pulled into the empty parking lot of the insurance company that was closed for the day, or more than likely the entire Christmas holiday.

Ten interminable minutes passed; fifteen and nearly twenty, before they saw two tall teenagers headed their way. Both were walking with what looked to be a practiced cocky swagger, again imitating movie machismo. One was cradling something in his arms. Could it finally be Snowflakes?

"There they are, Cole," she whispered as though the pair coming up the street could hear what was being said inside the truck. "It looks like they've got Snowflakes wrapped up in something, but how is she able to breathe bundled up like that? Please God, don't let her suffocate."

Cole eyed the pair suspiciously as they approached the driver's window, stopping a few feet away. He was right. They were just pimply-faced kids. The leader, the one with the mouth, couldn't have been a day over sixteen but he looked like a player for sure. The second boy was about the same age. Cole eyed the dark jacket wrapped tightly around something in the ringleader's arms, presumably Snowflakes. If the dog was in there, she was dead, because no way would an animal be that still. For one thing it would be fighting to get out, to breathe; whimpering.

"We've got your dog, but the rules have changed. We want the money first and then we lay the dog down over there in this jacket and you can go and get it after we leave. We talked it over and that's the way this is going to go down."

Cole watched him closely as he spoke. "How come the dog's not moving?"

Cole knew the sound of his voice would have been enough to activate the dog, even if she'd been sound asleep up until this point. There was no movement from within the jacket. No way was there a dog in there.

The ringleader was not often at a loss for words it seemed. "He's sleeping, all nice and peaceful. Now give us the money or we take off and you won't see your dog again. I'm serious, man."

Cole's gaze never wavered. "So am I. Let me see the dog. Show me that she's alive and well or I don't even start to reach for my wallet. We talked it over too," he said sending Elsa a brief glance and was glad to see her nodding, ready to back him up, "and those are *our* rules."

The ringleader seemed momentarily indecisive, his bluster failing him when he needed it most. This was clearly not going according to plan. He was beginning to panic. It was all right there in his eyes. It was plain to see that he'd suddenly become an unsure sixteen-year-old boy again and didn't know what to do.

The second boy was antsy, obviously a follower and looked ready to take to his heels at any moment.

The ringleader tried again, jutting out his chin in a show of false bravado "You said you'd give us the reward if we found your dog. We did, and now you owe us, man. I'm going to snap her neck in about two seconds if you don't pay up, right Jerome?"

The second boy, now identified as Jerome, had panic clearly written across his face. He didn't have to say it, he just wanted out of here although he nodded and gave a barely audible "yeah". Maybe ringleader would have something worse in store for Jerome than what he'd just threatened to do to the dog if he didn't back him up.

"Again, a dead dog is worth nothing. Show me the dog is okay and the reward is all yours, no problem. Do it now."

"I don't trust you," the ringleader said, his eyes darting from Cole to Elsa and back to Cole.

Clearly, it appeared that the boy had endured a hard life, and it showed in his level of mistrust; his anger. His entire demeanour said: don't mess with me, but underneath there was a scared little boy.

"You have no reason not to trust me," Cole told him. "I've been straight with you all along. So give me the dog and I'll give you the money.

That was the deal and that's what's going to happen. Period."

"No, man. No money up front, no dog."

Cole unsnapped his seatbelt and the ringleader and his shadow took it as a threat, suddenly no so brave. They backed up a few steps although Cole made no attempt to get out of the vehicle.

Just then a police car rounded the corner, unaware of the standoff going on in the parking lot, continuing on its way down the street. But it was too much for the teenagers. The ringleader quickly shook the stuffed toy out of the jacket, then both shot across the street and up the alley.

Cole let out a long, exasperated sigh. "That went well."

"All the way over here for nothing," Elsa moaned. "I was so sure we were going to get Snowflakes this time around. Damn those kids, I could ring their necks."

"Putting up lost dog posters with a five-hundred-dollar reward is bound to attract people who are just out for a buck. I'd say those kids have been in trouble with the law before. Did you see how fast they disappeared when they saw that police car? I think they set a land speed record."

"Can we cruise around the neighbourhood again to see if we can, by some miracle, spot Snowflakes? You never know, we might get lucky this time around. Sooner or later, she has to show up, if she's even over on this side of the city anymore."

"Sure thing, that's a good idea. Maybe we'll even take a run out the Shediac Road a ways. Animals will fool you with how far they can travel although she did seem to be sticking pretty close to this area. Also, if she had an idea to try to start for home, she'd know she was going in the wrong direction if she went that way, but you never know."

A half hour later there were still no results from their latest search efforts. "I'm sorry, Elsa, I've got to go home. I have livestock waiting and there's barn work to do. I'll have my phone on and we have to continue to hope that someone will see her and call us or take her in if she's cold and hungry. You know Snowflakes. She's a people magnet. She's already had two families who looked after her before she left of her own accord."

Elsa sounded as though she was on the verge of tears again. They'd never been too far away throughout any of this. "She's trying to find me, Cole. She wants to come home."

He reached over and took hold of her hand. "I know she does, sweetheart, and we will find her eventually. It will just take time. At the moment though I don't think there's much else we can do unless we get another call. If we do, let's hope it's better than the last one. It'll be dark in another hour or so, but we'll come look again first thing in the morning, as soon as it's daylight."

"It seems like it's going to start snowing any minute."

He glanced out at the heavy sky. "I can see that, but it won't be much, not a storm, thank God. She's probably holed up somewhere nice and warm. She might have even gone to someone's door, or maybe back to that older couple we had tea with this afternoon. That's entirely possible too. They fed her good food so she would have every reason to want to make a return visit. And they promised to call if they saw her again now that they know who her owners are. It's just a matter of us being patient."

Elsa sighed and he could hear how tired she was. After a good night's sleep they'd both be fresh and maybe walk the streets again calling the dog's name. If she was still in that area it had to produce results sooner or later. He started to pull his hand away to shift the truck, but she held on, actually raising it, and holding it against her face for a moment before she let go. He couldn't believe she'd done that, but the show of affection felt very good.

He hadn't gone a half-mile before his cellphone rang again and he activated his hands-free device. "Cole, have you decided whether or not you're coming over for Christmas Eve? You know your father and I would love to have you, dear."

"I'd love that too, Mum, but I don't think I'm going to be able to make it this year. I'll drop over sometime tomorrow."

"But we don't want you to be alone on Christmas Eve."

He smiled. "Well as it turns out I won't be alone on Christmas Eve," he said as he turned and winked at Elsa, and she smiled.

"Oh?" was all his mother said, curious but not pressing for information.

"Elsa will be with me. We're just headed back to my place and she's going to help me do the barn work."

There was a pause on the other end of the line while the information sank in. "Elsa! How wonderful! Is she there with you now by any chance?"

"Sitting right here beside me in my truck."

"Cole, I'm happy to hear you say that, and your father will be too. Does that mean the divorce…."

"We're not going to talk about that, Mum. Okay?"

Sandy Donahue backed off the subject immediately. His mother wasn't one to push her way into other people's business. He knew she liked Elsa, although she knew her daughter-in-law could be a handful at times. She was not in favour of the divorce, believing they could resolve their differences.

"I understand, son. Can I say hello to Elsa?"

"Sure, just hold on and I'll switch you over. So I'll say good-bye, see you tomorrow and let you talk to Elsa. Bye for now."

Once Elsa was set up on the hands free, she and Sandy had a great catch-up conversation.

When he pulled into his yard, again, they had already said their good-byes.

"I love your mother, Cole. She's so sweet, and I know she looked after Snowflakes when you were working. I really have missed her you know. From some of the horror stories I've heard from friends about their mothers-in-law, I realize I won the jackpot with Sandy. Remember how well we got along?"

"I certainly do remember. You told me one time you were closer to her than you were your own mother. I'm glad you're going to start seeing her again; go to lunch together."

"I feel bad that I didn't get back to her when she called me a long time ago, but we're okay now. And you're right, I always was closer to your mother than I was my own, although of course, I love my mother very much. She's just not the hands-on type is all, but I'd do anything for her. My father too."

"I know that," he said letting the words drop like a bomb, and he knew she knew what he meant.

Phoebe and Senator Randolph had been a thorn in his side since day one, and that included the evening she'd brought him home to meet her parents. If they had come right out and said take this one back, he's not suitable, they couldn't have made it any plainer they believed their daughter was scraping the bottom of the barrel.

But as time went on and he and Elsa fell more deeply in love, well at least *he* did, he'd thought they might soften toward him. The

Senator had even offered him a decent job as he put it, and that would be *anything* outside of the agri industry. Certainly something other than working with cattle, at the handling level. But Cole hadn't been interested, getting dirty at work was a way of life for him. He had no intention of changing his lifestyle, for anyone, let alone those two who thought they were better than everyone.

In actual fact his family were more secure, financially, than hers, but they didn't wave it in anyone's face. They didn't turn in the same circles, so they were of no use to the Randolphs socially. The phoniness of the whole thing drove him crazy. If by some stretch of the imagination he and Elsa did get back together, he refused to have anything to do with her parents. He'd rather spend time in a nest of rattlesnakes. The snakes would be friendlier and more trustworthy by far.

But their daughter was an entirely a different matter. From her blonde curly hair and huge cornflower blue eyes to her turned up nose and the stubborn tilt of her chin, she was the most exciting woman he'd ever met.

* * *

Dusk was beginning to slowly gather around them as Cole pulled into his yard and shut the truck off. After all they'd gone through so far, he couldn't believe they were returning home empty-handed yet again, but that's the way it had worked out. He started around the other side of the truck to help Elsa down, but she had already scrambled out and retrieved her overnight bag. She stepped aside as Cole got his bag of groceries out of the back and both started for the house.

"Okay, are you ready to come to the barns with me or have you changed your mind?" he asked once they were inside, and he'd flipped on the lights. "You could stay and cook supper if you want while I do the work. It's up to you."

"I want to come and help out at the barns. You've done nothing but help me for almost twenty-four hours looking for my dog, the least I can do is swing a shovel for a little while."

"Sounds good and then we can throw something together later to eat. I've got mac and cheese in the freezer that Mum sent over, and you know how good Mum's mac and cheese is."

"I do remember. Too bad we didn't have some garlic bread to go with it. Now that would be a treat."

"In the freezer behind the mac and cheese, so we will have that treat."

"I guess you can tell how hungry I am. I could probably eat everything in the freezer and have room left over for dessert."

"I'm right there with you. We haven't eaten enough today to keep a kitten alive, so we'll have to make up for it later. I'm glad to see you with an appetite, Elsa. You need to put on a few pounds."

"You want to fatten me up? You probably could, you're such a good cook. Anyway, mac and cheese sounds good," she said, giving a start when her cellphone rang. She glanced at the caller ID. "It's my father. Okay, here we go," she said as she pressed TALK. "Hi, Daddy."

"Elsa, it's now almost four thirty and I distinctly recall telling you to be here no later than three-thirty. Are you on your way?"

She took a deep breath. "Actually I'm not on my way. It's not going to be possible to attend your event."

The pause on the other end of the line was only momentary before the storm broke. Senator Randolph was a tough taskmaster, absolutely fierce when anyone went against him, and he enjoyed that reputation. He was used to people falling all over him because of his position. When that didn't work, his fiery bluster usually brought the more recalcitrant into line.

"Why in thunder not?"

"Daddy, it's no good getting upset. I've already explained why I won't be there. We still haven't found Snowflakes. We've spent hours looking and we don't have her yet."

"You're missing this very important engagement because of a *dog*? I don't believe what I'm hearing."

Cole watched Elsa. He could hear the Senator all the way across the room. Voices were getting raised but maybe this was the showdown that was needed. Elsa was a grown woman and her mother and father had way too much control over their daughter's life. They acted as though they still had a say as to what her decisions should be. The problem was that Elsa didn't seem to be able to see it, or were her eyes slowly beginning to be opened? He hoped so. It was about time.

"Snowflakes is not some *dog*, she's my pet and I love her. She's out there right now on a winter night alone, cold, and probably hungry. I can't go to some … party and just forget about her. I'm not made like that."

"You have put your mother and me in a very embarrassing position. As I explained to you before, and you already know, the invitations indicated that the *entire* family would be receiving our guests, all three of us, not just your mother and I. You are on the annual Christmas card, so you are expected to be here. You know that very well. Responsible people keep their commitments no matter what, Elsa. Now, I want you to listen to me very carefully because I don't want there to be any further misunderstandings as to how I feel about this. We have Santa coming at seven-thirty for the children, and if you must miss the meal, we at least expect you to be here to hand out the gifts and spend what remains of the evening with our guests."

"But Daddy…."

"I don't want to hear *but Daddy*!" he shouted. "I want to hear that you'll be here."

"I won't be there. I will be here, waiting and praying that someone finds my dog."

"I'll buy you a damned dog! There, problem solved. Be here no later than seven o'clock. You know the dress is semi-formal and I believe you and your mother have already shopped for the proper attire."

"Daddy, listen to me. It's a Christmas party, losing Snowflakes is real life happening and I'm needed here."

"Needed where? Where are you now?"

"If you must know, I'm at Cole's."

"You're still at Cole's."

"That's right, and this is where I'm staying until I find Snowflakes."

"So is this all about a dog, or is it about that no-good ex-husband of yours?"

"Cole is helping me find Snowflakes."

"How did the dog go missing in the first place? I thought it always stayed in the house."

"I told you, she was stolen out of Cole's truck."

"And how did the dog get *into* his truck?"

"I've been all over this with both you and Mother. Cole was looking after her for me while I was in Fredericton on business."

"Your mother or I could have looked after it."

"You hate animals!"

"We could have worked something out that was better than having to ask *him* for anything. You did the rebellion thing, hell you even married him, but I thought you had come to your senses when you asked him for a divorce. You finally did something smart for a change."

When the Senator got his ire up, he wasn't nice.

"Daddy, Cole Donahue is a good man. Just because he doesn't do what you want him to doesn't mean he's not a nice person. And just because we're getting a divorce doesn't mean he's terrible, any more than I'm terrible."

"Elsa, why in the name of God you want to spend your time with a man who actually enjoys wallowing in cow shit is beyond me. You were brought up to want something better in life than that. You could have had any number of decent men, but no, you had to try to get at us for some unearthly reason, so you chose the likes of him."

"It seems to me, Daddy, that you and Mother eat your fair share of steak, you even host barbecues so why do you look down on the people who raise the beef that you eat?"

"Because none of those people are good enough for my daughter, that's why! You're a Randolph. It's time you started acting like one, and that means getting as far away as you can from Cole Donahue and his bunch."

"I'm sorry you feel that way, but if you'll excuse me, I'm about to go to the barns and help Cole shovel *cow shit*. Merry Christmas, Daddy."

* * *

Snowflakes stared at Brutus, the neighbourhood bully, and knew there was little chance of escape with no alleys to get to quickly enough, and Brutus had murder in his eyes as he'd finally cornered his elusive quarry.

"Brutus!" came the woman's angry voice, and the big dog immediately deflated, knowing he was in trouble for jumping the fence yet again. "You come here, you bad dog. Come here!" Brutus obeyed, slinking up to his owner who promptly snapped a leash on his collar. They started away, and if dogs could glare, Snowflakes got a withering one from Brutus.

Snowflakes wasted no time skedaddling either, tearing across the open area past backyards, one of which obviously belonged to Brutus. She didn't stop until she spied the open driver's door of a delivery van, jumped inside, and scurried as fast as she could down in back of the seat, hiding. Minutes later the driver returned, hopped in, pulled the door shut and they were on their way. Bob the deliveryman was cheerfully unaware of his tiny stowaway.

Chapter Twelve

Cole stared at Elsa with disbelieving eyes. "Elsa! I've never heard you speak that way to your father before. I'm shocked."

She coloured. "I know, it was very disrespectful, and I should be ashamed of myself, but you should have heard some of the things he was saying to me."

Cole folded his arms, leaning back against the kitchen counter. "I did hear what he was saying, and I've heard most of it before. That old record has a great big crack in it."

"Well he was way over the line with all of it. The things he said about my dog were completely heartless! I love my father, of course, but I'm very angry with him at the moment. He should not have spoken to me like that or said those things about you. I will not tolerate it. He may not agree with everything I do or how I live my life. I try to give him as much latitude as possible, but he does not have to be nasty and rude. We might be getting a divorce, but he has no call to disrespect you, Cole."

"Don't fight with your father on my account, sweetheart. He and I have never gotten along, but I sleep just fine at night without his good opinion of me. It doesn't matter what he thinks of me, but it does matter what he says about my family, and he knows enough not to say it to my face. I won't stand for it. My family is every bit as good as his."

"I know, and I'm very sorry about that. I think Daddy gets so caught up in things he doesn't know what he says sometimes."

"Elsa, I know you love your father, and you should, but he knows exactly what's he's saying, at all times, and he knows how damaging it is. He's used to getting his own way because of who he is. He doesn't care who he hurts to get it, but what Senator Randolph wants doesn't mean anything to me. I'm glad he's done well for himself. I'd be the first person to tell him that, but he needn't bother waving it in *my* face, using it as a way to look down on me and my family, our way of life. I'm sure your father is a good man, but he needs a reality check, badly. It's not going to happen though, because all of the yes men around him are unlikely to do that. Anyway, I don't think you have to worry about Christmas with the folks this year. I doubt too many people stand up to him the way you did, and it probably isn't going to sit very well … for a while."

She grinned although it was a half-hearted attempt. "You're one to talk. You've gone toe to toe with him enough yourself, that's why he doesn't like you. You don't let him push you around. To Daddy that's an unforgivable sin, so

I'm not sure how things are going to play out from now on."

"He'll blame it on me. You're his daughter and I corrupted you is how that goes. Just give him time, he'll get over it. It's too bad everything had to blow up at Christmas though, that doesn't make for very good memories."

She put her phone away but stayed rooted to the spot looking uncertain. Her eyes welled up again as her emotions continued to run high after the loss of Snowflakes. He crossed the room to take her in his arms. "Elsa, you just stood your ground, that's all. You didn't attack him. He should understand that you'd be upset over losing your dog, and not push you like that. Everything is not always about him and when he starts to calm down hopefully he'll see that."

She laid her face against his chest, which he loved. He had to admit he was disappointed that her arms remained at her sides and not around him, which he would have loved even better, but half a hug was better than no hug at all. The best thing would have been a kiss, but he knew theirs was not supposed to be a kissing relationship anymore. Not officially anyway. Those days were past, apparently, and that was just plain stupid because the attraction between them could not be ignored, well by him, he should say. He resigned himself to being content to comfort her as he would any friend, and not get carried away. If he did step over the line that Elsa herself had drawn, she'd likely be out that door in a heartbeat, accusing him of trying to get her to call off the divorce. Whether she liked to admit it or not she was a lot like her father. She could be just as bull-headed, although few people could hold a candle to Senator Randolph in that regard. There wasn't a strong enough word for how much Cole disliked that man, but if he found the right one, he'd use it for his mother-in-law as well. If you knew one, you'd met them both.

"Don't be too down on yourself, Elsa," he continued when she still hadn't spoken. "He had it coming because of some of the things he said to you, but just let things cool off and he'll be back. He might even apologize, who knows? He has to remember it's your life and that means you get to decide what's best for you. You don't have to jump every time he speaks. You don't take orders from your father, or your mother either, for that matter. It was a Christmas party, not a military engagement with the freedom of the country at stake. The world will keep turning whether you attend that party or not. Besides, you had a perfectly legitimate reason for not being there, and they could have simply explained that to their guests who I imagine would be very sympathetic. And for what it's worth, I'm proud of you for standing up for yourself. Now, I'm sorry but we really do have to get down to the barns. You're sure you want to do this?"

She stood back, her chin tilted. This was the sassy Elsa he'd first met all those years ago, the girl he'd fallen in love with; the woman he still loved with every fibre of his being.

"Of course I'm going to the barns with you, Cole, why wouldn't I? I'm not afraid to get a little dirt on me."

He smiled. "Atta girl, but I think you'll find my barns are clean, well as clean as they can be considering that they're … barns. But there's not a lot in them right now, the herd stays outside. They just go inside for shelter in bad weather. They were in last night for instance to get out of that cold."

"What about calves?"

"When they're just babies, they're in for a few days in the calving pens, and then they're outside where they need to be, with the herd."

They set off toward the barns located in back of the house, walking the short distance down over the hill to where the outbuildings were located. The animals were lowing noisily, growing impatient for their supper.

They passed where the white face cattle were gathered to be fed, one animal eyeing them balefully.

She stopped in her tracks, gazing at it. "How come that cow is so much bigger than the others? She's huge!"

Cole chuckled. "Look a little closer, Elsa, that she is a he. He's out with the herd right now because all of the cows and heifers are already bred."

"What's his name?"

"Luther, and he's two and a half years old."

"Oh, just a baby, but what a big baby!"

Cole leaned against the top of the fence watching the bull watch him. "As a bull he's halfway to hitting his prime."

"He's certainly big enough. Will he get much bigger?"

"He'll fill out a lot more. A five-year-old Hereford bull weighs about 1,800 pounds but I don't think he'll be here quite that long. Maybe another year or so and then I'll need to change bulls for the sake of the bloodline."

She was also watching the bull. "Are you hungry, Luther?" she asked the animal who now regarded her with keen, unblinking eyes, obviously sizing her up. "Is it okay to go inside the fence? I mean he won't attack me or anything, will he?"

"No, don't go in there, Elsa."

"Why not? You're here with me and he looks like a big teddy bear. You won't hurt me will you, Luther?"

"He's a good quiet bull, that's all I'd have on the ranch, but don't go in with him, okay? He's used to me because I got him as a baby, but he might not be too friendly to you. A bull is a bull so give him lots of room, and plenty of respect."

She frowned. "No problem, I'll stay on this side of the fence. So how big is your herd?"

"Just over a hundred head."

"You said the cows are going to have calves, so are they … artificially inseminated? I don't know a lot about cattle ranching, other than I went to your father's ranch for visits when we first started going together. We didn't talk much about the cows when I did. I have heard though that's how ranchers are increasing their herd these days."

He smiled. Why her sudden interest in anything to do with cattle? He certainly hadn't been able to interest her before. True she'd never really been around them even though he'd been foreman of his father's ranch for years. After they were married, she'd made it clear that anything to do with cattle stayed at the back door when he got home. She'd showed zero interest in anything to do with animal husbandry.

But horses were another matter, those had interested her right away. He'd taught her to ride, and she was a natural. She'd taken to the sport with a vengeance but switched from western to English at the insistence of her parents. As her reward they'd purchased a twenty-thousand-dollar jumper for her, although she didn't compete anymore. Serendipity Rae was kept at the prestigious Halimeda Stables in Salisbury, and Elsa rode there now. Anything to keep her away from an actual working ranch, which by its very name, The Donahue Cattle Company, was not something that blended very well with the upper crust Randolph way of life. If she had insisted on riding, and she had, then they had to make sure she at least participated on their terms.

"Artificially inseminated? No, we do it the old-fashioned way around here. That's where Luther comes in."

"Oh, right."

He smiled to himself. "Come on, I've got to get these cattle fed, I'm running late and they're hungry. I'll get the tractor going and get some round bales out to them."

"What do you want me to do?"

"Well, you told your father you were going to shovel … manure … in so many words, so that's what you can do if you like."

"How many cows do you have in the barn?"

"At the end of February we'll probably have a full house, like I said, with mammas and their babies. Right now, there's only the one and she's not feeling too good. The vet is keeping an eye on her for the time being. We're not sure what's ailing her at the moment, so I'm keeping her away from the herd. After I feed and water her, you can clean her pen out if you want."

"Can I go right in there with this one?"

"Oh sure, she's quiet enough. Come with me and I'll show you where to find a shovel and the wheelbarrow."

After Cole had finished tending to the cow in the barn, he left her to her work and went about feeding the herd. He had just shut off the tractor when he heard a shriek from inside the barn. Elsa! Had that cow head-butted her or something? He wouldn't have thought so when she had no calf with her to protect, but….

Jumping down off the tractor he hurried into the barn just as Elsa was getting up off the floor. "What happened?" he demanded. "Are you hurt?"

She stood holding onto side of the pen, a woebegone expression on her face. The cow standing in the far corner seemed unsure about what to make of the screeching stranger in her enclosure.

"I slipped and fell into a big soft cow pie, well two or three of them all plopped together. I sat right in it, and I imagine I'm covered in it."

He checked out the area in question and sure enough she was covered in it. Her backside was sodden and stained; most of the sloppy manure still clung to her jeans.

He couldn't help but chuckle. "The cow has loose bowels because her temperature is up, but boy when you sit in something, sweetheart, you sure do a good job of it. Come on up to the house and let's get you changed out of those jeans. Is there another pair in your overnight bag by any chance?"

"No," she replied mournfully, laying her face on her arms, still leaning on side of the pen. "No jeans, just a pair of pyjamas, a change of underwear; stuff like that."

"Well come on then, pyjamas it is. I'll put those jeans in the washer and get them clean before they're stained for good. But first, I've got to get the rest of that manure off your butt. It's packed on there pretty good. How did you happen to slip and fall anyway?"

"It's the cow's fault. She was crowding me, and I kept backing up, too fast as it turns out. I stepped into a pile, slipped and down I went. I don't think she wanted me in her pen."

"She won't hurt you, she's just curious. Anyway let me get a rubber glove and I'll ... uh ... remove the rest of the manure. Actually," he said, his eyes twinkling, "I wish I had a camera."

"Don't you dare laugh, Cole Donahue! This is not in the least bit funny!"

But it was too late, and he couldn't help the belly laugh that bubbled up from deep inside and he had to give it voice or rupture something trying to hold it in. He stepped away from her, roaring with laughter. "You do look pitiful from back here and that got me to thinking. What would Senator Randolph say about his daughter dripping in cow ... manure? Maybe now's a good time after all to drop into his party. Hey, I'll put a rubber sheet on the seat of the truck, open the windows, and drive you there myself. I know you'd be a hit of the party. Come on, I dare you to do it," he said with a smile, really getting into it. "I can just about guarantee that everybody there would talk about that for the rest of their lives, and it would for sure end up on Facebook. You'd probably break the Internet. The video would probably trend and then you'd be a celebrity. So what do you think? Do you want to do it?"

"You are so hilarious, Cole! Hahaha! No I don't want to do it! But I think I have a better idea, maybe I should take some of this and rub your nose in it since you want to laugh so bad. How'd you like that? If it's so funny what happened to me, maybe you'd like to get in on the joke. Now *that* would be a good picture for Facebook. So what do you think, Cole? Do *you* want to do it?"

"You rub my nose in that and it'll be the last thing you ever do, so don't even try it!"

She reached back, removed a glob from her jeans and threw it at him anyway. It caught him on the side of his face, and she laughed at his horrified expression.

"You little...,." he scolded her, moving quickly out of her line of fire, and then the two of them were laughing as he caught her by the shoulders and thereby stopped any further missiles from being launched in his direction.

"Cole, you looked so funny when that hit your cheek, but it was only a little splatter. I got the whole pie, or several pies by the feel of it."

"Okay enough fun. On second thought I don't want all of that up at the house, or all over the barn for that matter, so you'll have to take your jeans off down here. I'll carry you up without them, so you don't get cold. You'll need a shower too because the moisture has probably gone clear through to your underwear."

She looked at him saucily. "I suppose you'll want me to take those off too so as not to get any on your coat while you're carrying me."

He felt that old familiar tightening when Elsa was anywhere near. Now talking about taking clothes off, hers and potentially his, he wasn't sure how far he could carry her anyway under those circumstances, let alone walk up to the house himself. But practicality won the day.

"Here, let me pull down your jeans from the back and we'll see how bad it is. You are decent underneath, aren't you?"

"Yes, I'm decent underneath," she snipped, "just pull the darned things down and get it over with. And leave whatever's on under the jeans where they are, please. When they do come off, up at the house, I can take care of it myself. Thank you."

She unfastened the button, unzipped them and he lowered her jeans that were literally dripping with the stuff. There was only a small stain on her white bikini briefs. He could carry her in his arms without getting covered in anything.

Her sweater came well below her bottom anyway, so she was well covered when he scooped her into his arms and started for the house. To balance herself he supposed, she put her arms around his neck and held on. He should dunk her in the water barrel for splattering him with manure, but it would be inhumane to do something like that in December. If it were summer that's exactly where she'd be cooling her heels, in the nice deep cold water barrel.

When they got to the house he deposited her onto the softwood plank floor, and she tugged at the hems of her sweater in the interests of modesty.

He was dying to chuckle because it did look pretty funny, still, but he wisely kept it to himself. "I know you know where the bathroom is, and of course, the shower. If you want to go right there I'll grab your overnight bag and bring it to you since your hands are full keeping the sweater pulled down over your butt."

She pulled an unladylike face in response to that last remark, then made her way down the hall. She closed the bathroom door with unnecessary gusto behind her. Still smiling he retrieved the bag and opening the bathroom door a crack, set it inside and received a muffled thank-you for his efforts. He wasn't even up the hall when he heard the shower going. A little clean up himself was in order too so he went to the kitchen sink, took a wad of paper towels, some soap and water, and made quick work of the stain on his cheek, then washed his hands thoroughly. Stinking stuff. You just wait, he said to himself, I'll get you back good one of these days, little Miss Elsa, and he could think of any number of ways to exact that sweet revenge.

He had the mess cleaned off her jeans and them in the washer when she eventually emerged from the bathroom, thankfully without using up all of the hot water. He remembered that Elsa's showers could go on indefinitely and drain an entire tank of hot water. He was grateful there was still enough left to run the washer because that load certainly had to be done in hot water.

When she finally made her way into the kitchen, he had supper ready. However she looked pretty delicious herself, so sexy with her damp curls, freshly scrubbed face, and red and white flannel pyjamas.

"Come on and have a seat at the table, Elsa. I'm just ready to dip."

"I have to say it looks heavenly and I love that there's bacon on top with the melted cheddar. I'm even more famished now that I smell this. Absolutely divine!"

"I passed famished a few hours ago so this stuff isn't going to last long."

He dipped each of them a generous portion, then sat down as they began to hoe into a plateful of mac and cheese, and enough toasted garlic bread to feed a family of five. Conversation was discouraged given the enthusiasm with which they attacked the food. It wasn't until the edge off their appetites that they felt the need to talk.

"I'm sorry, Cole," she said licking garlic butter from her fingers. "I said I would help you. I'm given the simplest job in the barn, shovelling manure, and I end up wearing it."

"I thought you were going to say you were sorry for throwing cow dung at me."

She smiled slowly, looking up from beneath lowered lashes. "I'm not sorry at all I did that. You deserved it for laughing at me, mister."

He chuckled, enjoying this side of her. "Maybe, but you did look pretty funny. I've been going to the barn my whole life and I never saw anyone get that much manure on them. Those must have been very big cow pies."

"The biggest."

"They had to be because they covered your whole butt and then some."

She laid down her fork purposefully, her eyebrows hiked. "Are you saying now that I have a big butt?"

"No!" How had he managed to get into the dangerous end of the pool with so little effort, the place where sharks swam? "What I mean was it had to be big to cover all your butt, no wait a minute. I mean that was a big pile of manure for one cow. They usually aren't that big."

She watched him, her blue eyes dancing. "What, my butt or the cow pies?"

He looked heavenward in comical pleading. "Help!"

She laughed. "It's okay, Cole, it was a rookie mistake falling into it like I did. I should have known that cow wouldn't hurt me, although she is very large. It made me nervous when she started crowding me like that."

"She probably thought you had a treat for her."

"Well I didn't, but as it turns out she had one for me. Where are my jeans now?"

"In the washer. A good hot wash will fix them up just fine, we'll dry them, and they'll be good as new. I don't think they're going to stain, let's hope not anyway."

"Great, thank you. I appreciate you doing that for me," she said before she put the last forkful of casserole into her mouth and watched him as she chewed it thoughtfully. "This is so good!"

"I'll tell my mother you enjoyed it."

"Your mother's a fantastic cook and it's been way too long since I had some of her mac and cheese. So good! Not meaning to change the subject, but I wanted to ask you something."

He never took his eyes off her. "Ask away."

"Don't ranches usually have names, like at the entrance or something? Your father's does I know."

"They usually do. The truth is I haven't thought of a good name yet. When I do, I'll put up a sign. I'm not one of those big outfits though, but I still should have a name for the place. Why, did you have something in mind?"

She thought for a moment, then grinned playfully. "Maybe."

"Is it printable?"

"What do you mean is it printable? Of course it is. I happen to be very good at naming things. I was the one who came up with Snowflakes, remember? So about this place, I was thinking of Lone Valley Ranch, that's what struck me as we were driving in here. I think the lay of the land is beautiful, and you are alone here in this valley. I don't see anyone else around."

Her words were only too prophetic. He was indeed alone in this valley although he didn't need to be reminded of the fact. Was this where he begged her to reconsider the divorce? They'd already had that conversation, although he hadn't begged. He would never beg anyone for anything, let alone for a woman to love him. And he certainly wouldn't beg to stay married to a woman who had decided otherwise.

But they were having a pleasant meal together, an impromptu version of Christmas Eve. It wasn't quite what he'd had planned, which was nothing, but he still didn't want to rock the boat. She was only trying to be helpful and decided he should take it in kind.

"Lone Valley Ranch, hmmm it has a nice ring to it doesn't it? I'll certainly take it into consideration when the time comes."

"Thank you, but who knows, maybe you can come up with something better later. It was just a thought. And whoever comes to live here with you might have something to contribute in that regard as well, so I guess you should keep your options open before you make a final decision."

Now where had *that* come from? He saw it for what it was, another fishing trip, but why would she even care? There very well could be somebody else someday, if he and Elsa continued on their way out of this marriage and things were finished for good. He'd thought a time or two about asking Mary Ellen Branscombe out. She was that pretty little

246

waitress down at the diner in Hillsborough, but he'd never quite gotten around to doing that. Not that Mary Ellen hadn't made it plain she'd be receptive to an invitation. It was just that, well, maybe it could wait a bit. He wasn't divorced yet anyway, and he didn't think it was right to get back in the game before his marriage was actually officially over. There was plenty of time for dating when he had the rest of his life to himself. He dreaded that day when his divorce from Elsa was final. He didn't want to think about it.

"Whatever that means, Elsa," he said trying to keep his tone light, but that's not the way it came out. It came out like it mattered way too much, but then again it did, confound it!

"It means we both have to move on, Cole. It doesn't help to get our hopes up. The dice has been cast as they say."

The mac and cheese suddenly began to churn in his stomach, but he did not want to be drawn into anything heavy on tonight of all nights. They were having a fairly good time, but of course it was a penchant of Elsa's to keep everything real. Well everything was already real enough, no need to double down.

As if sensing his shift in mood she changed lanes. "I can't believe we haven't had one single solitary call about Snowflakes all day, that shakedown attempt notwithstanding. I thought I was going to be sick when I saw the bundle wrapped up in that kid's coat. Thank God it was only a stuffed toy. I just hope wherever the poor little thing is right now, she's warm and fed. Hopefully someone has taken her in for the night and we can get her tomorrow."

Elsa's cellphone rang, startling her and she jumped from her chair and rushed to grab her purse and answer it.

"Hello?" she said bravely, seeing as how it was a call from one of her parents, she wasn't sure which until they spoke.

"Elsa, I'm on the upstairs telephone, taking time away from our guests to call you. I am very angry with you at the moment, first of all for the way you spoke to your father. He had you on speakerphone so I'm glad there was no one else here except me to witness your blatant disrespect. Quite frankly, I am shocked at your behaviour. You wonder why your father and I want you to get a divorce, it's because of this. You come within a mile of that man your good breeding goes right out the window. For some reason, which I cannot fathom, you want to be around him. So for that reason I'm telling you that you have to make a decision, him or us."

"Mother! That's ridiculous!"

"You think I'm not serious, Elsa? This is no joking matter. I am not saying that your father and I don't love you with all our hearts, both of us. We do, but what I am saying is that we will not put up with any more of your impudence. The way you've spoken to both of us today is reprehensible."

"Mother I am not a child, stop scolding me as if I were!"

248

"That's right, you are a grown woman and that's why I expected much better of you. I can't believe I'm having to have this conversation with you, but...."

"You remember the part about my dog being missing, right? If it weren't for that I'd be at your house right now, attending your Christmas party. You remember Snowflakes, right?"

"Of course we remember the dog, but we are your parents, not some dog, and when you make a commitment, we expect you to honour it. I've already had several people asking for you, wondering why you're not here. We've been telling people you're under the weather, but you putting us in this difficult position is a slap in the face. So make your decision and let us know what it is."

Elsa closed her eyes wearily. "Mother I'm not going to dignify that ultimatum with a response. You are my parents! I love you and Daddy, and I will always put you both first, above everybody else. I always have."

She glanced over as Cole got up from the table, dropped his dirty dishes in the sink, grabbed his coat off the hook on the wall, and left, grim-faced.

Chapter Thirteen

Snowflakes was having a much-needed nap curled up on an old coat in back of the passenger seat in Bob's white delivery van. As a matter of fact,Bob's last stop took a little longer than expected. Snowflakes, in the mood for a snack, took the liberty of helping herself to a portion of the Christmas dinner arranged on a lovely glass plate. She didn't take much really, just most of the turkey and a bit of delicious stuffing for good measure. Oh and a bite of two of a sugar cookie, and then it was time to bunk down again out of sight and sleep off the impromptu yuletide feast. So nice of Bob to bring something to nibble on in case anyone happened to drop by needing a drive.

Generous to a fault, Bob Boxford and his wife, Sue, were very busy at Christmas, preparing plates for seniors and shut-ins who might not otherwise have a Christmas dinner. In fact Sue cooked no less than five turkeys, and she and Bob paid for all the birds and trimmings out of their own pocket. Then Bob delivered the tinfoil-covered plates on Christmas Eve, just in time for the big day. And then of course there were the mouth-watering sweets that accompanied the meals. At last count Sue Boxford baked in the neighbourhood of thirty dozen cookies, Bob happy to do the trimming. The pair thoroughly enjoyed this festive season activity.

Each meal as well came with a small, wrapped gift, a cake of fancy soap for the women, and a bag of sugar-free candy for the men, just in case some might be diabetic. Each box also contained a frozen chill bar to preserve everything until it reached its intended destination. It was a labour of love, right from the minute they got things rolling in October when they began to buy the gifts, to the deliveries on Christmas Eve. It was an exciting and busy time in the Boxford household. There were a few new recipients on their list this year, and all looked forward to Bob's visit. They all wished he and Sue the merriest of Christmases, some with little holiday mementos of their own to pass along to the generous couple.

Bob and Sue were always ready to help others at their own expense. They loved giving back to their community, which in fact ranged across the entire city of Moncton. Both were now retired and since they had never been blessed with children of their own they considered these seniors to be their family.

It had been a long day for Bob and as he neared the end of his deliveries, he was looking forward to his easy chair in the living room of the modest home he shared with Sue. A quiet Christmas Eve in front of their lovely, decorated tree. However when he climbed in and pulled the last Christmas box toward him, he was dismayed to see that its corner was torn. The foil was partially ripped away, and some of the meal missing. He was perplexed. How on earth could such a thing have happened? He certainly couldn't deliver it in its present condition. Had Sue dropped it by any chance when she was helping him carry their precious cargo out to the van this morning? No, she'd never allow it to be loaded in that condition.

He could see his easy chair getting a little further away because this meal would have to be replaced. He couldn't disappoint the last senior on his list who was eagerly awaiting his arrival. Sue would have to make up a new plate, but she could easily do so because she'd simply take from their own Christmas dinner to replenish the one that had been damaged. Vandalized? Good lord, were their rats in here or something? And then he spied a little white curly leg protruding from the back of the passenger seat. A dog had to be stretched out in back of the seat, sleeping!

Climbing all the way inside was no easy feat considering his painful arthritic hip. He pushed the curtain that separated the cab from the cargo area, all the way to the side. Snowflakes raised her head lazily, her eyes winking as she tried to come awake from a most wonderful nap.

"Well what do we have here?" he asked kindly. "I do believe I've picked up a passenger somewhere along the line. Hungry, were you girl?"

Snowflakes was fully awake now and she cocked her head sideways and smiled her adorable little smile. Her tiny pink tongue lolled as if to say I'm sorry I stole some of that meal, but I just couldn't resist. It was really good too by the way, my compliments to the chef. You wouldn't happen to have an extra sugar cookie, would you?

Reaching ahead he ruffled the little halo of white curls on the top of her head and Snowflakes licked his hand in response. A good scalp massage went a long way. He won her over instantly, and she was relieved there were no hard feelings about the turkey dinner thing.

"I think you'd better come home with me," he told her good-naturedly. "I know Sue would love to meet you. Besides, you're putting us to a little extra effort so the very least you can do is stay for a visit. I don't know about Rascal though, he might not like to share his house, not even for a few minutes. We'll see if we can't get on his good side. But don't worry, sweetie, whatever way it works out, I won't put you out on the street with night coming on. That wouldn't be right. We'll think of something so you'll have shelter."

With Snowflakes now ensconced in the front seat riding shotgun, Bob called Sue on his cellphone and told her what happened to the last turkey dinner. After having a good laugh, she assured him she'd have the replacement dinner ready by the time he got home. She also told him she was looking forward to meeting the little scamp, whom Bob said was called Snowflakes. She reminded him that Rascal might have something to say about the whole thing, but to bring her along anyway for a hello, if only for a few minutes.

Snowflakes stood with her paws on the door vinyl looking out the window, she was seeing a whole new part of town, one that she truly hoped was Brutus-free. Completely refreshed now she was full of vim and vigour, and most certainly the Christmas spirit. When they pulled into the yard where the Boxfords called home, Snowflakes was almost dancing with anticipation, as if sensing yet another adventure in the making. Someone was making those Christmas dinners and cookies, and she was looking forward to meeting whomever it was.

That adventure wasn't long coming either when Rascal met her at the door with a fierce growl and vehement territorial barking. He actually bared his teeth, the ultimate unfriendly gesture. You would think the devil himself had come to call. And despite the fact that Snowflakes was about the prettiest little girl dog he'd ever seen, there was no softening of his heart as he angrily warned her away. The terrier made it patently clear that she was not welcome. Christmas or no Christmas, he wanted her curly white butt off his doorstep. That's what the barking said, each word enunciated very clearly.

Snowflakes tried not to take it personally. If the truth be told she didn't like the looks of him either, all spikey hair and sharp teeth. She barked three sharp little barks, and what she said to Rascal was: Get a grip!

Bob scooped Snowflakes up in his arms not a moment too soon. "I wondered if Rascal might not want any competition, but I had no idea he'd be that unwelcoming. Okay, no worries, I'll put little Snowflakes back in the van and figure out what to do with her before I get back home."

"I was thinking about that dear. Your friend Melvin Hoyt over on West Main Street lost his wife a few months ago and I know he's been terribly lonely. Why don't you take Snowflakes over to him?"

"But look at her, she's so well taken care of, she must belong to someone and they're probably looking for her. She has to go back to her real owner."

"I completely agree with you, dear, but I know Melvin would love the company if only for a day or so. After Christmas he could take her out to the SPCA and they would know if she's been reported missing, but at least Melvin wouldn't be alone over the holidays. I invited him over here for the evening, but he says he has something he needs to do tonight. Nevertheless there's still the rest of the holiday season to get through."

"That something he needs to do tonight is his Santa thing. He doesn't do it as much as he used to, only one or two special bookings, but it's only suppertime so he should be home. My last stop is right in that area anyway, so I'll give it a try. The poor little girl can't stay here, unfortunately, so wish me luck getting Melvin to take her."

Snowflakes was only too happy to accompany Bob as he made his last delivery, this time sitting on the seat as pretty as could be. She hoped when they were finished they wouldn't be returning to the house with that hateful little terrier. Snowflakes was a lover, not a fighter, but she knew a turf war when she saw one. She'd learned a thing or two during her days as a stray. Then, just as now, she'd rather hightail it to safety than stay and duke it out. She knew she'd lose, because despite the fact that her teeth were needle sharp. She didn't have a nasty bone in her body.

She sat and waited patiently while Bob carried the Christmas box into the tall apartment building. After ten minutes she began to wonder if he would indeed return, or what if like before someone opened the door and took her before he got back? Bob, where are you, she thought worriedly. Then at last she saw him walking toward the van, his topnotch of curls every bit as white and fluffy as hers. She knew she had found a kindred spirit in him, and Sue too for that matter, a lady with a kind, soft voice. She instinctively trusted them both. Rascal was another matter altogether, and well named although she could think of something better to call him.

Soon enough they pulled up in front of a small brick house a few streets over from Moncton's West Main traffic circle. Bob went round to collect Snowflakes off the seat, slipping her inside his roomy jacket. They looked almost like twins Snowflakes thought as they walked together, both white, curly, and aglow with the Christmas spirit.

A man in his early seventies came to the door when Bob finished knocking. Once again, here was yet another white-haired friend, although this man had a very impressive white beard that tumbled luxuriantly to the middle of his chest. Could it be? Snowflakes stared at it because she'd never seen one so splendid. She had a soft curly one herself, maybe an inch long at most, but nothing to compare with these outstanding chin whiskers. Wow!

"Hi Melvin," said Bob with a smile. "I've brought a furry friend to help you celebrate Christmas. I found this little stray in my van, almost polished off one of my Christmas dinners, she did. I'd take her home myself as a matter of fact that's what we'd hoped to do until the local shelter opens after the holidays. It didn't quite work out that way. We tried, but Rascal got his nose out of joint and made a terrible commotion. So we were wondering if maybe you could look after Snowflakes, at least until after Christmas. What do you think?"

Melvin shifted his half-glasses further down his nose so that he'd have an unobstructed view as he studied the little dog, and not unkindly.

Again Snowflakes' topnotch got a sound ruffling, which she had come to understand was an encouraging sign. If someone didn't like her, they usually showed their teeth, well, dogs did anyway.

"Lost are you, pup?" the man asked her before returning his attention to Bob. "Where do you think you picked her up? Or more to the point, where were you when she got in?"

Bob shrugged. "I've been all over the city today doing deliveries so it's hard to say when she climbed aboard. My driver's door sticks sometimes so I leave it open, and at some point, I got me a stowaway. Snowflakes is her name, it's on that little tag hanging from her collar. So do you think you can help me out? Sue and I thought you might like some company over Christmas."

The head ruffling continued, and Snowflakes sighed with delight when Melvin smiled at her. "I am alone now with Elaine gone; my first Christmas without her. My daughter in Fort Saskatchewan was going to come so that we could spend Christmas together. But her daughter, my granddaughter, is about to have her first baby and wants her mother with her. So you're right, I am batching it. I'd love to have this little beauty stay here with me, even if it's only for the holidays. I imagine by the look of her she's somebody's pet. This dog hasn't been on the streets very long. She's in too good a shape. So sure, you can leave her with me. I think we'll get along splendidly."

"Great! You need some company, and she needs someone to look after her, so this works out well all the way around."

"Will you come in for a minute, Bob? I know you're probably tired, but I wouldn't mind a bit of conversation. I'd offer you something to eat but I know Sue's likely got something waiting."

"There's no problem. She won't mind if I'm a little late. It is Christmas Eve after all. Didn't you tell me you were doing a Santa gig tonight over in Riverview?"

"That's right. I don't usually take anything on for Christmas Eve. I should say I didn't when Elaine was alive, but the lady who booked it was most persuasive. They're paying me very well, so I was not inclined to turn it down. It really is quite a thing; there'll be a lot of children there so I'm looking forward to it. It's actually very well organized, all of the gifts are wrapped and labelled, all I have to do is be Santa and the elves do the rest. Poor old Santa needs all the help he can get these days."

Bob laughed. "Poor old Santa looks to be in fine fettle, just round enough in all the right places and I see you have your Santa suit all laid out too." He got up from the overstuffed armchair to take a closer look at the outfit resting on the sofa. "You must have paid a mint for this thing. Very fancy, right down to your black Santa boots."

"It's all custom made."

"By the elves?" Bob couldn't resist asking, then had a good laugh at his own joke.

Melvin's eyes twinkled. "Maybe. Those Santa suits are made in a little place just north of sixty, so who knows? It's a man and his wife who retired there. He was a shoemaker, and she was a seamstress."

"Sounds very *North Pole like* to me," Bob chuckled. "If I see a sleigh parked outside, I'm going to start believing in the jolly old gentleman again."

"You wouldn't believe what that cost me." He nodded toward the suit. "I figured if I was planning to get into this on a professional level, I was going to look as close to the real thing as I could."

"If there's such a thing as a Santa award, you should be nominated, Melvin. You'd win it hands down."

Melvin laughed, and his stomach did indeed jiggle like a bowl of jelly, but that was beside the point. He was a dead ringer for Mr. Christmas in every way that mattered, except for his hair and that was a bit sparse on top. Nevertheless that's what white wigs were for, and he'd even sprung for one made from human hair to wear while he was in costume. No detail was too small for the perfect Santa.

"It's all about the Christmas spirit, eh Bob?" he winked, and Bob agreed.

"So what are you driving for a sleigh this year?"

"I got a nice little SUV last week. I should have ditched that old station wagon of mine years ago. It finally gave up the ghost and I had no choice but to get something else."

"And let me guess, it's red."

Melvin smiled again, his eyes doing a merry jig. "Of course."

Just then Snowflakes sashayed over to the sofa and hopped up on the Santa suit, turned three times to determine comfort, then settled down with a sigh on one generous red velvet leg. Bob reacted quickly before she could cause any damage to the expensive trousers.

Melvin waved a dismissive hand. "She's fine, what's a few more white hairs going to matter, hers … or mine?"

"It's a good thing poodles don't shed."

"Then I should have been a poodle because it's getting a little draughty on top."

Bob enjoyed Melvin's infectious sense of humour. He promised to stay longer next time as he headed for the door and was soon backing out of the driveway and headed for home.

Melvin looked at the poodle, surreptitiously watching him from across the room with one eye open. "Well, Snowflakes, why don't you come and sit on old Santa's knee and tell me all about the adventures you've had during your time on the lam? I'll bet if you could talk you'd have some tales to tell, wouldn't you?"

Snowflakes, always in good humour, hopped down off the Santa suit and up onto

Melvin's knee in the wink of an eye, turning once before settling down, obviously comfy.

"Well, what you do you have to say for yourself, pup?"

Snowflakes cocked her head to one side, smiling her adorable smile, complete with her tiny pink tongue.

"You're a sweet little one, that's for sure. I'll bet you're a hungry little one too, aren't you, one stolen turkey dinner aside. Which tells me that maybe we should go for a walk before it gets much darker. I would imagine you need to make room for supper, don't you?"

On cue she jumped down and went to stand at the front door, looking back as if to say, well, come on. Let's go.

"Hold on there, pup. I've got to get my boots on and my coat and hat. I don't come fully dressed like you do, except for that good-looking red sweater you've got on. My favourite colour."

Snowflakes barked her insistent bark, reserved only for more dire situations.

"Okay, I'm coming," Melvin sang out happily, pushing his arms into his jacket and not bothering to zip it. He pulled on a woollen hat, one that Elaine knitted for him several years ago but was still serviceable. "Just a minute, I'd better get a leash on you before you decide to run off and I don't have time to look for you tonight. This is Santa's busiest night of the year. I'd also better grab a plastic poo bag or the city will be after me."

Melvin tied a length of blue nylon cord to Snowflakes' collar and once both were completely ready for the road, off they went. Sure enough they hadn't gotten half a block away when Snowflakes made a deposit on the frozen grass beside the sidewalk. Melvin dutifully scooped and disposed of it in the next available garbage can.

The walk then proceeded in a more orderly fashion with Snowflakes trotting daintily ahead of her temporary master, and Melvin enjoying having a friendly, furry little dog on the other end of the makeshift leash. It was amazing how quickly one became attached to a critter. He was already dreading the time when he would have to say goodbye. But then again, he continued to reason, if she wasn't a stray, or reported as missing, maybe he'd be able to keep her. Straight on the heels of that wishful thought was the realization that of course she belonged to someone who loved her, and he had to take whatever steps necessary to put the two back together. Didn't he? Whoever that someone was, he believed they'd be mighty grateful to whoever brought the dog back home. He wondered how it had become lost at all.

He'd heard of cases where dogs who were no longer wanted, for one reason or another; were simply let go on the streets to fend for themselves. That was a most unwelcome thought for the dog's sake. But if that were to be the case, it would certainly be a stroke of good luck for him, as possible scenarios continued to tumble through his head.

It occurred to him that Snowflakes could probably take care of herself all right. She was small, but those were some sharp teeth in that tiny mouth. He didn't know but that the small ones could fight the best. But there'd be no fighting tonight. It was Christmas Eve, and she would be tucked up in a nice warm bed instead of out on the streets with all their nighttime perils. He thought about the ruined Christmas dinner and had a good chuckle. He was cooking a turkey tomorrow, and Snowflakes could have all she wanted; there were even going to be sugar cookies.

He chuckled again as he watched the poodle trip along as though she didn't have a care in the world. Maybe she was thinking about her adventure in the van, who knew? Or was she thinking about adventures that still lay ahead, such as when she was on her own while he was off playing Santa in Riverview. A hungry dog was not concerned about etiquette, although it did cross his mind that his house might not look the same when he came back if Snowflakes had separation issues and tore up cushions, slippers, shoes, et cetera. An unhappy dog, even if only left alone for an hour or two, could be a destructive force of nature. Animals did not understand the word temporary. Assuring them you'd be right back had no effect whatsoever on the outcome of that enforced alone time.

Anyway, he wouldn't worry about spilt milk before the carton was even out of the fridge. Snowflakes was an independent girl, he could tell. No pouting sessions for her. Sometimes you just knew these things.

They weren't back in the house five minutes before Melvin realized he should have gone in the other direction and stopped at the convenience store to pick up a bag of food for Snowflakes. How stupid could he be, he chided himself. He guessed he'd find out quickly enough if she did have separation issues, because he knew those little legs of hers had enough exercise for one night. She had to be tired, so he warned her to be a good dog before setting off in the direction of the convenience store before it closed.

When the front door closed behind Melvin, Snowflakes hopped up in the recliner and stretched out for a good long snooze, the fire slowly burning down in the brick fireplace and safely contained behind wire mesh screen. This house was nice and quiet, a good chance to get some shuteye and then she noticed the tree in the corner. My goodness! The lights actually winked off and on. She'd never seen the likes of that before. Elsa's tree had the usual million tiny lights that just shone, without blinking, with big gold bows on each bough and matching frosted ornaments. Everything was one colour, white, which was a tad boring, but whatever. She gave her full marks for good taste in everything else, for example ... dogs. To each their own, but *this* tree, with its wide variety of unusual baubles was interesting. Right near the bottom, within reach of a tiny white paw, was a miniature Jack in the box that seemed to pop in and out of its own accord. Hmmm. Did the Jack pop out, or the box fall away, and if so, how on earth did it get back into place to repeat the process? This demanded closer examination. After all, she might not be by this way again before she went back home.

Hopping down off the chair she approached the tree, watching the ornament carefully to make sure there wasn't some nefarious trick involved, like say the box going sideways to poke her in the nose. That wouldn't be funny at all. Inching closer she didn't take her eye off the ornament. What *was* making it work? She got closer still and wouldn't you know it, the thing stopped moving. Now that wasn't fair! She sat back on her haunches and waited. Sure enough, as though recovering from a much-needed rest, the spring-loaded ornament flicked again, Jack popping up with a glint in his tiny painted eyes.

Okay, now she had to see what would happen if said ornament should be, say, dabbed a bit with a curious paw. She held one little paw aloft as if in a gesture of warning, but Jack just kept on popping. So be it, she'd pop back. There was nothing like a little tree game to put everyone in the Christmas mood. Whack! She hadn't meant to hit it quite that hard, but off the ornament came, rolling along the floor, Jack still jumping out of the box in a most annoying fashion.

Going closer she nudged it again with her paw, but if the toy were frightened at all, you'd never know it, carrying on as though he hadn't just been knocked out of a tree. Now this was starting to be fun. Game on. Jack popped; Snowflakes swatted. Jack was getting quite a ride around the room when the door opened just as Snowflakes began to bark at the thing, having a grand old time. This was turning out to be quite a Christmas after all.

"Hey you little devil!" shouted Melvin as he hurried into the living room to rescue the tiny intricate ornament his sister had given to him many years ago. She'd sent it to him from Germany, that's where Norine was living at the time while her husband James was in the service.

Snowflakes had the look of a dog who'd been busted, trotting to the other side of the room, and hiding behind a chair until Santa Claus calmed down. Thank goodness though that when she peeked around the corner of the chair, Melvin was laughing.

"There, there now. No harm done, Snowflakes. There's no need to hide behind the chair. The ornament wasn't broken. I got here in time, but I can see where you'd find it interesting. It is quite a little marvel, isn't it? I usually put it higher in the tree in case it got knocked off. I had no idea I would be having such a special guest come by.

Snowflakes was finally coaxed into the kitchen where Melvin filled a small dish with dog food, and the poodle set about dipping into another light snack.

"You do like to eat, don't you? If I were you, I'd start watching my waistline, that belly of yours will only stretch so far."

His good-natured tone reassured the dog, and she looked up at him lovingly, knowing that all was forgiven. She gave him yet another imploring look which when translated into human meant, you need to water me now.

A bona fide dog person, Melvin got the message loud and clear. "You'll be needing some water," he said as he went to the water cooler and filled a bowl with fresh spring water.

Snowflakes thanked him with a dainty lick to the hand, a universal sign of canine trust rather than a tasting. All was well in her world.

Melvin knew he could really get to love this poodle, despite the fact that he usually preferred larger breeds. There was just something about this spirited little dog that tugged at his heartstrings, and it really was so wonderful to have a pet around the house. It was a sharp reminder of how lonely he'd been over these past few months. Elaine was the love of his life. No matter how much he'd prayed that the outcome would be different, that somehow Elaine would turn a corner and recover despite the doctor's grim diagnosis, she'd still died. The pain of losing her might dull over time, but it would never go away completely. At times he wondered how he'd made it through these terrible past few months. He missed her so much; pined for her. She was that kind of woman, everyone who knew her, loved her.

He recalled meeting Elaine Seely at the roller skating rink while they were still teenagers. He'd bumped into her, he wouldn't admit it was on purpose, and caught her when she went off balance. Cokes, French fries, and lots of conversation followed, and it wasn't long before they'd become a couple. Marriage seemed like an obvious choice from the very first, and she'd been a good wife, understanding the long hours his job demanded as an inspector with the Department of Agriculture. He'd loved the work and they'd even had their own little farm for many years until he'd retired, and they'd moved into Riverview to be closer to services, hospitals and the like.

That they'd had so many years together was a blessing, there was no other way to describe it. Nevertheless he was far from ready to let her go when the time came. And that, to his everlasting dismay, had been way too soon because of her cancer. He couldn't help but think how much Elaine would have loved this poodle. She always favoured tiny breeds. Now Elaine, he felt like saying, I've been completely won over. I never knew small dogs could be so much fun.

There was still time to relax a bit before he set off on his Santa assignment, so he picked up Snowflakes and settled her down on his lap. He smiled because it felt as though she belonged there even after so short a time together. She did seem quite content to stay with him and of course he wanted her to do just that and enjoy her new home. He pulled the folded sheet of paper from his pocket that he'd found on the way to the store. A missing dog poster for Snowflakes, the little white poodle. He studied it for long minutes, deep in thought, then crumpled it into a ball and tossed it into the dying fireplace embers. A second later the paper burst into flames and within a minute or two was fully consumed and quickly reduced to ashes.

Chapter Fourteen

"Elsa, are you there?"

"I'm still here, Mother and I'm sorry. I'm sorry I won't be there. I'm sorry you're left to explain my absence. I'm sorry about everything, okay?"

"And the way you spoke to your father was outrageous. You really hurt him, Elsa. He is not used to be being treated with such disrespect, and by his own daughter!"

She sighed, knowing she should go after Cole, no make that *wanted* to go after Cole. She felt like she was in a war, one in which she wore a piece of each uniform and was being shot at by both sides. Of course, her father would consider speaking her mind an insult to him, but she *had* been rude."

"You're absolutely right, I had no call to say what I did to my father. But he could have been a little more reasonable with me too, under the circumstances."

"You stood us up, how do you think we feel? This Christmas Eve gathering is to be an annual highlight on our social calendar, and I thought you understood the importance of it to us. Your father has been a senator for seventeen years, it's not like these types of events are something you've never been exposed to before. You know very well what's expected of you because of our position in the community. We have standards to maintain. And then there's Cole...."

"Leave Cole out of this, okay? Just please do that."

"But Elsa, your father and I have discussed this, and it would be a bad idea for you to change your mind about the divorce. You've come this far it would be disastrous for you to turn back now."

"For whom?"

"For any of us, especially you. The proceedings are well underway, so it would be silly to change your mind now. I'm sure the judge would take a dim view of it if you suddenly started backtracking and later realized your mistake and wanted to go ahead with it again. You'd only be making things difficult for yourself. We just don't want you to make a second mistake while you're trying to undo the first. You have to listen to us because we only want what's best for you."

Elsa let out a weary, exasperated moan. Would this nightmare never end? She was worried sick about Snowflakes as darkness continued to gather, and now it was snowing, although thankfully not hard. Through the kitchen window she could see the big flakes falling lazily through the air, backlit by the dusk to dawn light. The very last thing she needed was to go several rounds with her parents over some stupid Christmas party. If she heard one more single word about it, she was going to scream! And of course she'd stuck her foot in it and her mother was miffed, her father was angry, and Cole didn't look too happy with her when he grabbed his coat and left to go ... where? Yes, this was a *wonderful* Christmas Eve. Come right down to it she would rather be at the party with an artificial smile in place, saying all the right things expected of the Senator's daughter than going through this. At least she knew the rules to that, and in the long run maybe it was just easier. But in her soul, she was tired of it all, could suddenly see how it sounded and looked to Cole. Her ears were now open to the way he'd been hearing and seeing everything. Yet he had loved her through the worst of it, tried to be a good husband.

"Mother, I've said I was sorry, and I am, so let's leave it at that. I don't want to get into the whole divorce thing, not tonight of all nights."

There was silence on the other end of the line as her mother digested her words. "Your father hasn't been himself since you smarted off to him, I think you owe him an apology too."

"I said I was sorry."

"An apology to him, directly."

"Mother, I'm not coming over there tonight. I'm already in my pyjamas."

"At Cole's house."

"Yes, at Cole's house."

Her mother sighed heavily, dramatically, and there was a wealth of unhappiness in the sound. "I understand you're not coming, but if I can pull your father away from his guests for a minute or two will you speak to him … civilly?"

Elsa knew that if her father was in a poor mood her mother would have to live with that during Christmas, so in the spirit of the season she would try to smooth things over. Besides, she could go about the rest of her evening with a relatively clear conscience. She truly did owe him an apology for her part in it.

"Of course, I'll speak with Daddy."

"Thank you. Just wait on the line and I'll ask him to come upstairs."

It took so long for the senator to come to the phone that she began to wonder if he intended to speak with her. At last she heard the receiver being picked up and braced herself for yet another blast. Senator Randolph was not known to be a gracious loser, and she knew she was in for more bluster before he deigned to accept her apology.

"The first thing I want to know is if you placed this call yourself, or are you simply apologizing because your mother called and asked you to? Your answer will determine what I have to say to you next."

Great, nailed right out of the gate. She guessed her mother must have told him she'd made the call herself, so to keep peace in the family she went along with the subterfuge without committing herself or implicating her mother.

"Daddy, the important thing is that I want to say I'm sorry for being flip with you on the phone. That wasn't very nice, and it is Christmas after all."

"Hmmph!"

"I love you Daddy, very much, and I'm sorry it didn't work out that I could be there tonight. I'll make it up to you, I promise. I was not very respectful with some of the things I said, and I do regret speaking to you like that. I truly do. Now, am I, your only child who loves you with all her heart, forgiven?"

There was a brief pause, and when he spoke, she could tell he'd softened somewhat. "Of course I forgive you, Elsa. I love you, darling, although I'm still bitterly disappointed. But I was a bit hard on you too so let's call it a draw and start afresh tomorrow. Okay?"

She was relieved that the storm appeared to be abating, well the one at her parents' house anyway. The one here she guessed was still building, but one apology at a time. "Okay. I love you, Daddy. I'll be by sometime tomorrow. All right?"

"We'll look forward to seeing you, now I must return to my guests. I'll tell them you send them your good wishes for the holiday season, along with regrets that you couldn't be here."

"That would be fine, thank you. Merry Christmas to both you and Mother."

When the call came to an end, at long last, she dropped her phone back into her purse. Grabbing her coat she shoved her feet into her hiking boots and started out, pyjamas and all. She saw the light on in the barn and went there first. Sure enough there he stood, leaning on the rails of the enclosure for the sick cow.

"She's not worse, is she?" Elsa asked reasonably as she walked up, but her heart sank when he didn't turn his head.

"No, I'm just checking on her like I do every night."

"Well that's a relief that she hasn't taken a bad turn."

"Yes, it's a relief."

She stood there also leaning against the rails within arms length, but he might as well have been standing there alone for all the attention he paid her. It was time to take the bull by the horns, have the conversation they should have had a long time ago.

"Cole…."

"What?"

"I'm sorry."

"What is it you're sorry about this time, Elsa?"

That stung and she could tell this wasn't going to be easy. So be it, he was already miffed at her. Now was as good a time as any to lay all of her cards on the table.

"I'm sorry you heard what I said to my mother, about putting them first. That's probably what you're upset about, right?"

"They're your parents, what else were you supposed to say?"

"So why did it upset you then?"

"Because I guess the truth hurts, that's why."

"Like you say, they're my parents."

"And I'm your husband! Where did I come in the scheme of things when we were together, hmmm? Was I third, fourth, maybe, if I was lucky? It certainly wasn't first, or a place of any importance."

"You knew the score when you married me, Cole."

"What, that I was going to be shoved aside and should learn to like it? That I would always come after everything else in your life? Elsa … what do you want from me exactly, or more to the point what did you want from me when you married me, because it certainly wasn't to have me stand by your side. I just never knew my place, that's what was really the problem, wasn't it? I was so damned lucky to be part of the great Randolph entourage, no matter how low on the totem pole I was."

"Like I said before, I think it's important that we have an amicable divorce and remain friends."

"Amicable divorce my ass! You say that because it suits you, and your parents; everything all neat and tidy. No loose ends or messy scandals. You know, there's one question you've never really given me an answer to, and that's why you're divorcing me. Oh, I read the papers, irreconcilable differences, but what does that even mean? Why don't you call it what it really is, freeing you up for something better?"

"It means we couldn't get along. All we did was fight, Cole, so if that means freeing me up for something better than fighting all the time, then yes. You can call it that if you like."

"We fought so much because you started in on me before the ink was even dry on our marriage documents. Push! Push! Push! Cole, do you have to wear jeans? Cole now, please don't mention what type of work it is you do. Cole, dear, remember to use the small fork for dessert and the large fork for the main course. I felt like I was in finishing school, and yes, your damned right we fought, because you couldn't get your way. I was fighting just to be me, the man you said you loved. Only you weren't comfortable trotting the real me out in front of extended family and guests. I was a little too rough around the edges, wasn't I? And why did we have to attend every single engagement on your parents' social calendar anyway? Why weren't we allowed to settle in and make our own lives? But even though we had our differences, I thought we could have worked them out if we gave it half a chance; stepped back far enough to remember why we got married in the first place."

"It wouldn't have made any difference."

"I think it would have if we had tried to resolve our differences; you ease up on me."

"So why are you saying this now? You never even fought back when I asked you for a divorce. I had you served, and you were like *all right, I guess this is the way it's got to be.*"

"So it was only a ploy for me to tell you, for the millionth time how much I love you? How important you are in my life?"

"It was not a ploy, that was never my intention in any of this. But if you loved me so much, why didn't you at least try to talk me out of it? I don't seem to recall having that conversation with you."

"Would it have made any difference? I mean would you have called off the divorce if I had dropped to my knees and begged you?"

"Why didn't you?"

"Because why would I fight to stay married to a woman who doesn't want me? I'm not desperate. If you'd loved me like you told me you did, you wouldn't have done it in the first place. I always thought, through all of this, that you'd wake up one day and knew you'd made a mistake and fix things. I loved you enough that I was waiting for that."

"Cole, at the end of the day, what's love got to do with it?"

"How about everything?"

"We were too different, you and I."

"You always told me that's what attracted you to me. Who wants a cookie cutter version of themselves? Differences are interesting; they can work."

"Not all of them."

"Okay, what differences are you talking about that you felt you had to end our marriage rather than try to live with them?"

"Let's start with the house. We couldn't agree on the type of house we wanted to build. I couldn't get you to go along on even one single thing about it."

"I agree, we should have been clearer about the house. When you said a big house, I thought two-stories, four bedrooms or so that we'd fill with children someday. Isn't that a big house? But no, you had to have a mansion just like your parents do. I never wanted to live in a house that … echoes. But I did, because you lived there. I tried to make peace with it."

She pushed back her hair, a nervous gesture because the low-hanging curls were nowhere near her eyes. "You didn't exactly grow up poor, Cole. What's wrong with having a show of wealth?"

"Do you see my parents living in some ante bellum mansion acting like overlords? No, they live in a modest farmhouse. Like them I wanted something homey, not humungous. I've got nothing to prove to anybody."

"Your parents' place is beautiful as far as that goes. It might not be a mansion, but you didn't grow up in a shoebox either. Maybe you should try to be more like my father, he…."

He turned on her, his eyes burning with fury. "What did you just say to me? Try to be more like your father? That is never going to happen. I'm my own man, heavy emphasis on

280

the last word. Man. I'm not some lap dog you can order around and try to make over into something more acceptable to the snobs in your life. And since we're talking about your father, why don't you tell me the truth behind you filing for divorce. Differences over what we wanted in a house, or having a few disagreements aren't it, and you know it."

"I don't know what you mean."

"The hell you don't! I've always felt your parents were behind you asking me for a divorce. They wanted to get rid of me right from the first. If it wasn't for them, I don't believe you would have gone ahead with it. I'm right, aren't I?"

She turned away, not wanting him to see the look on her face that would reveal he'd hit a bull's-eye. She could never tell him the things that were said about him behind his back, that he was a joke, a cattle rancher trying to mix with the elite of federal politics. Some of her family's friends were polite, nice to his face, even engaging, as he'd witnessed on more than once occasion. Others, the more overt snobs, looked at him with open disdain. Like at the barbecue when Cole and her father had the set to about Cole's choice of attire. She had been pleased that Cole had stood up to her father, but in the long run it had become more and more obvious that she was married to someone who just did not fit in with their way of life. Had her teenage rebellion become a dead albatross around her neck? She'd wondered about that at the time, but loved him enough to marry him, hoping in time he'd fall into line. That somehow, he could remould himself. He never had, and now perhaps she'd felt it was in his best interest to go on his way without any further embarrassment; maybe avoid the conversation they were having now.

"Elsa, I asked you a question."

She sighed, wishing they were doing this in the nice warm kitchen rather than the barn where a pair of pyjamas under a coat simply wasn't warm enough.

"Cole, I don't want you to be hurt in any of this."

"You don't want me to be hurt! Don't you think I've already been hurt?"

"Okay then, hurt any more than you already have been."

He moved so that she had to look at him, his eyes full upon her now in a blazing dark flame. She could feel their burn.

"I'm right about your father and the part he played in the divorce, aren't I? Your mother too."

She turned away again.

"Answer me, dammit!"

She whirled to face him. "Okay. Yes! You're right, Cole! It was their idea, and they're paying for it. There, do you feel any better knowing that? I don't believe you never suspected it anyway, you're not stupid."

"If that's a compliment, keep it. I don't need it."

"I'm just being honest."

"Okay, good idea. Let's do the honesty thing. I wasn't good enough, was I? You got me home, after we got married, unwrapped me, and said 'what was I thinking?' He was okay to have a fling with to push my parents' buttons because it was fun to see them so pissed off. But why not take it a step further and marry the guy, really get them going? You've always been playing that cat and mouse game with your parents since I've known you. It's like you're kicking against the restrictions of your life, being told to toe the line, but you went and took it too far and then didn't know what to do with me. You didn't know when to end the game. Have I got it just about right?"

He certainly had some of it right, she had a rebellious nature and there was just something about the relationship she had with her parents that she enjoyed pushing their boundaries of tolerance. Had she forgotten about Cole in all of that? No, she hadn't. Some of what he said was so true it hurt, badly, but what was her hurt compared to what she had caused him to suffer?

"The least you can do is answer me, Elsa. We never talked about this, not really. Maybe I didn't want to hear you say it, I don't know. I know you loved me, a man can't be that wrong about the woman he's making love to."

"I won't deny there's chemistry."

"There's a lot more than chemistry between us, and you know it. I think it's terrible that your parents force you to choose between them and me. You'll always be their daughter, so I don't know why they're so threatened by a man in your life, but you swore before God to be my wife and I take that seriously. I thought you did too. You can be both you know, their daughter and my wife. It's not an either/or situation."

It *was* an either/or situation. Cole would absolutely blow a gasket if he knew her father had tried to stop the wedding just before she walked down the aisle. But she'd had her way and gone on to marry Cole Donahue, ranch foreman, despite her parents' vehemence that he was totally unsuitable. And it was true that when she'd gone home in tears after one of her and Cole's arguments, over the new house, her parents had been adamant that she get a divorce. They'd pay for the entire thing and support her through it. She'd been furious with Cole at the time, so she'd gone along with it, although she'd thought better of it later.

She could have called it off at any time, but the argument her father made held water. His courtroom expertise as a lawyer worked her over, explaining to her that Cole simply didn't fit in with her lifestyle and never would. She'd just been promoted to the vice-presidency of Profit Line, and how could a man who worked with cattle dovetail with her professional aspirations? The corporate functions he would be expected to attend with her, many of them black-tie events where boots and jeans just wouldn't cut it? Her career was important. Her father had used his influence to help her along in that regard, and surely that was worth something. Had it been a mistake to marry Cole in the first place? Probably. But the game had been taken far enough when she agreed with her parents that a divorce was in the best interests of everyone, especially Cole.

"Let him go back to his own kind," her father had insisted the night she had gone to their house to talk on the pretense of wanting to visit her parents. "You'd be doing that man a huge favour," and us … and you, were the unspoken words.

Still, it wasn't as neat and tidy as it sounded. Nothing in life usually was she acknowledged ruefully. As in any divorce there were casualties. She refused to consider that, wishing she had a tough political hide like her father in order to deal with the inevitable fallout. In her case she was dealing with the corporate world, and to that end she strode forward, striving to achieve that very level of success she had always pushed against; pretended to dislike. But really, wasn't she still playing games even now? She sought success and social acceptance yet resented her parents for accomplishing those very same things. She loved Cole yet hobbled him at every turn when all he'd ever tried to do was just be himself. She'd been trying to live in two worlds for too long. One of them had to stop long enough for her to get off.

She was aware that Cole was waiting for a response to her earlier logic; knew this discussion was far from over. It had only just begun with a hundred miles of painful revelation between them and the finish line.

She looked at him sadly. "Sometimes choices do have to be made, Cole. I chose to marry you, and yes, it was a mistake. I never should have drawn you into the drama that is my life. The Randolphs turn in different circles, don't you see at all that you didn't fit in?"

His face had turned to stone. "Fit in? You mean I don't have the right pedigree. I don't have a university degree. I've only been working like a man since I was twelve years old, but that doesn't count for anything in your world … to you."

"Well my parents…."

"I'm not talking about your parents! I'm talking about you! Do you mean to say that everything between us has been some stupid game? That you didn't have any feelings for me at all, other than someone to play with? Mess with my mind? Did you talk behind my back the same as everyone else did? Don't think I wasn't aware of that at all those lavish get-togethers."

"I never talked behind your back!"

"No, but I was an embarrassment to you, wasn't I? I was the man who didn't dress right, the man with no fancy credentials. The man who worked with cattle, not just pushed paper around and stayed nice and clean. How silly we must have looked together, you the golden delicate princess and me, the country clod who should have been parking cars for those events, not hanging out in the big house. Thank God,

286

you got me all cleaned up nice for the wedding so at least I didn't embarrass you then. What a farce!"

"Our wedding was not a farce, Cole. It was a very special day."

"A special day like what, a birthday? We stood before God, Elsa, before *God* and made our vows, and all the while you had a divorce lawyer on retainer. The truth is coming out, isn't it? That whole idea of us getting married was just a lark to you because you never had any intentions of making it work. It was just an … experiment, to see if I'd come around. Dress different, speak different, act different … *be* different, but I didn't. I stayed the same way I was when you met me, thinking that was the person you were in love with. But really, I was just a work in progress, someone to try to make over once the rebellion foolishness was over and we had to settle down to the real thing. And it didn't work out because you never really wanted it to, never mind how stubborn I was about it. And when it didn't, well then run to Daddy and cue the divorce lawyer.

"I honestly believed you loved me, Elsa. That we'd get through the rough patch, but it wasn't long before even I could see that things were never going to change. That wasn't the end game because you were still climbing. You were getting right into the same groove as your parents and a country hick could only put a monkey wrench in those plans. So I was out before I held you back any more than I already had."

"It's not like you, Cole, to be so dramatic."

"I'm not being dramatic, I'm just facing things I didn't want to face before, maybe seeing you for the first time for the way you really are. How foolish it was to think you'd come to your senses because you loved me."

"You're making everything sound so ugly."

"It is ugly. I feel used, Elsa. I was used, wasn't I? You were just playing games until I didn't amuse you anymore."

"You were not used, Cole! We had a good time together and don't pretend you didn't."

"I'm not pretending I didn't have a good time because I did, where I was wrong was in assuming that you felt the same way. You certainly gave a good performance that you did, and all the time you were just trying me on for size; having fun before you shucked me off and found someone who was better husband material for a Randolph. I can only imagine how happy the Senator and Mrs. Randolph will be when the divorce is final. You've certainly given them a good scare by being here tonight with me, but then that's all part of the game too, isn't it?

"And you know what? I fell for it again tonight because I loved you. I always thought there was hope for you and me; that there was a chance you'd wake up one morning and realize you couldn't live without me and call off the divorce. That finally, you loved me as much as I loved you and there weren't going to be any more games. But no, it's full speed ahead, with a little detour here and there just for the amusement of it all. Well you've made a fool out of me for the last time."

"Cole, you make it sound like I have no feeling for you at all, and I do. I will always have good memories of our time together. Just because something has to end, for whatever reason doesn't mean there weren't good times. Isn't that a little like throwing the baby out with the bathwater? Why not be friends, celebrate what was good about our marriage."

"As soon as I think of something maybe I'll give that a try."

"I get the feeling you think I'm a terrible person, I'm not. I'm not heartless, I care a great deal about other people's feelings."

He threw up his hands, aghast. "Do you even hear yourself right now? How can you stand there and say you're not heartless? What you did to me was a pretty heartless thing. I know you're not a terrible person, you're just so caught up in everything you don't even seem to see that I was just collateral damage; a means to an end. I have a heart and you've been walking over it for a very long time, but no more."

She felt as though she was going to be sick to her stomach, the mac and cheese and garlic bread now having fully turned on her. She wanted nothing more in this world right now than to feel his arms around her. Maybe there had just been too much truth telling.

She knew she wasn't a bad person, just ambitious, socially conscious, something that had been ingrained in her all her life. As for her time with Cole, he had been a walk on the wild side, something very different from her over-protected upbringing. Had been like a breath of fresh air. Even now her heart did the same old flip flop every time she saw him. Did she love him? Cole seemed to think not and judging by her actions she could not blame him. But yes, she did love him, she honestly did. Nevertheless she had started them down this path of no return, engineered by her parents, and she knew she had to suffer the consequences. If nothing else, she was brave enough to stand up and take what she had coming to her.

But was it too late? Dare she think they could find a way out of all this mess? She reached tentatively and touched his arm, feeling the same energy she'd felt the first time he'd asked her to dance at that cowboy bar nearly twelve years ago. She would never forget that night. It was more than just the rush of something forbidden. It was more like being fully alive for the first time in her life. It might have been teenaged rebellion, even at eighteen, but the truth was she couldn't get enough of it; enough of him. She'd been in denial for so long she was starting to believe there was no other way. But laying the wound bare tonight had told her everything she needed to know. She wanted him, at any cost. No longer would she allow her parents to dictate the terms of her life. She'd been so worried about Cole fitting into her life, wasn't it about time she tried to fit into his? She loved his parents, but whereas before she'd always thought sadly that they weren't socially acceptable, now she was finally seeing the whole thing for the refreshing new direction she needed in her life.

She knew her words tonight were a knife that went straight through his heart and inflicted a mortal wound to them as a couple. But for her now it was like at long last, after a never-ending journey through a dark valley, the sun had come bursting through. She also felt it in her gut that her epiphany had come just a little too late.

Turning to finally face her, his eyes were obsidian, frighteningly devoid of any spark of life. "You disgust me, you, and every other snob I've had the misfortune to meet over the almost seven years of our marriage. Come on, I'll drive you home and then I never want to see you again, except to sign anything that will put you out of my life for good."

Chapter Fifteen

"Cole, don't say that. I know I deserve to have you angry with me but being hateful is not going to accomplish anything. I mean it when I say I want us to still be friends."

He stopped and turned toward her with an incredulous look on his face. "You're actually serious, aren't you?"

"Of course I am. I wouldn't have said it if it wasn't true."

"Why, Elsa, because you never play games with somebody's feelings? You and I both know that isn't true."

She grabbed hold of his arm. "I don't want things to end like this, it doesn't do anybody any good to part as enemies. I don't want to be your enemy, Cole."

He stopped dead in his tracks, but at least he didn't snatch his arm away. "You know what? What you want is not always everybody's priority. I think a dose of your own medicine would do you the world of good."

"And just what is that supposed to mean?"

"What is that supposed to mean? Let me ask you this. Can you imagine a world where you can't get your own way all the time? A world of fair play and honesty?"

"I play fair, most of the time."

"Well there it is, *most of the time*. That just might be the most honest thing I've ever heard you say."

"You know very well what I mean."

"Do I? I think the truth has a way of coming out no matter how hard you try to disguise it, or stop it, or twist it around to your own satisfaction. The truth is you've been jerking me around for years because you knew I loved you. You felt safe to do or say whatever you wanted to because good ole Cole would take it in stride."

"You're really angry."

"You bet I am! Can you blame me?"

"Are you angry with me?"

"Bingo!"

"Or my parents?"

"All of you, and I'm surprised that you'd even have to ask. More games I suppose, and I'm sick to death of the whole thing."

"Cole, it's Christmas. Come on!"

"I don't care what time of the year it is. You stand in this barn and admit that not only didn't I not fit in with all of your high falutin' ideas, but that you had a plan to get rid of me, all of you, you *and* your parents. I'm not surprised with them, but I thought better of you, Elsa. You presented yourself in a much different way when we met, and even now the way you talked to your father tonight? Sometimes I think

293

you can't make up your mind as to who you want to get at more, them or me. But for all you pretend not to like about them, you're just as bad as they are, maybe worse. You led me to believe you thought differently, but at least they were always up front with me. I could see the first time I ever laid eyes on them, that they knew I was wrong ... for everything; that I wasn't good enough for their daughter. Their expressions and frozen smiles were all too clear. It was like reading a book."

There was nothing more she wanted to do at this moment than to wrap her arms around him and hold on for dear life, but she'd failed him in so many ways. She felt the burden she'd been carrying all these years lightening a bit by coming clean about a lot of things, but she'd hurt him in the process. She knew he loved her desperately, and she also knew that love gave her power over him. She'd always felt she could bring him back without too much effort if she'd wanted to; like say, decided against the divorce. But their conversation tonight had changed everything. She could feel it clean through to her bones. He'd always warned her, don't push me too far or you won't like what happens. At the time she'd accused him of threatening her physically, but now she understood there was a final line to be crossed and she just might have done that. The thought of Cole having nothing more to do with her, completely cutting her out of his life, was terrifying. Her moment of atonement had come.

Still, her strong-willed streak was a powerful force, an inner blaze that saw her push things to the limit just to stand back and watch the explosion. However in doing so she might lose the only man she had ever loved. She couldn't allow that to happen! But Cole was right, and it became crystal clear in that moment that she was indeed a game player; a very selfish one. She routinely put her own feelings ahead of his and realizing what he'd said about her was actually true, she felt shame wash through her like battery acid. But to admit that to him threatened everything she knew and trusted about herself and her way of life.

"I can't help how my mother and father think," she continued on blindly. "I am their daughter, not their keeper. Their views are black and white with very few grey shades. They see the world in a particular way and when it's not to their liking they try to rearrange it. Get rid of what doesn't work."

His face hardened. "Well thank you very much. I guess I was just so much garbage to be gotten rid of. Everyone and everything is dispensable."

"You make them sound like horrible people, but they're not. They do a lot of really good things."

He rolled his eyes. "I'm not saying they don't have good in them, what I am saying is they're phony snobs. Unless they decide you're of their class, you're nothing to them. In my opinion life's too short to waste any of it around people like that. You know the day you had me served with divorce papers I felt like a ton of bricks had fallen on me, as I'm sure you can understand coming out of the blue like that with no justification. I do remember one thought that went through my mind though, and that was thank God I don't have to be around Senator and Mrs. Randolph anymore. Honestly, that's what I thought. They are controlling and … puffed up. Again, I know they're your parents, but your mother is more concerned with appearances than she is about people and their feelings. Your father is a stuffed shirt. I don't need people like that in my life. It's enough to know they exist at all."

"It hurts me to hear you describe Mother and Daddy in that way."

"You used to agree with me once upon a time, but now you've decided you want to be just like them. I was your husband, a man you were supposed to love, honour, and cherish but you cut me loose fast enough when it suited you. I was never anything to you but an embarrassment. But I like who I am, where I come from, and I will never change for anyone. And I was a good husband to you. I loved you, cherished you, provided for you, but that wasn't enough, was it?"

"Cole, you are a gorgeous hunk and any woman with red blood running through her veins would agree with that, but you could have met us halfway.

"See? Us! I married *you*, Elsa, not them, and I think I met you more than halfway."

""Okay then, meet *me* halfway. All I asked is that you dress appropriately for certain events instead of always doing the down home thing."

"By the down home thing, you mean being myself? My comfort zone includes jeans and boots and a good shirt. Never in this universe would you have talked me into a pink cardigan tied over my shoulders and dressed entirely in white, including white loafers."

"You're overstating things just a little. It wasn't always a white outfit, that was just during the summer."

"Any time of the year! That's not in my wheelhouse, sweetheart. I ride horses, not golf carts. You brought the wrong man home from the dance, but the thing is, you knew very well what I was all about right from the start. I never misled you in any way. You probably thought it'd be funny to drop me into the buttoned-down bunch we socialized with, but it backfired, didn't it?"

"I don't know what you're talking about."

"Oh yes you do, but now you've told me things here tonight that make it impossible for me to continue with you ... in any way, and that includes as friends. I'm dead serious, Elsa, I want you to get your things together and I'll take you home to your mansion. If you want to go in your pyjamas that's up to you, or nothing at all if that's what you want. You can take your wet jeans with you and if I get a call about the dog, or hopefully find him for you, I'll bring him by. I'll make sure to call first so as not to interrupt any very special plans the Randolphs probably have laid on for the holiday season. Wouldn't want to interrupt the cocktail hour."

"No!"

"No! What does that mean, no?"

"It means no, I'm not going until I have a chance to explain everything, to finish saying what I have to say."

"You've already said enough and so let me explain where *I'm* coming from. I'm don't want you here. There, is that plain enough? I want you gone, and since I'm the only taxi out of here, I'll drop you wherever you want to go. So it's either that Christmas soiree at your father's mansion, or home to your own mansion on the hill. Take your pick, but it's a one-way trip, lady. I don't want you back here."

"Why are you so angry?"

"You're a smart woman, figure it out."

"You weren't this pissed off about the divorce!"

"I was at first if you care to recall, and then I decided I'd be a nice guy about it. Let things settle down and maybe you'd come to your senses, but no more. I've had it with all of your game playing. I'm done letting you jerk me around. There, does that explain it for you adequately? I don't have a college education, but I think I can express myself fairly well without the fifty cent words."

"Say what you want, but I'm not leaving here until I've said *everything* I have to say."

"Is that your final word?"

"Yes, it is!"

"Fine, then I'm going to call the police and have you removed from this property. And I'll thank you not to make a big scene when they get here because I offered to drive you home and you said no."

He turned on his heel and started away and she knew a moment of real fear. She had never seen Cole like this, angry yes, but he'd turned to stone in front of her. Everything she'd been able to say in the past to bring him around simply wasn't working. Call the police? She'd die of mortification. Elsa Randolph sitting in the back of a police car, thrown off the property of her soon to be ex-husband. Unthinkable! And it wasn't only the embarrassment. She knew if she left here like this she might never see him again and it frightened her in a way she'd never experienced before. How could she have thought that even with a divorce pending he would ever really be out of her life for good? Way in the back of her mind, safely tucked away, was the belief that he could never bring himself, divorce or no divorce, to totally say goodbye. He just loved her too much to ever do that. But the absolute truth of things rose up in front of her to douse her with ice-cold reality.

Wasn't it possible for him to meet someone else and move on? Share a bed with another woman? What had she been thinking? She'd openly flirted with the idea, even taunted him with his moving on after the divorce. But she knew when it became final, she was the one who would have the hardest time dealing with it. It had not sunk in until this very moment the dangerous game she'd been playing, and she'd lost. She'd somehow thought that by remaining as friends she'd still see that special look in his eyes that was reserved only for her. No, the reality was she'd have to see herself replaced in his affections by another woman. But that look had been extinguished tonight anyway, and she had no one to blame by herself.

Hurrying out of the barn she quickened her step to catch up with his long-legged stride. Somehow, she had to turn this thing around before it was too late, if it wasn't already too late. A feeling of love for him came over her, squeezing her heart so tightly it almost took her breath away. He was her Cole! She couldn't lose him!

"I'm not going out of here with the police, that's for darned sure," she found the strength to hurl at his back.

"No, it wouldn't do for you to be seen in the back of a police car, would it? Whatever would Mother and Daddy think? But then again maybe that would be another amusing pushback. Hmm?" he asked over his shoulder.

"Cole, listen to me," she managed, winded, once they'd reached the house, the large flakes of snow clinging to their clothes.

"I'm done listening to you, Elsa. I've heard enough. The bottom line is that I got mixed up with a bunch of snobs and they wanted me out. Thing is, I didn't think you were like them when I married you, not really. I thought you were better than that, but you went right along with everything at my expense. You became one of them right in front of my eyes and I was too stupid to see it coming until it was too late. So go back to *your* kind and leave me alone."

He opened the door, and she slipped inside before he slammed it shut. "That's what happened yes, I admit it, and I feel terrible about it."

"I can imagine how terrible you feel. You told me you wanted a divorce without us even trying to talk things out. Now that I look back, you probably goaded me into those arguments so you'd have an excuse to justify things. But tell me this, it's something I always wanted to ask but didn't have the stomach to before now. Is there someone else in the wings waiting for you and me to ... finish up? I get that Matt isn't suitable, somehow.... I notice he didn't jump when you wanted him to come and help you find your dog, so I guess he isn't senatorial son-in-law material either. Does the search continue, or do you have someone more acceptable lined up?"

"You're being deliberately mean."

"Maybe, but you didn't answer my question. Was there someone else all along? You used the first excuse that came to you to divorce me, irreconcilable differences, but since you've decided to be honest for a change, was there another reason? Were you running around on me and didn't want to besmirch the good Randolph name? I'm surprised the good senator didn't try to have our marriage annulled. Even he knew we scorched the sheets well enough to make that a laughable excuse, although I understand there are other ways to go about it."

She thought about their lovemaking, she and Cole, which no matter how much they argued, never seemed to bear the brunt of their marital discord. There had been no disconnect in the bedroom, not really, only a few dry spells when tempers flared. So she wondered how he could think she was plying her favours elsewhere. She had not so much as looked sideways at another man despite the fact that their divorce was in the final stages.

"I was never unfaithful to you, Cole."

Was that relief she saw in his eyes? She hoped so because that meant that it mattered; that this wall that had been instantly erected around him might not be a permanent fixture after all. Please God, she prayed. If it was too late for them to stay married, she desperately still wanted to be his friend. She could not stand the idea of his terrible opinion of her coming between them like this, although she knew she'd earned every word of his scorn.

"But Cole, can you say the same thing? I heard rumours about you on the town a time or two."

"I did go out with the guys once or twice but there was never anything more than that. I should have though, seeing as how I was being tossed aside like I was. I'll bet that would have worked out perfectly for your little team. Something concrete to hang their hat on; add that to my list of crimes."

She was profoundly grateful that no other woman had shared his bed since they'd gotten together so many years ago. Even before they became an official couple she believed she was the only one as far as he was concerned. All through university he was waiting when she came home for visits, leaping into his arms. They'd gone together for five very long years because she wanted to finish school first and then start her career before walking down the aisle. He'd waited for her patiently, proud of her because she wanted to continue her education.

And then five years married before she'd asked for a divorce, so Cole had been on her radar for a very long time, and honestly, she couldn't imagine it any other way. Had she really understood what she was doing when she agreed to what her parents had demanded, still caught up in their control over her? Had she realized at all what she'd done to him? The harsh truth was that she'd been so focused on the wrong things that other than superficially, she hadn't really understood the depth of his hurt. Now, the haunting look in his eyes when he talked about it, told her she hadn't even begun to fathom his pain. What she had done to him hit her with full force and the impact nearly staggered her. She had played fast and loose with his love for her, and it was a despicable thing to do. Still, she resisted acceptance.

"Honestly, Cole, there were a lot of things in play and sadly you got in the way of them. It never meant that I didn't care for you. Sometimes maybe it's better to cut ties before you hurt the other person too much, I don't know."

"Bullshit!"

As much as she willed them away tears sprang to her eyes, and she made no attempt to brush them off. "You were miserable in my world, Cole. Admit it! It wasn't all me, or my mother or my father. You didn't even try to cooperate."

"I did try to cooperate, but did you honestly think I would want to become a clone of your father? Isn't one enough? I'm sorry," he said, "that last remark was uncalled for. Yes, I could see the differences, and I know I'm probably not the easiest person in the world to live with, but I was trying to make it work because I loved you. How would you feel if I came home one day and just announced I wanted a divorce? You wouldn't be hurt? And what if I told you, finally, that my mother and father thought it was a good idea if you were out of my life because basically, you weren't good enough for me? Engineered the whole thing? Treated you like a second-class citizen. Would that sting a little do you think?"

"Cole, you've always been such a big tough guy."

"Not that tough, Elsa. I have feelings too, just because I don't show them all the time doesn't mean I'm not hurting. You hurt me; it got to be a game with you. Knock me down then; test my love by coming onto me to prove you still had me wrapped around your little finger. You play games with your mother and father, and they play games with you. You're all there in the trenches together just digging away at each other. I was a threat not only to their precious reputation as social bigwigs, but eventually you too as a rising young executive. Vice-president at twenty-nine, what's next?"

She looked at him not even trying to stem the flow of tears. "I've been offered the presidency."

"President at thirty. Wow! That's got to be some kind of record. Boy, that divorce came along just in time because you'll need someone decent on your arm for all of *your* social engagements. At least now I won't be holding you back from your upwardly mobile climb. Congratulations!"

Her tears were still flowing, dripping off her chin, and she swiped at them angrily. "It doesn't matter, I probably won't be taking it."

"Why not? Really, I think it's very impressive and I mean that. I was always very proud of you."

She shrugged. "Not that impressive. Profit Line is a relatively small company."

"Don't sell yourself short, being offered the presidency is a major accomplishment. And now you can sit up in your big empty mansion on the hill with no cowhand husband to embarrass you, and no children running around that want looking after."

She lowered her head into her hands. "That's an awful thing to say."

"I know it is," he said, his tone gentling slightly, "but since we're into telling the truth tonight, isn't that just about right? You are your mother's daughter. It's all about the image. Everything has to be just as you think it should be now that you've settled down and finished sowing your wild oats with the likes of me. Straight to the top."

"There is nothing wrong with a woman having a career."

"I agree wholeheartedly. If you recall my mother has a very fine career as a school principal. But mind you, she didn't ditch her husband or forego a family just so she could reach the top of her profession."

"You make me sound horrible."

"You're not horrible, Elsa. I never said you were, but you've done some questionable things. You play fast and loose with other people's feelings to get what you want; toss people aside when you're done with them."

"I know I've made a lot of mistakes. I know I didn't do the right thing by you, because that's what this whole argument is about right now. I know I played some stupid games, okay? I'm a sassy person by nature. You know that. You even said you liked that about me."

"That's right."

"Up to a point."

"That's exactly it, up to a point. You have to care about the fallout, or even be aware of it. Are you telling me you'd do things differently if you had a chance to hit rewind?"

She cried all the harder, her head bowed. "Yes, Cole, I would," she finally managed. "I've been such a fool about things but the worst of it is how I hurt you. You're such a good man, a sweet man, and I should have broken up with you long before it ever got to the marriage stage. I should not have asked you to live such a restricted lifestyle, one that's completely foreign to you, and then wanting out when you didn't change in the way I thought you should. All I cared about was what I wanted."

"Or stand by me after we were married. You have to pick a side, Elsa."

"I know that, and I should have picked you, stood with you, been proud of you, not apologize for you. I know I sold you short. I know I never should have asked you for a divorce; that was selfish and unnecessary. I listened to my parents when I ought to have stood up to them in favour of the man I loved. Can you ever forgive me for what I did?"

"You hurt me, Elsa. I appreciate your honesty tonight, but it hurt pretty bad at the time; it still does and probably always will."

"I'm sorry. Maybe I should never have danced with you that night at the cowboy bar, remember?"

"Ha! Do I remember! How could I forget? I knew you and your girlfriend were out for a walk on the wild side and I was only too happy to accommodate you. And it was quite a ride while it lasted, wasn't it? I guess we should look back on our time together, not as a mistake, but remember the good times and the happy memories."

"There were plenty of those."

"So what's ahead for you now, Elsa?"

"I'm serious, I said I was going to turn down the presidency, but in truth I have already turned it down."

"Elsa," he grinned, "you're going to have to work on the honesty thing a little more."

"Hey, I always tell the truth, it just takes me a little while to get around to it sometimes."

"So why did you turn it down?"

"I don't know, I've been dissatisfied with my life for a while, I would say the last year in particular. I'm getting what I wanted, maybe faster than most because of who my father is, but I'm not fulfilled. Life at the top isn't as much fun as I thought it would be. I feel empty; alone. It's not what I imagined at all."

"And what had you imagined? I know what you used to tell me you wanted to do with your life."

"Children?"

"Yes, children."

"That's right. I got so caught up in everything I lost sight of what was really important. I listened to the wrong advice. It's so crazy. I mean here I was the vice-president of a growing company, making important corporate decisions every day. Then let my mother and father control my life as though I didn't have the brains to do it myself. When I say it out loud it sounds awful. So I decided to make a few changes starting in the new year. You know I always looked at January first as a really great jump off point for new and exciting things."

"What changes are you thinking of making?"

She sighed. "It's a little frightening, but I have actually resigned from the company. After that business meeting in Fredericton I tendered my resignation, effectively immediately. My father will be livid when he finds out, but whatever. I won't be going back after the holidays. That's why I was late getting home, I stopped by my office in Moncton to clean out my desk. I just wasn't happy, Cole. It wasn't fun anymore. So I'm going to take some time off to think about what I really want to do with my life. And maybe next time I won't get so caught up in everything that I'll make such bad choices. So you really forgive me for all of the crap I put you through? I'd be grateful if you could find it in your heart to do that for me."

He took her in his arms. Her heart sprouted wings and soared, even did a few back flips. Nothing mattered more than being held by him, it was just sad that she'd realized too late what was most important.

"Of course I forgive you. I'm sorry I said I was going to have the police take you away, I think you know I would never do that."

"I don't know," she teased. "You sounded pretty serious. I thought maybe I was going to spend Christmas in the big house or something."

"Nah, I care too much for you to do something like that. But speaking of the big house, tell me, Elsa, honestly, you actually like living in that big old ugly chrome and glass mausoleum?"

She laughed. "Honestly?"

"Yeah, honestly. You worked with the contractor to build the house of your dreams. Big dreams, big house I guess."

"And all of it without any input from you."

"That's right. I wouldn't want to take credit for that thing, believe me. I hated living in it. But were you really happy living there, especially after I moved out?"

She snuggled closer. "I hate that house with a passion now. It feels like a museum, or some public building downtown. All that white on white and chrome, and way too much glass. Ugh! I guess it's one of those things in life where you say to yourself later, what was I thinking?"

"You've had quite a few of those moments I think."

She punched him playfully in the arm. "Yes, but I have enough insight to learn from my mistakes. You know, I'm still sick about losing Snowflakes, but it has brought us back closer again. I always want you in my life, Cole. I can't imagine not having you with me."

"You know there are words I would give anything to hear you say to me."

"What, that I love you? You know I do, with all my heart. I have never stopped loving you. There's no place in the world I'd rather be than standing here in your arms, lying in your arms, sleeping in your arms…. Seriously. It's like I've come home."

"Well I'm going to ask you to put your money where your mouth is, Ms. Randolph. Never mind the divorce, it's probably too late to stop it now anyway, but why don't you sell that big house of yours and come and live with me here, on a cattle ranch? I might be in the market for someone to help me run it. Let's go back to where we started, on the wild side. What do you say?"

Chapter Sixteen

She looked at him in surprise. "Sell my house? The one that I was involved in the designing of, right down to the smallest final detail?"

"That one, the glass palace."

She tried to stifle a laugh. "That, I will have you know is an outstanding piece of architecture. I know you're not a fan of minimalism, but it is a lovely home. It was amazing what that architect was able to achieve with glass and chrome, and wood too, of course. And I think that beautiful country setting, with the amazing view makes it all the more impressive."

"You said you hated it."

She now wore a broad smile. Since Cole had left, or more to the point been asked to leave, she'd knocked around in that big old house. She could never remember being more lonely in her life, except of course if she included growing up in her parents' mansion. Now that she'd been in Cole's warm, comfy log cabin she had no desire in the world to return to what had once been their marital home.

"I do hate it, but I...."

"Put your money where your mouth is, Elsa."

Her old feistiness returned, actually it was never very far away. "Sell my home? You sell this one and move back there with me!"

"No chance," he said, and she knew by the expression in his eyes that despite the fact their conversation had taken a lighter turn, he meant every word he said.

"I'm just pulling your leg," she told him with a wink. "It goes on the market right after Christmas. There, called your bluff, Mr. Donahue. You didn't think I'd actually part with it when push came to shove, did you? Thought maybe I was still playing games. Well, I'll tell you, Cole, I'm through with that silliness. You're too important to me to risk losing you again."

"So you'll move in here with me?"

"I'd love to move in here with you, although it might be a teensy bit crowded once I get all of my stuff here."

"Great!" he exclaimed at her decision to move in with him, his eyes sparkling. "And this place is more spacious than it looks. There'll be plenty of room for both of us, you'll see, and we can add on if need be."

There were tears in her eyes again. "Cole, I know I'm repeating myself, but I am so sorry for everything I've put you through. I apologize from the depths of my heart. I was in way over my head. I bought into something that way down deep wasn't really me. I don't want that lifestyle anymore, any of it. Just being here with you, even for these few hours, and away from all of that, I've never felt so relaxed in years. I've found out that I really don't have the stomach for social climbing. The simple way of life is where I'm most comfortable. You told me I had to choose, and I choose you. I'm going to look at it like a permanent walk on the wild side."

"You're actually saying you want to trade in your business suits for blue jeans and boots?"

"You bet! I have lots of business training, a university degree that I should probably get some use out of, so I'd love to help you run this place. You say there might be an opening coming up? If so, I'd like to apply."

"I am accepting applications as it turns out and I have to say things are looking pretty good for you so far, considering the position has just been created."

She snuggled against him, wondering how she'd managed to live without this for so long. "Cole, thank you for forgiving me for the way I acted."

"Elsa, I wasn't exactly an angel either. We got into some pretty good scraps, and I said things I'm not proud of. I'd say we both have some apologizing to do. Do you forgive *me*?"

"Done!" she cried, holding on even tighter if that was possible.

"Elsa, I love you with all my heart. I never stopped loving you and I never planned to, even though I would have eventually moved on if we had actually gotten divorced."

She raised her head, pulling back at arm's length to study him, a twinkle in her eye. "How long would you have waited before you … moved on?"

He shrugged. "Oh I don't know, a week … maybe two."

"A week … maybe two?"

He laughed. "The truth is, Elsa, I never thought that far ahead. I was just doing one day at a time hoping you'd come to your senses about us. Before these last couple of days I must say I was about giving up hope."

She sighed, still studying his face. "Make no mistake about it, Cole, I love you. I know my actions didn't show it because I let a whole lot of other stuff get in my way, but I would have been a sorry woman if I'd gone through with that divorce. You woke me up. You really did. I've behaved so badly, and I played a dangerous game. Thank God it's not too late. I will go to my grave loving you. I might have moved on too, over time, but I know now I would never have found anyone that could compare to you. I gave you my heart when we got married, that part was very real, and nothing has changed."

He pulled her against him again, holding her tightly and it was a moment or two before either of them spoke. Cole was the first to lift his head.

"Did I hear you say thank God it's not too late with respect to the divorce?"

"You heard me right. My lawyer said there were still some financial details being worked out, and along with the Court's busy calendar, we couldn't expect the divorce to be finalized until sometime in January. When he told me that, last week as a matter of fact, something shifted in me. It really did. It was like the reality of it came up and stared me in the face, but I thought it was too late now to turn back for a lot of reasons. I'd look pretty silly for one thing, and I thought you just wanted the whole matter done and over with."

"So it's not too late? Is that what you're saying?"

"That's what I'm saying."

"So-o-o-o...."

"So, if you're in agreement, I'll call my lawyer right after the holidays and tell him to stop everything. That you and I have decided not to go ahead with the divorce. We're reconciling and intend to live happily ever after, as per our original intention. Is that what I should tell him?"

"That's what you should tell him."

They pressed against each other, as if by their solid grip they were establishing their eagerness to be one again.

"Elsa, I never thought we'd have another chance, and now this."

"Neither did I," she said, sniffing. "I thought I'd screwed things up too badly to ever find our way back together, but it seems I've been given a second chance."

"We've both been given a second chance. God, I love you, Elsa, and never more than at this moment."

"I have not felt so light, so happy, in a very long time. I wish I had the biggest most wonderful Christmas gift in the world to give you right now, Cole. One that says how sorry I am for all the hurt I caused, and that shows how very much you mean to me."

"You just did, with everything you've told me," he said, his voice wavering. "There is nothing I wanted more than to have my wife back. You had to come back to me, I couldn't go up there beating my chest and issuing you an ultimatum. I know you, it would never have worked, would it?"

"Sadly, no. That would have been entirely the wrong thing to do. We're both terribly stubborn, I'm sure you can see that by now, so I guess we have to figure things out on our own terms. But what scares me is that I might not have found my way back, in time, and that is something that will always haunt me. Again, if it wasn't for Snowflakes, I'd still be sitting up there in my glass and chrome palace, miserable, but too proud and stubborn to tell you so."

"Maybe we've both had to eat a little crow, but no matter. Now, are you serious that you want to help me run this place?"

"If you'll have me."

"Of course I'll have you, but I warn you, honey, I have no intention of making this into the biggest cattle ranch in the area or anything like that. I'm not in competition with anyone. I only want to do my own thing. I never wanted to be the biggest anything, just make a comfortable living. Besides, I'm the foreman at Dad's ranch, so this is really just a part-time thing for me. But a hundred head of cattle is nothing to sneeze at either."

"You worked a lot of hours on your father's ranch, has any of that changed? I mean has your dad downsized or anything?"

"No, if anything, he's gotten a little larger in the last year or so which keeps me very busy. And I seriously have been looking for someone from the area to help me here."

"Why not let that someone be me?"

"There are things you could do to help, but I don't expect...."

"I want you to teach me how to drive the tractor so that I can move the round bales, and when the calves start coming in what did you say, February or March, I imagine there'll be more than enough to do. I'm sure there are lots of things I can do to help there. What would your hired man be doing?"

"Well ... feeding, fence mending, there's always plenty of that to do after winter and of course barn work. There would also be some heavy lifting."

"I'm pretty strong."

"I don't want my wife working like a man. I can take care of that when the time comes. It's just to free me up a little is all."

"So there's enough to keep me occupied by the sounds of it, and the really heavy stuff *you* could do, which you would anyway, running both ranches. Cole, I know it could work, and it would be a new direction for me, a fresh set of challenges. You know I'd enjoy that."

"You could also take care of the computer end of things; orders, registration, work like that. You might want to reconsider because it will be quite hectic."

"I can do hectic, I had to keep a lot of plates spinning as vice-president. This is just another type of business, same skill set, well almost, and I can hardly wait to get started."

"That works out well then because the job's open immediately. You can start tomorrow if you want to."

"Those terms are acceptable, but there's one drawback that I should make you aware of right out of the gate."

He looked at her curiously. "What's that?"

"I'd have to cut back a bit when I started getting bigger."

"Bigger?"

"Bigger as in being pregnant. I want us to start a family right away, what do you say to that, Cole Donahue?"

"What do I say to that! Hot damn, yes! That's what I say. You know that's what I've always wanted, Elsa. Remember what we talked about back before we got married? Well these are the very things we're discussing now. We took a break, but we're back."

319

"I know," she sighed. "Having babies was always on my agenda, although unfortunately it kept getting pushed further and further onto the back burner. I'm almost thirty and you're thirty-five so we're not too late by a long shot to start making babies. It's hard not to think about all the wasted years though. Oh how I wish I hadn't gotten side tracked, we'd have children by now."

"No use crying over something we can't change. We're back on track now and that's all that matters."

"But about the job, I think a pregnant lady could do most of the work in the job description."

"Most of it, yes, but if there's any risk at all, you do not do it. I'll find someone else temporary, if need be, but before you get too far along you should be fine with most of those chores. And under no circumstances are you to go anywhere near that bull, or any other bull. Understood?"

"Yes sir!" she laughed doing a mock salute.

"I'm dead serious about that, sweetheart."

"I know you are and I have no intention of getting close to that much hamburger, or I should say *any* hamburger with a bad attitude. I promise you I won't take any chances, whether I'm pregnant or not. Okay?"

He grinned. "Okay."

She glowed as she breathed in the warm scent of him, an enticing blend of leather and maple firewood. "Cole, this is turning out to be the best Christmas of all. Bar none, except that I miss Snowflakes so bad. I want her here with us, then it really would be the perfect Christmas."

"We'll find her, Elsa. I've got a very good feeling about it. Do you think she'll like living here on the ranch?"

"She'd absolutely love it, I know she would; all those cattle to bark at. I think she was lonely over in that big house too. You might think differently when you start to feel crowded with all of us here together."

He chuckled. "One big happy family, but there's one important part of this equation that we haven't considered."

"Oh? What's that?"

"Your parents."

"What about them?"

"They'll probably take a bad one when they find out the divorce has been called off. Didn't I just hear you tell your mother not a half hour ago that they would always come first? I have to admit, that hurt when I heard you say that. That was a one-two punch to the solar plexus."

"I've been trying to play both ends against the middle for so long it comes as second nature to me now. I'm so sorry you had to hear me say that, it must have really hurt. Cole, they're my parents and even with all their flaws, I love them very much. And, thank God, even with all my flaws they love me very much and have always had my best interests at heart, although a bit too much at times. As of tonight though they do not get a say about our marriage. You are the man I love. I married you because I loved you and for no other reason, even though there were some hiccups along the way. I feel the same way today. There's no other man on the face of this earth that I want to be with other than you, and my parents are going to have to accept that."

"There'll be fireworks."

"It's likely. Knowing me I might even be disappointed if there weren't, but my parents and I need to have a very long talk about you and me. I will support you Cole in everything you do and say, but I have to ask that you try to meet them halfway too. There may just be a pink cardigan in your future after all, you never know."

"I don't think I'd look good in pink, but whatever. White loafers are out though, under any circumstances."

She laughed. "Seriously, I will just lay it out for them; tell them you are my husband, and I will not be swayed from the life we promised each other when we got married. And I'll also tell them I have apologized to you for the part I played in all of this. Besides, after the grandchildren start coming, I'm sure they'll begin to soften up."

"And what about when you tell them you're going to help me run this ranch? I mean down in the trenches? There'll be mega fireworks then. Get ready to run for cover when you make that announcement."

"They might just surprise you. Once they see how happy I am they could change their minds. Did I ever tell you that my mother actually grew up on a farm in hardscrabble?"

"Ahhh, no that little piece of information didn't came up in conversation."

"That's because she had such a hard time as a child. They were dirt poor. Her father died when she was six and her mother raised seven children on her own. They had nothing. Her mother died young too and her sisters and brothers were scattered to the wind, but my mother rose above her raisin' as they say, she reinvented herself and became Phoebe Langley, a beautiful young woman who was determined to marry well. She told me that herself. And so she did. She married Gregory Randolph when he was a newly minted lawyer with big aspirations. I know you're familiar with my father's political career, and that he eventually became a senator. So the last thing she wants is to be reminded of her sad past. Perhaps she thought us getting together would be like history repeating itself, who knows, and she wouldn't want that for me. Please don't ever bring it up to her, but I told you so you'd perhaps understand why she thinks like she does."

"I never knew. Poor Phoebe. Does your father have a difficult past too by any chance?"

"No, it's just as you know it, the son of a senator himself and schooled since he was in knee socks to follow in his father's footsteps. My father had it drilled into him that his family was better than most, and that the torch would be passed to him some day to keep the good Randolph name alive."

"So he's only playing to type. Well that's okay. Now about my parents, they will be over the moon when they hear we've reconciled. And they'll be so happy when the grandchildren start coming."

He studied her face and then lowered his lips to hers in a noisy kiss, the wet and wild kind. It was a full minute before they broke it off, both trembling and needing more.

He kissed her forehead. "What do you say I put another log on the fire, pull that rug in front of the fireplace and maybe we can get started on making those babies."

She beamed. "Cole, I can't think of a nicer way to spend Christmas Eve. Look," she directed his attention toward the window, "it's like Hollywood snow out there, big flakes falling so slowly. It would be the perfect night to hitch up a team and go for a sleigh ride… that is if you had horses here."

"Or to make babies."

She was still smiling. "Or to make babies."

She felt contented, happy, although the fate of poor Snowflakes weighed heavily on her heart. She wondered if she'd have to make peace with maybe never seeing her toy poodle again, no matter how many times Cole assured her that things would probably turn out fine. It seemed that every cloud, no matter how dazzling the silver lining might be, had a dark shadow here and there to keep everything real.

"Would you like a glass of wine, Mrs. Donahue?" Cole asked, winking at her, knowing she'd decided to keep her own name and he had always been perfectly fine with that. He'd just finished putting another seasoned maple log on the fire, the flames slowly starting to lick at its sides. It filled the candle lit room with the soft glow of firelight and Christmas tree lights.

"I'd love a glass, Mr. Donahue. I think some red wine would be nice because after all it is Christmas Eve. I meant to say too that Mrs. McIntyre put up a nice little tree for you, not overdone, but just right."

"I really didn't want to bother with a tree," he called from the kitchen as he popped the cork and poured two glasses half full, "but she said I should have one and so I humoured her. My mother's glad I have a tree too. I'll tell Mrs. McIntyre the next time she comes to clean that you liked her tree, or I guess you can tell her yourself since you're going to be living here. Elsa, I'm so glad we're together, sweetheart. You have made me a happy man tonight, and forever."

They sat cross-legged in front of the fire. Neither said anything for a few minutes, mesmerized by the crackling flames and the continued melting of any residual tension between them.

He moved closer and she relaxed in his arms as they sipped their wine, the dusk to dawn light still doing a superb job of highlighting the gentle fall of snow outside the picture window. If this was a movie there could not be a more perfect Christmas Eve setting, right down to the idyllic snowfall.

Still sipping her wine she made good use of her free hand, unbuttoning his heavy flannel shirt and pushing it aside so she could run her hand over the hair-roughened skin of his chest. He moaned audibly, adjusting to give her even better access. And then he got busy, setting his wine glass on the floor beside him he slipped his hand under her sweater, pausing at the confines of her lacy bra. She leaned into his touch, and he was reaching around to undo the clasp when there was a loud knock at the door and they both jumped, Elsa quickly pulling her sweater into place. Cole was busy righting himself as well. With an expletive under his breath as to someone's poor timing, he went to answer the door.

She couldn't help but wonder if perhaps her parents, despite her heartfelt apology to them for her absence tonight, might have decided to come and intercept any reconciliation attempts that might be underway between she and Cole. Well they were in for a surprise if they did.

She was nervous as she stood by his side while he opened the door, and it would have been a contest as to who had the bigger look of surprise on their face when they saw Santa Claus standing there.

"Melvin!" Cole exclaimed.

"Mr. Hoyt!" Elsa said, her mouth still open in surprise. "Aren't you supposed to be at my mother and father's Christmas party at the mansion?"

"I'm on my way there right now as a matter of fact."

She groaned. "Don't tell me they sent you here to pick me up and take me with you to the party. They'll stop at nothing! Well," she said laughing as she shook her head, "I'm afraid it was a wasted trip because I'm not going anywhere tonight. I'm staying right here."

"I think Melvin might be here to see me," Cole said when he could get a word in. "You said you'd stop by and visit my ranch when you got a chance. I guess tonight is as good a night as any even though it's quite a distance out of your way if you're supposed to be in Riverview."

Cole turned to Elsa. "Melvin was the agricultural inspector with the Province for many years in this area and he and I got to know each other quite well when he visited my father's ranch. As a matter of fact he and Dad are good friends."

Elsa chuckled. "And I know Mr. Hoyt because it was me who booked him for Mum and Dad's Christmas party."

Cole turned his attention back to his old friend. "Well don't stand out there on the doorstep in the snow, come on in! I didn't exactly expect you to show up in a Santa suit when you came for the tour, but it's a nice touch considering the season."

Melvin smiled as he stepped into the cabin and closed the door behind him. "You're both wrong, the reason I came…." He was stopped mid-sentence when a little white curly head poked out of his coat and gave Cole and Elsa an adorable smile, complete with her tiny pink tongue.

"Snowflakes!" Elsa shrieked. "I don't believe it!"

Snowflakes showed just exactly how pleased she was with the turn of events by giving a sharp little bark, actually several of them in rapid succession. Melvin set her on the floor, whereupon she turned around in a circle, stood up on her hind legs and pranced with her two front feet in the air giving her version of a happy dance.

Everyone laughed.

Elsa made a dive for the dog and gathered her in her arms and proceeded to get a sound face licking from her delighted pet.

Melvin smiled happily, an ideal Santa. "I understand your Snowflakes had quite an adventure while she was gone. I was asked to look after her by a friend of mine who delivered Christmas boxes. It seems the poodle stowed away in his van; even ate part of a turkey dinner along with a sugar cookie for dessert. He wanted me to mind her until after Christmas when the SPCA opened again. Anyway I was on the way to the store to get her some food late this afternoon when I saw one of your posters. I thought well, I'm going out later to a Christmas party, I'll just drop out to Shenstone first and make sure this little monkey gets home in time for Christmas. I made it with only a short time to spare too.

"She came to me at just the right time, you know. This is my first Christmas without my wife, Elaine, who died a few months ago. I was desperately lonely, and even though my friends suggested I get a four-legged companion, I always put it off. Now I'm completely sold on the idea. Snowflakes has shown me how great it is to hear the pitter patter of tiny feet around the house. I'm going to get a dog in the new year, and I wanted you to know that it was Snowflakes who helped me make that decision."

Cole shook Melvin's hand. "That's great to hear. Say, we're cooking a turkey tomorrow, why don't you come back out and have Christmas dinner with us? We're not having a big feast or anything, but we'd love to have you come and later we can give you a tour of the ranch. What do you say?"

Melvin grinned. "I was going to cook my own turkey tomorrow, but I could do it on Boxing Day instead. I'd love to come if I wouldn't be any trouble…."

Elsa gave him a kiss on the cheek. "You wouldn't be any trouble at all. We'd love to have you. After all, it's not every day that we get to have Santa come to our house for Christmas dinner!"

Everyone laughed, and Snowflakes, smiled her adorable smile and barked her happy bark.

Epilogue

One month later: After Elsa officially called off the divorce Cole and Elsa renewed their vows and took a second honeymoon to Hawaii. Both were blissfully happy.

* * *

Snowflakes was none the worse for wear after her hours on the loose, passing her veterinary check-up with flying colours.

Brett, having apologized to Wally, his old boss, was not only reinstated, but promoted, and he and Lelia were saving for a down payment on their new home.

Six months later: Elsa and Cole put up their new ranch sign, Lone Valley Ranch, standing back, arm and arm, looking out over their expansive property.

Snowflakes was loving her new role as ranch dog, and as per Elsa's prediction, did her best to keep every other critter in line.

Melvin Hoyt, aka Santa Claus, did indeed get a dog, a female golden doodle that he promptly named Jackie.

Phoebe and Senator Randolph had not been at all pleased with Elsa's decision to reconcile with Cole but were living up to their promise to their daughter to at least be tolerant of their son-in-law.

* * *

Eight Months Later: Lelia gave birth to Zoe Beryl, Brett present in the delivery room and overjoyed with the arrival of their new baby girl.

* * *

One year later: On Christmas Eve, Elsa unexpectedly gave birth two weeks early to her and Cole's first child, a son, Shane Coleton Donahue. Both mother and child were doing well. Senator and Mrs. Randolph were naturally disappointed though that Cole and Elsa would not be able to attend their second annual Christmas extravaganza at the mansion. After all, the invitations had already been sent....

Snowflakes had her own little bed next to the fireplace where she dozed comfortably when off-duty. She was still the life of the party, inquisitive and good-natured, but no amount of coaxing would *ever* get her into Cole's truck again.

The End

If you enjoyed this book, please leave the author a review.

Eden Monroe loves giving voice to the endless parade of interesting characters that introduce themselves in her imagination. She writes about real life, real issues and struggles, and triumphing against all odds. A proud east coast Canadian, she enjoys a variety of outdoor activities and a good book.

BWL Publishing

bwlpublishing.ca